CAMERON
KALE

Live the Bow Principle -
Believe God
Obey Him &
Watch Him Perform Miracles

Blessings
David Wtulaka PR 2013

CAMERON KALE

THE EVANGEL OF MARIAH CITY

DAVID WHITAKER

TATE PUBLISHING
AND ENTERPRISES, LLC

Published by Tate Publishing & Enterprises, LLC
127 E. Trade Center Terrace | Mustang, Oklahoma 73064 USA
1.888.361.9473 | www.tatepublishing.com

Tate Publishing is committed to excellence in the publishing industry. The company reflects the philosophy established by the founders, based on Psalm 68:11,
"The Lord gave the word and great was the company of those who published it."

Book design copyright © 2013 by Tate Publishing, LLC. All rights reserved.
Cover design by Allen Jomoc
Interior design by Mary Jean Archival

Published in the United States of America

ISBN: 978-1-62147-232-2
1. Fiction / Christian / Suspense
2. Fiction / Christian / General
13.02.11

This book is dedicated to my son,
Solomon David Whitaker

Solomon inspired me with some of his ideas to write more
creatively in some of the action scenes of the book. Thank you,
Solomon, for challenging Dad to write to your age group!

ACKNOWLEDGMENTS

I always give credit to my wife, Denise, for having the patience to put up with me when I am in the zone of writing. She forfeited many conversations while I was drifting into a creative world of my own making.

I have already mentioned that my son, Solomon, has been an inspiration to me in writing this novel. It has been his blunt, fair judgment and creative enthusiasm that helped me to get into the mind of a twelve-year-old as I wrote.

Thank you, my dear pastor, Steve Brown. It was through knowing you that I was able to depict such a close relationship of Cameron Kale to Pastor Kit Tyler. My season of being your Abishai was one of the great blessings in my life.

Thank you, Gary Coon, for your learned insights about writing a first chapter that either catches or does not catch the attention of the reader. I took this advice seriously.

Most of all, I give thanks to the Lord for allowing me the experiences of real life that made this fiction piece possible. If we live like Cameron Kale, daring to believe God and obey Him, we won't miss seeing that God is a God of might and miracles in our lives.

CONTENTS

Part III: Triumph over Evil

PREFACE

Cameron Kale, the Evangel of Mariah City is the story of a typical family with untypical experiences. The Kales, a practicing Christian family, experience the reality of spiritual warfare in everyday life. Beyond the daily earthly routine, Dr. Kale's life is more than earthbound—it is outer-worldly as he encounters the spirit villain, Ser Pentino, who is none other than Drawg, a grotesque demon spirit from hell. Dr. Kale outwits this dastardly demon through his living relationship with God. The Spirit meets Dr. Kale daily to enable him to overcome Drawg's destructive powers.

This fiction is full of fact, as it is an allegory of the Christian life. All of the spirit encounters are true to life experiences of the Christian who is confronted with the reality of spiritual warfare. It is the hope of this author that the reader will not only enjoy the excitement that surrounds this American family but also will relate to the real-life drama that has life-changing power for the Christian.

The evangel (the good news) is what God has called Cameron to share in Mariah City. It is the call of every Christian to share the evangel to all. Sadly, while Cameron does share the good news, he finds that it has not been his daily focus. He, like so many other Christians in Mariah City, settles for things of lesser value in the kingdom than sharing the evangel. Cameron learns hard lessons about the value of growing the kingdom of God.

PART I

The Calling

Chapter One

CAMERON KALE

It was Saturday morning, and the sun was just coming up as a passerby on an isolated highway noticed the guardrails on his side of the road were crumpled like a bent-up soda can. As he got out of his car, he noticed skid marks running up to the guardrails. Noticing a white tracker at the bottom of a steep embankment, he knew it must be a serious accident since the vehicle was upside down, and it appeared whoever was in the car was pinned inside. The hillside just outside of Mariah City was speckled with red and gold vehicles that morning as firemen, police, and paramedics covered the dismal scene. A small crowd of people was now waiting above whispering bits and pieces of what they overheard to each other. Rescuers used a Jaws of Life to open the vehicle. They removed the body from the wreckage, placed it on a gurney, and then moved the gurney into the ambulance. The lights were not on; the expected speed of the van toward the hospital did not happen. Was this a tragedy? Who was involved? Was it a friend or family? Mariah City was a small town, and everybody knew everybody. Any news was big news, and a car accident like this one would impact the community.

———◦◦◦———

The sun was shining through Dr. Kale's bedroom curtains at 7:00 a.m. Sleeping in on weekends rarely happened at the Kales' home, and it was no different this morning.

Turning and stretching from side to side, yawning as if there was little oxygen left in the room, Deni, Dr. Kale's wife, kiddingly yelled into the bedroom from the kitchen, "Hey, are you planning on sleeping the day away?"

Dr. Cameron Kale lived a busy life in Mariah City, Nevada, as a chiropractor and attended a small church. Deni worked at a local pregnancy center and always seemed to be at Dr. Kale's side, helping where she could.

Dr. Kale was thirty-five years old, a slim, 5'9" with brownish-red hair and blue eyes. He stayed fit by working out at the gym and looked more like he was twenty-five. He felt he needed to be an example to his patients, and knowing his body was the temple of God made him try to stay in shape as well. He often said his only temporal vice was his love for a car his parents gave him for graduation from high school in 1994 he fondly called "Old Blue." It was a racy-blue 1967 Z28 Camaro. Cameron often said his priorities were God; Deni; their twelve-year-old son, Cody; and Old Blue. He could honestly say that he was in love with Old Blue, but it was nothing like his love for his bride, Deni. Deni was a tall and slender blonde. Cameron's favorite compliment to her was in the form of a question: "Do you know you are beautiful?" They enjoyed spending most of their time with each other and Cody. They also liked to kid each other, which was just a good sign of a healthy marriage.

"Okay, I'm up."

Deni briskly walked into the room. "What are your plans today?"

"I told Amy Benson I would come in this morning and adjust her back. She said she is going on vacation, and she doesn't want to deal with the pain during her R and R."

"I wish you would adjust our schedules," Deni replied jokingly. "We need to spend more time together. It seems that we are always working and never have enough time for ourselves."

Cameron took hold of his lovely bride's arms and pulled her toward him. "I love you, Deni. You are right. I will try to make more time for you and Cody."

"Dad!" Cody rushed into his room with a panic. "It's Mrs. Benson. They are talking about her on TV. She was in an accident!"

Dr. Kale, Deni, and Cody ran into the living room and watched in horror as they realized a good friend and patient of his had been in what sounded like a serious accident. He didn't hear if she was still alive or not, but one thing was for sure: this moment quickly clouded over the sunny day that began.

Grabbing their coats, they climbed into Old Blue and screeched out of their drive on their way to Mariah City's Community Hospital emergency room to meet the ambulance.

"You guys stay here," Cameron said when they arrived at the ER. "I'll go in and see what I can find out."

Moments later, Cameron's eyes connected with a familiar face. It was Pastor Kit Tyler. The look on his face was not encouraging.

"Hello, Cameron. I don't have very good news. Our friend, Amy, is no longer with us. But she's in a better place."

As quickly as those words came from Pastor Tyler's lips to Cameron's ears, they stung like the venom of a serpent in his soul. He didn't know if it was because of how this would affect her husband, Scott, or because death for her—death for anyone— seemed so final.

"Cameron!" Scott Benson's voice rang out from the door that led from the curtain-drawn cubicle where Amy lay covered from head to toe on a gurney. Cameron hugged his friend but felt as though his knees would buckle from weakness and grief. Scott, on the other hand, seemed at peace and was strong and focused.

"I'm here for you, Scott," Cameron choked. "Whatever Deni and I can do, let us know."

Clem Mager, the police chief's deputy, came to the hospital to talk with Scott about some of the details of his wife's accident.

"Cameron, you know Clem Mager, Chief Bormand's deputy?"

"Sure, hello, Clem."

"Hello, Mr. Kale. I have heard some good things about you."

"I'm glad to hear that. Thank you."

Cameron wasn't sure why the police deputy was there but figured that he was no doubt on the scene and was there to pay his respects and do his job. Clem was a jolly but caring person who knew many people in the community through his job. He had only been a Christian for a short time but was not afraid to let others know about his new faith in Jesus Christ.

As Cameron said good-byes to Pastor Kit Tyler and his grieving friend, he walked toward his florescent blue Camaro, shaking his head.

"Cam, what happened?" Deni asked desperately. "Is Amy okay? Tell me."

His face gave the truth away—Amy was gone, just as Pastor Kit said. Their friend, so full of life and character hours ago, was now gone. Cameron could not deal with the reality of her passing. Struggling with the notion of death was something he had never come to terms with. Death seemed to end all things. Even so, the last words Pastor Tyler said before he saw Scott—"She is in a much better place"—seemed to stick in his mind.

"I know Amy is in heaven. She was a great Christian. I remember how she shared her testimony about asking Jesus to come into her heart and life and make her a Christian. She always said she was a poor manager of her own life, and Jesus did a better job. I know she is not just gone but gone to another place. But I"—Cameron bit his lip and stammered out his words—"I can't understand why we have to deal with death."

Like Deni, Cameron grew up in a Christian home and was taught that death is only falling asleep and going to be with the Lord. But Cameron spent too many hours growing up watching horror flicks and visualizing death as something morbid, spooky, and demonic. He learned in church and from the Bible that demons were real. Cameron always seemed to fear this thing called *death*. Since Cameron was an upstanding professional in the community, he could not tell anyone, other than Deni, that he had nightmares about an outer-worldly being, Ser Pentino, whose name was Drawg. Drawg was the ruler of darkness and had supernatural powers. Cameron believed that this being was not just a figment of his imagination but the same person the Bible described as Satan, the prince and power of the air and prince of death and darkness. Now a nightmarish reality stormed upon him like his night terrors with Amy's passing.

Bang, bang, bang, bang, bang!

Someone was pounding on his window. It was Scott.

"Scott, you scared me!"

"I had to tell you its okay. Amy is fine."

"What do you mean she is fine?"

"She's fine! She's with the Lord. I talked with the paramedics, and no one is really sure what caused her to go over that embankment. She went out early to town to pick up some food for her ladies meeting. But last night Amy made it a point to tell me that she was ready."

"Ready for what?"

"She said she was ready to be with the Lord. She was not afraid anymore to die."

"You don't mean—"

"No, not suicide. She meant whenever it was her time, she was ready to be with the Lord."

Cameron envied the unexplainable peace that Scott had at that moment. Superficially reassuring Scott that he understood, he drove off, pushing his nagging thoughts to back of his mind.

Cameron, Deni, and Cody arrived back home. Cameron noticed a car parked on the side of the road.

"It's Pastor Tyler. He must have taken a shortcut here."

"I wonder what he wants," Deni said, confused.

Pastor Tyler emerged from his vehicle with a smile and walked toward Cameron. "You left the hospital in such a hurry. I wanted to speak with you about something that couldn't wait."

Pastor Tyler's answer seemed like it took minutes rather than seconds to Cameron. "This may not seem like the time or the place, but I have been putting this off. I need an assistant, and I know you have been studying pastoral courses. I want your help. The Lord knows the church could use a dedicated and knowledgeable man like you. Give it some serious thought and prayer, and let me know just as soon as you can. Hurry, though, Cam. The Lord could come back any time."

Cameron responded with a half smile and a look of surprise. "Thanks for considering me. I will get back to you."

While Pastor Tyler drove away, Cameron, still in shock from the question the pastor asked him, could only hear his last words: *"Hurry, though, Cam. The Lord could come back any time."*

How many times had Cameron heard this over his lifetime? He knew it, but he wondered if he really believed it. Was he willing to live as though that were true? Stepping up to the responsibility of a pastor seemed like a tall order for a busy chiropractor and family man.

"What did he want?" Deni asked.

"He asked me to be his assistant."

"What did you say?"

"I told him I would think about it and get back to him."

"What do you want to do? Are you ready to take on that responsibility? What are you going to tell him? Cameron? Cameron?"

"Oh, uh, I don't know. Let's get some lunch."

Word of Amy Benson's accident and death spread like wildfire through Mariah City. No one could figure out why Amy lost control of her vehicle and ended up on the bottom of a hillside. Investigations were still being conducted by local and state authorities, as there was some suspect of foul play. The Christian community was talking about it because Amy was so well known by many in the community. She was loved and would be greatly missed.

The memorial service was being held at Mariah City Community Church, and the huge crowd that was expected to attend emerged as a testimony to just how important Amy was to so many people in Mariah City.

Pastor Kit Tyler came to the podium after most of the attendees were seated. "Friends, we will miss our dear sister, Amy Benson. I don't have to tell you what a dedicated Christian lady Amy was. This huge crowd, to date, is the largest crowd we have ever had attend Mariah City Community Church. Amy always said she was working on getting more folks to church. Well, Amy, you did it. You did it! We are thankful, however, that Amy is with our Lord and at peace. Therefore, this is really a celebration."

Pastor Tyler's countenance quickly changed from a hearty smile with gleaming eyes of compassion to a more sobering expression.

"Though Amy is with her Lord and is enjoying the bliss of heaven, she left behind those who sorrow. The Bible tells us that we who are left behind will not all sorrow. It goes on to say that someday, in the twinkling of an eye, we who know Christ will be changed from mortals to immortals, and we will be with the Lord forever. Take comfort in that, my Christian friends."

Pastor Tyler turned toward Scott. "Scott, we know this will be difficult for you. We know how much you loved Amy and how close you two were. I just want you to know that we of Mariah City Community Church will be with you and will be here for you. You are in our thoughts and prayers continuously."

Pastor Tyler never left out any opportunities to invite people for the Sunday services. He continued. "Folks, I want to offer many of you here today who are not members or regular attendees of our church to come out on Sunday. I want you to know you are invited. Many people just don't go to church because no one ever invited them. Well, none of you here can ever use that excuse again."

The crowd responded with laughter, smiles, and nodding of heads to show their approval of this warmhearted servant and of Mariah City Community Church.

As Pastor Tyler began to close the service and move the crowd to the cemetery for the intermit service, Cameron's love and compassion for his friend Scott made him forget about his emotional struggle about death. Cameron began to wonder what he could do to be a true friend to Scott.

He was also thinking about what God had in mind for Mariah City Community Church with so many attending this service impacted by Amy's life. He knew God was up to something. But what?

Chapter Two

CAMERON KALE'S VICTORY OVER THE ENEMY

It was 2:00 a.m. the next morning, and Cameron was startled out of his sleep.

He was a dreamer, and tonight was no different. Wrestling in his sleep, Cameron tossed and turned over the question Pastor Kit Tyler had asked him the previous day. It was this question that fueled the nighttime drama in Cameron's mind as he lay next to Deni, who slept without a stir. A host of ghoulish characters sat like a jury in the jury box at a trial, accusing Cameron of dishonesty about being prepared to be a minister of the gospel.

"You can't even handle the subject of death, and you dare to be a minister of God!" they droned. Another person who looked like one of Pastor Kit's deacons accused him of not being able to teach others about the purpose of death for a Christian. Still other faces he did not recognize screamed out as if to condemn him that he was not suitable to be a pastor.

"No!" Cameron yelled out. "You are all wrong! I am not guilty!"

"Yes," the clouded faces said. "You are guilty, Cameron. We are your accusers!"

"Who are you?" Cameron asked, panicking.

Like something out of a weird sci-fi movie, all the accusers merged into one face and came into bright focus out of the dark— it was Ser Pentino, whose name is also Drawg of the spirit world.

Cameron rose up quickly from his soaking wet pillow. "No, you are not my accuser!" Believing himself to be awake, Cameron was startled to see a figure in the corner of his bedroom with a light over him that did not come from any light receptacle or lamp. It was merely suspended over him. The figure was a small man, very well dressed in a business suit, with a soft voice. He smiled at Cameron.

"There is no need to fear me. My name is Ser Pentino. We have met before in some of your dreams. It is true. You have done no wrong. I have observed you over the years of your life, and you have always been a person who cares about helping others. You have been good to many people, like your friend, Amy, whom I have taken to be with me."

"No, you are lying," Cameron retorted vehemently. "Amy was a strong believer. She is *not* with you but with the Lord, who has prepared a mansion for her, and she will live eternally in joy with Him, who is Lord of all."

The man in the suit began to growl and cower as if he was in pain. He then jumped to the other side of the room as if he had the paws of a lion. "I am the accuser of the brethren. It doesn't matter what you say. I will make others believe you are no good. I will come against you, because you stand with my greatest enemy, Jesus, who claims to be Lord."

"He is Lord," Cameron proclaimed to Ser Pentino. "He is my Lord, and I will stand with Him for all eternity!"

Disappearing as a vapor of smoke, the haunting image immediately left Cameron's room. Cameron, whether he had been dreaming or was awake, realized he had encountered the enemy of the ages: Satan himself.

Deni began to awake. Although it was still only 3:00 a.m., she thought she heard Cameron's voice and the voice of another.

"Deni! Wake up! I have Pastor Tyler's answer."

"What? You woke me up now, in the middle of the night, to tell me this? Couldn't it have waited until the morning?"

"No, listen!" With a sense of urgency, Cameron poured out his heart to Deni with passion. "I dreamed I was before my accusers, and they became one accuser. It was God's enemy telling me I should not accept the pastor's offer."

"Cameron, have you been sipping brandy?"

"I need to tell you my dream. Well, it wasn't really a dream. I actually, uh, never mind—just know that God gave me strength tonight. He gave me strength to stand against the tricks and lies of the enemy and declare that Jesus is Lord. When I took my stand to obey the Lord, the enemy ran away."

Deni was concerned that Cameron might have been too stressed over Amy's passing but realized that he was making more sense and showing more passion for the Lord than he had for years. She listened intently.

"The enemy lied to me, telling me that Amy was with him, but I knew better. When I proclaimed the truth, his power seemed to melt away and have no grip on me. As I boldly told him Amy was a believer and with the Lord, who had prepared a home for her, my nagging fears about death left me. I felt the Lord's strength, and I knew Amy was okay. Deni, God wants me to stand for him and teach truth to those who need truth. He wants me to teach about Him, as well as be a comfort to others. I have been so afraid of everything, and now I know I have to stop being afraid and trust in the Lord. I am going to tell Pastor Tyler tomorrow that I will accept his offer to be his assistant."

"Cameron, I am proud of you. Tomorrow is coming quickly. Let's get some sleep, and we'll talk more in the morning."

"I love you, Deni. Good night." Cameron laid back into his pillow, turning his head toward the moonlit window, and stared at the starry night. "Thank You, Lord, for knowing my heart and hearing my cry," he whispered with a smile. "Thank You for being the Creator of the moon, the stars, and the Kale family too. Thank You that You *are* God and Lord and that You protect us from the evil one. Good night, Abba Father! Good night."

Chapter Three

CAMERON KALE, THE EVANGEL

"Good morning, dear," Deni said. "What makes you so bright and cheerful?"

"I had a good night's sleep!"

"Since when have you ever had a good night's sleep? You are always dreaming."

Cameron remembered his dream and his encounter with Ser Pentino but knew a change had come over him. He was different now. He had won a battle. He knew God wanted to use him to help others who wrestle with truth and God's enemy. Today was a new day.

"Cam, we have to get to church early this morning. I am helping the ladies with the potluck."

"That's okay. I have to talk with Pastor Tyler early this morning and give him the good news."

"What news is that?"

"You know, about becoming his assistant."

"You aren't serious about that, are you?"

"Don't you remember our talk last night? I told you God showed me in what seemed like a dream that I was meant to be called to preach the gospel."

"Cameron Kale, now I know you've been dreaming! When are you going to find the time to do all this? Are you sure? Do you really believe God wants you to assist Pastor Tyler?"

"Yes, I do."

"Well, I have not seen you this passionate about anything in a long time. I support you. Whatever you decide, I am with you."

Deni had always been a helpmeet to Cameron since they first dated thirteen years earlier. She always seemed to come alongside him to help whenever he needed it. While not many marriages are made in heaven, this was one that was close.

"Cody! Are you ready? We are leaving for church!"

He could hardly hear his parents over his iPhone plugged into special speakers blasting out some of his favorite tunes.

"We are leaving for church!"

"Okay, coming!"

———✿✿✿———

The Kales reach the church after a brief ten-minute drive to downtown Mariah City, only a block from where Cameron attended night school to complete his master's degree in biblical studies. Some of his professors were also members of Mariah City Community Church. Cameron met Pastor Kit sitting in his study.

"Good Morning, Cam. You know Jepson LaPlant, don't you, one of our newest deacons?"

Cameron turned to look at Jepson as if he had seen a ghost—it was the man who was in his dream as one of his accusers. "Uh, yes, good morning, Jepson. Beautiful day, isn't it?"

"Yes, sir. This is the day the Lord has made."

"Yes, it is," Cameron replied.

"Well, Cam, I am hoping you have an answer for me," Pastor Tyler boldly pronounced. "Did you pray and think over what we talked about?"

"Yes, Pastor, I have, and I am very happy to tell you that I believe this is what God has planned for me all along. Yes, I would love to be your assistant."

Strangely, Cameron noticed an odd expression on Jepson's face. He made a face like he had indigestion. The mood in the room clearly changed. Cameron felt it. He had experienced this before. Cameron could feel oppression in the room.

Pastor Tyler saw a look of concern in Cameron's eyes. "Cam, are you okay? Are you sure this is what you want to do?"

"No, uh, I mean yes, I do believe I am supposed to do this—I mean, I want to do this, or I believe the Lord wants me to do this, and I want it too."

Something was odd about Jepson. He couldn't put his finger on it, but Jepson seemed to react to Cameron's announcement of acceptance to become Pastor Tyler's assistant. He wanted to chalk up his feelings about Jepson to the fact that this man was an accuser in his dream last night, but it seemed so much more than that.

"Congratulations, Cam. Welcome aboard. This will be an exciting journey. I know the congregation will be excited about this new appointment. I will announce it this morning, if you don't mind."

"No, that would be great!" Cameron exclaimed.

The worship service began, and the worship team led the church in a set of well-known and heartfelt praise songs.

"Deni, Does it feel weird in here?"

"What do you mean?" she whispered. "You never talk about feelings. What's going on?"

"Nothing, it's just that it feels like what Pastor Kit said you feel like when there is spiritual warfare."

As quietly as Deni could possibly be, sitting shoulder to shoulder with other members of the church close by, she answered Cameron bluntly. "Dr. Kale, are you going on about your dreams again?"

"No," he whispered. "But God must be doing something big, because the enemy is not happy."

"May I have your attention?" Pastor Tyler announced at the conclusion of the worship set. "I want to share some good news with you all. Folks, I am happy to announce that I have appointed

Cameron Kale as my assistant pastor. Cam, come up here and share a few words with the church. Tell them why you are here."

The church applauded as Cameron made his way to the front and up on the platform.

"Thank you. It is good to see so many of you here who were at Amy's memorial. I see you took Pastor Tyler seriously."

Everyone laughed.

"I know Amy is pleased looking down from heaven to see so many of you here at church. I am happy to accept this invitation. It was really not expected, even though most of you know I attended Bible school just down the road between chiropractic appointments."

More laughter rang through the auditorium.

"I appreciate some of you professors who attend here and who have helped to provide a biblical education for me. You have invested in my life. But I want to share with you something the Lord made clear to me last night in a dream. Some don't pay attention to dreams, but I do. Sometimes God chooses to get our attention through dreams because He can't get our attention any other way."

Some *amens* came from the crowd.

"But last night God showed me that I have a responsibility to stand for Christ and to tell others how they need a Savior—the Savior, Jesus Christ. I am like many of you.

"Most of us are professional people in our city, but while we look like we have it together on the outside, we are a mess inside. We have fears, fiery trials, and phobias. Some of us are afraid to live, and others of us are afraid to die. I learned a lot yesterday from my good friend Scott, who lost his wife in that car accident. He comforted me when I should have comforted him. But he was confident about where Amy was. I have struggled with the idea of death most of my life. Today, though, I want to tell you that Amy is looking down on us and cheering us who know Christ to keep up the race toward our heavenly home. We don't need to fear death, or fear anything, if we know that Jesus Christ is Lord. He is our victor and our salvation. If you put your trust in Him and let him manage your life, like Amy used to say, 'He will come into your life and clean up your mess.' I wonder if anyone today would be honest and say they don't know Jesus in that way and want to receive Him.

"Is there anyone? Don't be ashamed. Come up to the altar, and counselors will meet you up front to pray with you and show you how you can know Christ like Amy did and like I know him."

In a matter of seconds, individuals and families began to slip out of their pews and come forward. Many were folks who attended Amy's memorial but had never been in Mariah City Community Church before. Over 100 people came forward to receive Christ as their Savior.

Deni sat with her hand over her open mouth, which was drawn into a smile that wrinkled her cheeks. Cameron was praising God and moved with tears as he saw the people come forward to receive Christ.

While it seemed that God was bringing some revival to this little church of 1,500 people, Cameron discerned a contrary spirit in the room. Looking through the crowd to some now-empty pews on the other side of the church, Cameron saw a small man dressed in a nice business suit—it was Ser Pentino. This time he was not startled but righteously angry that he would dare to show up in God's house and at a time like this. Cameron gazed at Ser Pentino and nodded his head to let him know he was not afraid but stood behind the power of Jesus Christ.

Filled with God's spirit and the gift of faith, Cameron looked again only to see that Ser Pentino had left.

—◦◦◦—

As the Kales made their way out of church, Dr. Cecil James, the president and a professor at the Bible university Cameron had attended, came up to congratulate Cameron.

"Cameron, Pastor Tyler could not have picked a better man. I always knew God had something special planned for you. Keep up the good work. If there is anything I can do to be of help to you, let me know. I mean that."

"I will, Dr. James. Thank you."

Driving home the long way for a Sunday afternoon ride in the beautiful sunshine of Nevada, Deni asked Cameron who the little man was dressed in the business suit.

Cameron turned his head toward her as if it was spring-loaded. "You saw him?"

"Yes, who is he?"

If Cameron doubted what he experienced that night in his bedroom with his accuser, he didn't now. "Deni, that was the man I have dreamed about. That is Ser Pentino."

"When I looked at him, he looked back at me, and it gave me the creeps. His eyes were like fire, and he made me feel uncomfortable."

"Don't worry. 'Greater is He that is in us than he that is in the world.'"

Chapter Four

BE ON YOUR GUARD

Cameron Kale actually slept through an entire night without a dream or any kind of bizarre spirit encounters. Seeing God's hand upon his life at Mariah City Community Church the day before, as well as seeing so many giving their lives to serve Jesus Christ, gave him a peace that surpassed understanding.

Cameron fixed some toast and coffee, letting Deni sleep in. He felt he had provided enough excitement in her life lately and that she deserved a rest.

"Good morning, Cam." Deni sleepily walked into the kitchen in her housecoat reaching for a cereal box. "You look rested."

"I am not used to that, you know." Cameron looked up from his newspaper. "Isn't it great? I feel on top of the world today. Like Superman. Sort of invincible."

"Yeah, well, maybe I'll find you a cape, and you can fly over to the grocery store to get some more milk."

Cameron chuckled.

Deni wandered over to Cody's room and shouted, "Code, time to get ready for school. You don't want to oversleep! You have a test today, remember? Cody! Wake up, buddy."

Deni thought it was odd that she didn't even get a typical acknowledging groan from him to signal to his mother that he was working on getting up. There was an eerie silence from Cody's room.

"Cody?"

As Deni entered the room, she saw his bed empty with blankets piled up on the floor. The room looked like a shipwreck of Cody's belongings, seeming as though they had been tossed around the room. Deni shrieked.

"Cam! It's Cody! He's gone!"

Cameron ran to the room and saw books and clothes and some of Cody's prize possessions on the floor. An autographed baseball and some broken model cars were crumpled and scattered around the room, as if a tornado had passed through it. It looked as if there had been a struggle.

"Cameron, call the police! Something has happened to Cody. He wouldn't do this. Someone has come in here!"

Cameron raced through the house as if he were a mad man. He checked the doors and windows. "Deni, the doors and windows are all locked! I can't figure how anyone got in here or how they got out!"

"What are we going to do, Cameron?" Deni asked, sobbing.

"I don't know. I don't know. I guess we better call 911 and tell them what is happening."

As Cameron went to pick up his cell phone from his desk, he heard a video call on his laptop. Someone was trying to Skype him. Cameron answered the call while Deni stood behind him. A face emerged.

"Hello, Cameron. You know who I am, don't you?" It was Ser Pentino.

"That's the man I saw at Mariah City Community Church in a business suit," Deni said.

"Cameron Kale, I have your son, Cody, with me."

"What have you done? Where is Cody?"

"Oh, don't worry. He is here, safe and sound. I will take care of him. You will get him back, of course, but first you must do something for me."

"What is it? What could I possibly do for you? Do you want money? I can go to the bank."

"I don't need your money. But I do need something from you."

"What is it? Anything—just give me our Cody back." Deni was so frightened that Cameron could feel her trembling behind him.

"Meet me tonight at midnight at the Mariah City Parking Garage on Main Street. Come alone. I will tell you then what I want you to do. I will have Cody with me, but don't try any tricks. They won't work on me anyway. I am the master of tricks. So you can't fool me." The call ended.

Cameron stood stunned, holding Deni close to himself. "Deni, I don't know what to do, but I know that I can't sit around and wait before something happens to Cody. I pray that he is alive. He has to be alive!"

"What about the police?"

"I can't call them. You heard Ser Pentino. He will know if I call the police. We can't take the chance that Cody could be harmed or even—" He could not get the word *killed* out of his mouth.

"Come on. Let's check out the parking garage downtown. Maybe we can find some clues as to where Cody is."

Cameron and Deni get in Old Blue and raced out of the driveway and onto the street, zigzagging from street to street until they arrived at the parking garage.

Driving through the maze of parking areas top to bottom, the panicked couple could not find any clues as to where Ser Pentino and their son might be.

—◦◦◦—

In an open space that once was used for storing pylons and tools below the parking garage, Ser Pentino and Cody were securely hidden from the possibility of anyone finding them. This room was sealed off and had not been used for years. No one really knew about this room, except, of course, Ser Pentino.

Ser Pentino, also known as Drawg, took the duct tape he had used to cover Cody's mouth off. "What do you have to say for yourself, young Cody?"

"You will never get away with this. My dad will find you and—"

"And what, young Cody? Do you think your dad has powers like I do? He is mortal. I am a spirit. I am the prince and power of the air. I rule the earth, you know!"

Ser Pentino loosened the bands he had used to bind Cody's hands and feet.

"You see, I am not so bad. Some might even dare to worship me. Some say that I am a devil and paint me with a red suit and horns. I am nothing of the sort. I am an angel. In fact, my real name is Lucifer. I was cast from heaven many millennia ago only because I emulated the God of the universe. I merely wanted to be like Him. It was just a simple compliment. But instead of respecting me, He was jealous of me and cast me and a third part of all of the angels in heaven out with me. He cast me to the earth to inhabit a serpent, to crawl on my belly. How humiliating. That is the God your dad, Cameron Kale, serves."

Cody countered Ser Pentino. "You are a liar. God is not like that. He is a good and gracious God. If He cast you out of heaven, it was because you were trying to be God."

"Oh, a bright one!" hissed Ser Pentino. "I know. I have seen you reading your Bible. It's such a shame that you believe these things only because you have been brainwashed by your parents."

"It's true that my parents taught me things about the Bible. But I believe them for myself. I am a believer in Jesus Christ."

"Yes, you are, and what a shame. You fool. You will die a shameless death like all the rest of those petty praising losers."

As Ser Pentino turned his back to Cody, Cody saw a large stick the size of a baseball bat and took the opportunity to grab it. Swinging the stick with everything he had, Cody grunted with all of his strength and watched what seemed surreal as the heavy stick flew through Ser Pentino as if it was a knife slicing through melted butter. His body separated into masses of disproportioned body parts and then came back together as if he had been untouched.

Cody jumped back in horror at what he witnessed and realized that some of what this serpent-man was saying was true. He was a spirit being. He must have been God's enemy himself. Cody froze lifeless at what he saw next.

Ser Pentino revealed himself in the ugly and demonic person that he was, Drawg, the spirit of the underworld. His body was a man's, but he had the feet and head of a lion. His face was grotesque when he opened his mouth. Out of it came serpents and dark ghoulish spirit beings that surrounded him like subjects before their king. He had an odor of brimstone and of rotting flesh. He was repugnant and horrible to look at.

Cursing and growling intermittently, Drawg stared at Cody as if he would devour this innocent young man. While Cody stood motionless in the dark, cold corner of the cement-block room, Drawg began to change before his eyes into the most beautiful being that he had ever seen. Staring as if he was in a trance, he saw a transformation of this being that defied description. The light and the beauty of this angel of light mesmerized him. Ser Pentino now revealed himself as Lucifer, the archangel of God, who had been cast from heaven. Cody seemed to be transfixed by this appearance. He could only hear words coming from the being that sounded cheerful, kind, and friendly.

Lucifer reached his hand out to Cody. "Take my hand, son. I will not harm you. Come to me, and I will give you rest."

Cody heard something, or someone, within himself speak: "He is transforming himself into an angel of light."

Cody had heard this inner voice as he was reading the Bible in his room. It was the Spirit. The voice became louder and louder within him.

"False apostles transform themselves into angels of light."

Suddenly, Cody came out of his trance. The Word of God spoken to him by the Spirit opened his eyes. He was no longer fooled.

"You are not good. You are the enemy of God. You are a liar and a thief and are trying to make yourself to be like Christ."

Lucifer quickly changed back into his human form, Ser Pentino. "One last time. Yes, you are correct again. I am a liar and a thief. I am the enemy of Christ, and because you belong to Christ, I am *your* enemy too."

—◦◦◦—

It was now close to midnight. Cameron left Deni with Pastor Kit Tyler so that he could meet Ser Pentino and find out how he could get Cody back. Pastor Tyler warned Cameron of the danger that he was in and that he would be better off contacting the police. Cameron insisted that he couldn't risk Cody's life. Cameron had not told Pastor Tyler everything he knew about this Ser Pentino for fear that the pastor would think he was losing his mind. He knew he would have to sit down with him and share with the pastor what had been happening in his life and about Ser Pentino being present at Mariah City Community Church the day so many people came forward to accept Christ as their Savior.

Cameron got in his car and headed back to the parking garage. Unaware, Ser Pentino had summoned his spirit messengers to find Cameron as he drove toward the garage. As Cameron drove down familiar streets, the streetlights began to dim. Things seemed so much darker in the city that night. He couldn't figure out why everything looked so dark. He turned down a street he thought was only a few streets from the parking garage, but it became a dead-end. A little confused but thinking that he was just stressed from this real nightmare experience, he turned around and headed back onto another street that became another dead-end street. Cameron stopped the car and rubbed his face and shook his head.

"What is happening? I am so confused. I am feeling so overwhelmed that I don't know what is happening to me. I feel so weak. I don't know if I can handle this. I am so afraid that I will never see Cody again! I don't know what to do." Cameron began to sob. "I don't know if I have ever been so weak." In a brief moment of seeming despair and silence, he remembered the Bible's teaching that "strength is made perfect in weakness." Cameron felt cast down, depressed, and deeply discouraged but not forsaken. He bowed his head and prayed.

"Lord, I know you are with me. I am not forsaken. You have a plan. I need your help. You are not the author of confusion. I know that you know where Cody is. Would you take me to him,

Lord? I pray that you will give me strength to stand in this evil day against the schemes of the evil one. I pray it with authority in the name of Jesus Christ. Amen."

Cameron felt like he had stepped into a phone booth, put on the Superman suit, and could leap a tall building with a single bound. The Spirit gave Cameron amazing strength and focus.

Turning his Camaro around, Cameron sped out of the dead-end and onto another street that was familiar. Speeding near the parking garage, Cameron asked the Lord again, "Help me find him, Lord. You see where my boy is."

Cameron remembered a room that he used to play in with his friends as a boy. They were not supposed to play there, but it was a cool place to hide out and hang out as a kid. He remembered that the room had been sealed off by cinder blocks just behind the number one painted on the wall of the first level of the garage. Cameron screeched into the garage and headed toward the big blue number one painted on the wall.

He could hear an inner voice. "He's there, Cameron. He's there."

Cameron dropped his gearshift into the next gear and headed straight for the wall. Cameron whispered a prayer: "Be all right, Cody. Be all right." Within seconds, Cameron smashed through the concrete block wall with Old Blue and braked to a stop inside the large room that he remembered.

No one was there except Cody sitting in the opposite corner of the large room with his head bowed into his knees.

"Cody!" Cameron pushed his car door open and ran through the crumbled blocks to grab his son. "Are you okay? Are you hurt? Where is Ser Pentino?"

Cody bear-hugged his dad. "Dad, I will never make fun of you again when you tell us about your dreams."

"I'm glad, son. I am so glad you are okay."

"I am, now that you are here. Dad?"

"What, Cody?"

"The Spirit was here too. He is the one who saved me."

"He saved me too, Cody. He saved me too."

Chapter Five

MAKING CONNECTIONS IN GOD'S KINGDOM

Cody was now safe and heading back home. Neither Cameron nor his son was too concerned about the beating his dad's car took plunging through the cinder-block wall in the parking garage. What was important was that dad and son were together and Cody was safe.

"Dad, I'm sorry that I didn't believe you when you told mom and me about Ser Pentino. To be honest, I thought you were going crazy."

"Don't worry about it, son. I understand. There were times I thought I was crazy too."

"You know, even though we are taught that these things are true in the Bible, we really don't believe like we should. My Sunday school teacher, Nick Sarren, said that God's enemy is stalking us and wants to destroy us."

"He's right."

"But he also taught us that we can't fight this enemy with physical things. They don't work against him. I understood that, Dad, when I was with Ser Pentino."

"What do you mean?"

"When his back was turned to me, I hit him with a huge stick I found in the garage."

"What happened?"

"It was not like anything I have ever seen. The stick went through his body, but it didn't hurt him."

"I believe you, Cody. The Bible says that the only weapons that work against him are the words of God. When we speak the truth and believe it, the enemy cannot stand. He will run away from the truth."

"That's good to know, but why didn't we really believe it when we read it in the Bible?"

"That's a great question. Sometimes our faith is weak and God has to stir things up in our lives so that we will believe Him. I guess that is what happened to us. We have a patient and loving God. Sometimes He uses tough love, bringing difficult trials into our lives, so that we will pay attention to Him and trust Him."

"Well, Dad, I am thankful to learn the truth, but I hope I don't have to learn it that way again."

"Me too, son."

Cameron and Cody arrived at Pastor Tyler's home. Pastor Tyler and Deni had been in constant prayer for several hours as they waited to hear something.

Deni ran out of Pastor Tyler's house as they drove up. "Cody!" She grasped Cody and kissed him. "Are you okay? Have you been hurt?"

"Mom, I'm okay. Dad saved me."

She grabbed Cameron and kissed him like a schoolgirl. "I love you, Cameron Kale. You are my hero. My Superman."

Cameron blushed, thinking it had been a long time since he had blushed from his wife's kiss.

Pastor Tyler spoke up. "Good job, Cameron. A hero indeed. You'll make a great assistant pastor. Of course, I knew that before I asked you."

"Thanks, Pastor Tyler. But really, all the credit goes to the Lord. Right, Cody?"

"That's right, Dad!"

"What do you say we go home? It's late, and we could use a good night's sleep."

Cameron and Deni knew the only way they could truly find their home secure and keep Cody safe was to pray and ask for the Lord's protection.

Cody could not remember how Ser Pentino got into their house or how he was able to get him to the hidden room in the garage. It all seemed a blur to him. Cameron, Deni, and Cody prayed together that night and asked for the Lord to watch over Cody. They realized how important it was for them to pray together. This was not a common practice in the busy Kale home but would become a habit from now on!

As Cameron and Deni turned off the lights by their bed, Cameron could only think about what Ser Pentino said: "*I want something from you.*" Cameron knew he had Cody only because the Spirit intervened, but thought to himself, *What did Ser Pentino want?*

———

Early the next morning, Cameron was surprised to wake up with the knowledge that he did not meet Ser Pentino in his dreams that night. It had been a calm and restful night.

Cody walked into Cameron and Deni's bedroom. "Good morning, parents."

"Good morning, Code. It looks like the Lord answered our prayers, didn't he?"

"Yeah, he did. I had a pretty good night's sleep, considering what happened yesterday. It all seems like a dream. Like one of your dreams, Dad!"

"I know. I was thinking the same thing. Well, we can all thank God this morning that Cody is safe and at home with us. We also need to pray that God will protect us from Ser Pentino. Now that I have accepted God's call, His enemy has targeted my family and me. We shouldn't be afraid, but we need to stay close to the Lord and seek His protection from this evil person."

Deni drove Cody to school and gave specific instructions to Cody to stay with his friends and not go anywhere outside of the school until she came to pick him up.

Cameron drove to the clinic to start a busy day of seeing patients.

Amy Thompson, Cameron's secretary, called into Cameron's office. "Dr. Kale, your first patient is here. He's a walk-in. He says he knows you."

"Thanks, Amy. I'll be right in." Dr. Kale entered the exam room where his patient Jepson LaPlant was waiting.

"Hello, Cameron."

"Jepson! What are you doing here?"

"Well, the back is a funny thing. I heard that you are the best in town when it comes to fixing a hurting back."

"Thanks for that encouragement. Sure, I can help you." Let's take some X-rays and get a look at that back. The X-ray tech will be in to see you, and I will be back in a few minutes."

Dr. Kale came back into the room after he had a chance to read the films.

"Well, looking at the X-ray that was done, it looks like your back is injury-free. You might have some muscle tension moving your vertebrae that is causing your pain. Let me have a look." He lowered Jepson on his table and began to examine his back. "So have you had things that are stressing you?"

"Well, if you must know, I have been tense about things at the church."

"Yes, you have some tight muscles in the lower region of your back and some in the upper back too. Church? What tensions, if you don't mind my asking?"

"Well, you know, I am a deacon, and I'm a little stressed over the politics at church."

"Politics? There are politics in the church?" Cameron was using his keen sense of humor.

"Well, there are politics in every church."

"What politics have you so stressed?"

"It's Pastor Kit Tyler."

Cameron paused his exam. "Whoa, Jepson. If you have problems with the pastor, you need to talk with him directly."

"Well, that's the problem I have. We have. Several deacons have approached pastor about different things." Jepson wasn't specific but was deeply troubled about the things he told Cameron were troubling him. "He's going off the deep end, Cameron."

Cameron wanted to be a good listener to Jepson, but he did not want to be a participant in gossip, particularly gossip about the pastor. "You can't be serious. Pastor Tyler has been a tremendous blessing to the Kale family. My life has really been blessed by him."

"Yes, I know he asked you to be his assistant. I knew you might not understand. Why would you? Pastor Tyler has become your new boss."

"Well, I trust him and have no reason to think anything different about him. I'm just concerned that you think of him the way you do."

"Not just me, but several of the deacons are concerned about him."

"Breathe out…" As Dr. Kale pushed down on Jepson's spine, there was a cracking sound. "There. The lower back looks a little more aligned."

Jepson thought his crunch on the back was a little firmer than necessary. "*Ouch!*"

"There. The upper back looks better too."

"Cameron, I know you don't like what I am saying, but you have to at least listen to what the deacons have to say. Someday you will have to answer to us."

Cameron was about ready to give Jepson an alignment he would never forget but stopped in his tracks. "Have you ever studied the Bible? I mean really studied it? Your role as a deacon is to be a support in ministry to the pastor so that he can give himself to prayer and the ministry. You act as you are judge and jury of this man. The pastor is God's shepherd and leader. The pastor will answer to God for his actions, but we are to lovingly respect and support and follow our pastor as long as he is obedient to God's Word."

Jepson didn't have anything to say but a "thank you" for the adjustment.

Chapter Six

THE TRUTH WILL SET YOU FREE

Appointments had been slow all day, so Cameron left early, thinking that he would swing by the church and talk with Pastor Tyler. He needed to pick up his job description and discuss with him exactly what he would be doing to assist him. He also wanted to find out how the pastor had been doing. He wondered if Pastor Tyler was having a difficult time with his deacons.

"Hello, Cameron."

"Good afternoon, Pastor."

"Call me Kit. Seeing that we are going to work together, we can be on a first-name basis."

"Okay, I will do that, Pastor. Pastor—I mean Kit—how are you doing?"

"Great! God is good. How are Deni and Cody? That was quite a scare, Cameron. I am thankful it all worked out and that everyone is safe."

"I know you are upbeat and positive, but the life of a pastor is not always easy."

"You are right about that."

"Since I am going to work with you, it would help me to know how things are going at the church—I mean, in the ministry and leadership."

"Cameron, have you been talking to my deacons?"

"Well, one of them came and talked to me today."

"Jepson?"

"Yes, how did you know?"

"Well, he has been after me to retire for months. He says the other deacons feel this way too, but they have said nothing. He says that they trust him and he is speaking for them."

"What is all this about? Why does he want you to retire?"

"Well, he thinks I am old and senile and that he knows how to run the church better than I do. He's of the notion that the deacons are my bosses and that I am not listening to him. I didn't want to start your new job out telling you these things, but perhaps it will be better if you know upfront what you are dealing with. There are men in the church who are really not men at all."

"Huh?"

"What I mean is, they are letting their wives run the church and make decisions for them. They are Jezebels, Cameron."

"What, sir?"

"You know, they have the 'spirit of Jezebel,' the prophetess who came after Elijah and many other of God's prophets."

"Yes, I know who you mean."

"Well, Cameron, there are women—and men for that matter—who have the Jezebel spirit in the church. They are usurping authority that does not belong to them. They will come against any leadership that is godly and promote their self-agendas. You have to watch out for this. The Jezebel spirit is in the church, and it will ultimately destroy it if we give into this wicked anti-God spirit."

"Who are they? I mean, if you don't mind, sir."

"Well, you could easily recognize them, but I will tell you who they are. Sally McPherson. She has the sharpest tongue in the West! Watch your p's and q's around her. She will head you off at the pass and chop you off at the knees if you are not careful. This one loves to tell everyone the latest news and loves to spread her concerns to other church members. She is wonderful at spreading discord. Then there is Rita Ranting. There could be no better name for this one. She is a ranter, for sure. Everything in the church belongs to her. Of course, she earned it, if you know what I mean."

"Pastor, we don't earn anything. It is all by the grace of Jesus that we have anything."

"Tell that to Rita Ranting. There is Dawn Tharston, Tom's wife."

"Yes, I know her."

"She wants to be pastor. Cameron, I sound like a crabby, old, senile fool right now, but I have to tell you the truth, son. You will have some women, and men too, who want to be the person God did not call them to be. They will challenge you on everything because they believe they can do a better job. Take these challenges as blessings because God allows them in your life for good to grow you in your faith. But remember to be as wise as a serpent, not just as harmless as a dove. You cannot be an effective pastor as a doormat. Love people. Be patient with them. But let them know you are the man God called you to be and never, never yield to the spirit of Jezebel.

"Well, Cameron, through the power of this unholy trinity of women, their husbands—John, Henry, and Tom—have brought me tremendous grief. And Jepson is the ringleader of them all. You would not believe all of the demands that have come to me only through Jepson. He is their spokesperson."

"What kinds of demands? What do they think you are not listening to?"

"Do you remember the message I preached about what I believe God wants to do here in Mariah City, beginning right here at Mariah City Community Church?"

"Yes, I remember that sermon very well. In fact, it was the one I felt that God was calling me to be a part of. It was really my first call to the ministry."

"Yes, I remember you told me that after that service. I never forgot it. God showed me that He wants to use you in this church. God has bigger things planned for you here more than you even know. I believe that, Cameron. I believe it even more after I heard you share the gospel in church this past Sunday and a hundred people gave their lives to Christ. You are going to be part of the revival that God has planned for this church and for this city."

It was hard for Cameron to see this concerning himself, but considering the experiences of the past few days, it was making more sense to him.

"I have shared with the board my desire to see Mariah City Community Church expand its ministry to reach the community and that I needed someone like you to head up outreach in our church. I know you are the man for the job."

"Well, I don't see the problem, Pastor."

"Cameron, the reason Jepson has been trying to get rid of me is because I wanted to ask you to come on board. Jepson somehow thought he would be my assistant someday.

"Did he ever say anything to you about this?"

"Well, God gives some of us discernment. Jepson became a deacon because he was elected by the church to handle church business. He was willing to take on the job. He is not the sort of person I would trust with this church ministry. If I didn't think the church might toss me out and believe Jepson's senility claims, I would make him resign as deacon. But he has become a listener to everyone in the church and has become a busybody. He always seems to know what everyone is doing and gets in the loop of everyone's conversations. He offers to help others so that they can secure their trust and then spread some form of gossip about what is going on in the church, or the church according to Jepson."

"I had no idea."

"You don't know the half of it, Cam. Watch your back. Jepson is jealous of you, and I am not sure what he might do to get rid of me—and you—and try to secure this ministry for himself. You are a greater threat right now, because Jepson has seen what happened on Sunday. He does not joy in what happened like I do. He only sees this as a threat and a challenge to him. It will be more difficult for him to make a case to get rid of you because of what the church saw and heard on Sunday."

"That is interesting. He didn't even mention what happened on Sunday."

"I had to tell you the truth. Just remember that the truth will set you free. Keep your eyes on the Lord and don't be threatened by Jepson. Remember that we do not wrestle against flesh and blood but principalities, powers, the ruler of the darkness of this world, and spiritual wickedness in high places."

As Cameron left for home, his thoughts were going a hundred miles an hour. It was difficult to process all that he had heard that day. While some of the information was quite troubling, it was also a revelation to him and confirmation of his calling. Indeed, the truth was quite revealing and made Cameron free to see more clearly the scope of what God had planned for the Kale family in Mariah City.

If it was clear before, Cameron's calling was even clearer now that he was to carry the evangel to Mariah City.

Chapter Seven

TEMPTED TO GIVE UP GOD'S CALL

"Cameron! Cameron!" Deni was calling Cameron from the bedroom as she was stretched across her bed, writhing in pain.

"Deni, what's wrong?"

"I don't know. I'm hurting so badly. I can't stand the pain."

"Do you have the flu? When did this start?"

"I came home while you were still at work. I had some lunch and sat down to read my Bible. I am so happy about what God is doing in your life. I just felt like reading. And then—" Deni's explanation was interrupted by striking pain in her abdomen and lower back.

"I am calling the ambulance. You need to get to the hospital."

Cody overheard his dad and stayed back in his room, asking God to help his mom and his dad too. He could hear the siren and see the ambulance lights as the emergency vehicle pulled into the Kales' driveway.

"Dad, the ambulance is here!"

"Thanks, Cody. Send them in here."

The paramedics came into the master bedroom and began to check Deni's vitals while they asked her a series of questions. She tried to explain, but the pain was so intense that she could not finish her sentences.

"We need to get her to the hospital, Dr. Kale."

Deni was placed into the ambulance on a gurney and the ambulance pulled out of the drive. Cameron and Cody drove to the hospital behind it.

While Cameron tried to keep his mind on the road, he couldn't help feeling helpless as he thought about his life partner. She was in pain, but he felt it too. As he wrestled with emotion and doing his best to keep it at bay, there was another thought trying to make its way to take Cameron's mind captive: He had not seen or heard from Ser Pentino in days. He couldn't help but wonder what he was up to. He was certain, though, that he had not seen the last of his nagging enemy.

As the ambulance pulled up to the emergency room, Cameron remembered that he had just been there not even a week ago when Amy was brought to ER by ambulance. Cameron mustered up all of the courage he could to not think that the outcome for Deni could be like Amy's. He could not bear the thought of losing Deni. He needed her and now even more as a co-laborer in ministry.

Deni was rolled into the ER. While several ER doctors examined her, Cameron filled out some paperwork and kept Cody as comforted as he could. What was only minutes at the hospital seemed like hours.

In a very short time, Deni's condition was getting worse. The doctor examining her came into the waiting room to brief Cameron about her situation.

"I'm not sure what it is, Dr. Kale, but I have some good ideas. We are doing blood testing now and have her on an IV drip. We should know something soon. It looks like a strand of virus that we have only seen in the past few days."

"Can I see her?"

"Well, under most situations, I would say yes, but we can't take the risk if she has a virus that you will be contaminated too. If it is what we think it is, you and your son both will need a vaccination. I will have someone bring you and your son something to drink. It may be quite a wait."

"Thanks, Doctor."

As Cameron and Cody sat in the waiting room, the nurse brought Cameron some coffee and Cody a soda pop. "I hope you like Sprite."

"It's my favorite. Thanks."

"Thank you for the coffee. I need it."

After sitting through several episodes of *Monk* playing on a *Monk* marathon, Cameron and Cody were getting restless waiting to hear something.

"Cody, I'll ask the nurse if she has heard anything."

"Okay, Dad."

As Cameron got up, there was a blasting noise of sirens coming toward the ER with another emergency case. Cameron and Cody looked on with curiosity. As the medics ran the gurney through the hallway on the other side of the glassed-in waiting room, Cameron gasped, as he could see that it was Pastor Kit Tyler.

"Cody, wait here. I have to see if they will let me in to see Pastor Tyler." Cameron met a nurse in the hallway and asked her if he could see the patient that just arrived. "Ma'am, I'm the associate pastor of that man who just came in. For all practical purposes, I am the only pastor that he has."

"Sure, come on back." The nurse led Cameron into the room where Pastor Kit laid on a gurney.

"Pastor."

Struggling to breathe, Pastor Tyler tried to speak through the oxygen mask fastened to his face. "Cam—er—on."

"Don't try to talk, Pastor. I am here with you."

"What…what are you doing…here?"

"Deni is here. She got sick earlier. The doctors are with her."

Pastor Tyler struggled to breathe out a prayer. "Lord, God… please deliver us from evil."

The pastor's cry through the mask sent chills down Cameron's spine. He was scared. He felt alone. He felt helpless. Two people close to him were struggling, and their outcomes were not known.

Cameron didn't know what to do. He lost his sense to help his pastor. He felt so weak like he did the day he tried to comfort Scott. Now the thought of death came back to haunt him. Not his own death, but that of his wife and perhaps his pastor too.

The doctors told Cameron to wait in an empty room and said they would let him know when he could come back to be with the pastor.

Cameron did as they said and sat down in an empty room and didn't bother to turn on the lights. He sat there with his head bowed into his hands and knees. He sat in silence with his mind filling with a thousand thoughts. It seemed like one of his nightmares, but this was reality. Nearly exhausted, Cameron began to feel as though he could fall asleep. Though he did not hear the sound, someone closed the door, not knowing that Cameron was in the room.

In an almost dreamlike state, Cameron opened his eyes to see a bright fluorescent green-like glow in the corner of the room. He had seen this before in his dreams. First, he heard a voice.

"Cameron, give up this folly of assisting Pastor Tyler. Give up the idea of sharing the evangel. It will only bring grief to you and your family." Soon a familiar face emerged from the green light. It was Ser Pentino. "Cameron, you didn't think you would not see me again, did you?"

"No, I—"

"Remember I told you I wanted something from you? You were able to rescue your son, Cody. I was not able to convince you to give me what I wanted then. But I will convince you now."

"What do you want from me, Ser Pentino?"

"I want you to give up the idea of assisting Pastor Tyler. I want you to stop spreading the evangel—what you call the 'good news' about Jesus."

"You can't ask that. It is not yours to ask."

"But it is. And I have made sure that you will give me what I want. You see, your wife is very sick, and your pastor friend is very sick too. They have both contracted a strange virus. The doctors just call it another strand of virus. I call it one of my better death potions. Your partner and pastor will die before this night is over if you do not give me what I ask."

"No. It isn't true. It isn't possible!"

"Oh, it *is* possible, and it *is* probable. Do you want to take the chance that you could have helped two very important people you love but you chose not to and they died because of you, Cameron? Tell me, what will it be?

"You fancy yourself as some sort of superhero, Cameron Kale." Ser Pentino laughed. "Let's see you smash your way out of this one, Superman. You are no match for me. You are weak and incapable of helping those close to you. You are a joke, Cameron. You have no strength. You have no choices here. Who's going to help you now?"

Talking to himself, Cameron muttered, "I can't let them die. These past few days have been nothing but a battle. My own family's lives have been threatened, and my pastor's life is in jeopardy, not only by this virus, but also by those who want his ministry to end. Why would anyone want to hurt Pastor Kit? I can't believe this is happening to him." Calling out to God in anguish he cried, "Lord, I don't think I can handle this. I am too weak, and Pastor Kit has too many enemies." Cameron repeated what he said: "He has too many enemies." He repeated the word *enemies*. "The enemy!"

Chapter Eight

KNOW YOUR ENEMY

The Bible says that God establishes the thoughts of those who trust in Him.

It also says that the spirit of God intercedes for us when we do not know how to pray. He intercedes with groanings that cannot be uttered. Cameron began to think about the enemy. Ser Pentino was the enemy of Christ. Cameron began to feel a sense of strength he had not felt since he found Deni lying on her bed in pain.

"Lord, I come to You seeking forgiveness. I have sinned because I did not come to You when I found Deni sick. I did not pray over my family. I began to fear like I did when Amy was hurt. I failed to trust You, Lord."

Cameron knew the Lord had forgiven him. He immediately felt strengthened as if he had been pumped with steroids.

"Lord, forgive me that I could even entertain the thought of giving up my call to serve You. I know You will not let anything happen to Deni or Pastor Tyler. I pray in Your name, Lord, and by Your authority. Bind Your enemy and heal my wife and pastor. Lord. You are the Great Physician. I believe You have the power and desire to heal them. I am not putting You in a box, Lord. I know You have Your timing. I know You have a time for us to die, but I sense that this is not what you want. I pray in Your name to heal them, Lord. Heal them. In Jesus's name."

"Dr. Kale? Dr. Kale?"

Cameron could hear voices just outside his door. The doctor who led him to this empty room opened the door.

"Dr. Kale, you need to come. You won't believe it. Your wife, sir, and your pastor friend. They are both okay."

Cameron jumped from his seat like a runner out of his starting blocks. Wiping tears of joy from his face, he ran in to get Cody.

"Dr. Kale, we led your son back to see his mother. They are both okay."

Cameron rushed in to see Deni sitting up on the bed with a smile and reaching out to hug him.

Pastor Tyler was in the bed on the other side of the curtain, sitting up and smiling too. "Kale, I don't know what happened, but the docs say this was a miracle."

"Pastor Tyler, it was a miracle."

"You didn't know what you were bargaining for when you signed up with me, did you, son?"

"No, sir. I really didn't. But I am learning more every day how to be a better soldier of Jesus Christ. I know one thing. The battle gets easier if we first know who the enemy is."

"Cam, you sound like the Apostle Paul now."

"I will take that as a compliment."

"It is. What do you say I let you preach on Sunday and share that very thought? I could use a rest."

"Consider it done, Pastor."

Sunday morning came quickly, and Cameron had taken some time to study some passages of Scripture that related to his topic of knowing our enemy.

Just before the morning service, Cameron was sitting at a desk in a small office that Pastor Tyler gave to him so that he could study when he was at the church.

"Nice digs, Dad." Cody said, walking into the office.

"You like it?"

"It's okay. It could use some paint and decorating."

"You think so?"

He just smiled. "Do you want me to pray for you that God will help you with your sermon?" Cody decided that he was going to pray for his dad every time he had to preach.

"I would like that, Cody."

Cody wrapped his arms around his dad's neck and prayed. "God. Help Dad with his sermon. Let him say the words you want him to say. Be with him and help him, Lord. Amen." It was a simple prayer, but without a doubt, Cameron thought, it was heard by the Lord.

Cameron's sermon was upbeat and kept the attention of his audience. Not unlike the week before, Cameron detected a countering spirit in the large, high-ceilinged auditorium. He could not explain the feeling that he had other than the Lord was giving him discernment about the spiritual climate in the church. Cameron knew he had the gift of discernment, and he could discern that much of his audience accepted his message on the surface but that there was a disconnect somehow between his message and those who were attending that day.

"Paul says that we are to know our enemy," Cameron said. "In Ephesians six, he tells us that we are not to be tricked by our enemy. That tells me that we have to know who he is. I don't mean his name, but his character. We often think that we are battling people, but it isn't people we deal with—it is God's enemy using men and women who come against what God is doing in our lives. We know that not every sickness or physical trouble we encounter is the work of the devil, but oftentimes he can use sickness or our physical situation to bring difficulty in our lives. Remember that God will allow troubles in our lives to develop us, but the enemy of God uses them to destroy us."

As Cameron preached on, he could not help notice Jepson LaPlant in the congregation scooting around in his seat like a child moving about in the sandbox. He could not sit still. Something was troubling him. *No doubt he is most likely troubled with me*, Cameron thought. While the thought was fleeting, Cameron kept to his topic.

"Everyone here at Mariah City Community Church ought to know that if you are committed to Jesus Christ, you have an enemy. He hates you because he hated Jesus first. I also believe if you are committed to serve Jesus Christ in sincerity, you will get a dose of the enemy's troubles in your life. If you have no troubles, you may wonder if you are committed to the Christ you say you serve."

Jepson continued to act as though he was writhing in pain listening to this sermon and finally got up and left the auditorium. Cameron could not help notice his speedy exit.

Following the sermon, Pastor Tyler thanked Cameron. "Cameron, another great one. We certainly cannot do the work God has called us to do if we can't see what the serpent is up to."

Cameron continued to shake hands and greet friends and visitors who came to hear him since they heard about his evangelistic sermon the week before. It became the talk of the town in the city's churches.

"Deni, get Cody, and I will be there in just a moment. I have to get my books in my study."

"Okay. Don't take too long. We are supposed to have lunch with Pastor Tyler."

"I'll be right there."

As Cameron rounded the corner of the hallway in the offices of the church, he stopped short as he saw Jepson in the deacon's office sitting and talking quietly to a small man in a pinstriped suit. A sickening upset came to Cameron's stomach. His mouth opened wide as if the doctor was telling him to say "*ahh*" during a checkup. His face turned pale, and he suddenly turned aside so that he could not be noticed. It was Ser Pentino—Jepson knew about Ser Pentino!

Cameron could not help but think that Jepson was in some type of scandalous, heinous association with the prince of darkness himself. He was telling the congregation that they should know their enemy, but he did not actually mean know Ser Pentino personally. Cameron left without being noticed by either of the two persons talking in the deacon's room. He quickly came out to his car to meet Deni and Cody.

"Let's go!"

"Cam? You look like you've seen a ghost."

"Something like that. Ser Pentino!"

"Cameron, no!"

Cody piped up. "You saw him? Ser Pentino?"

"Yes, I did."

"How could you see him, Dad? We are at church!"

"Son, you are more likely to see the devil in church than any other place."

"Cameron? How? Where?"

"I will explain more later. Let's get to the restaurant to meet Pastor Tyler."

—✦✦✦—

The Kales were seated at a table at the new Fire and Ice restaurant in the area. The cozy ambiance of lighted candles on bright white linens adorned with different shades of blue dinner napkins set the atmosphere for a nice lunch. Waiters and waitresses waded through the crowds with ease, as they had mastered their craft of customer service and restaurant etiquette. A nicely dressed hostess led the Kales to their seats. Pastor Tyler had reserved a table but had also invited Scott Benson to have lunch with them. Since Scott was dealing with more alone time in the absence of his life partner, Pastor wanted him to join. Cameron was anxious to talk to Pastor Kit as he was being seated.

"Cameron, are you okay?" Pastor Tyler asked.

"Oh, I am fine, Pastor. Hey, Scott. Glad you could join us."

"I am too, Cameron. Deni, how are you? I heard that you had quite a scare a few days ago with some strange virus."

"We both had a scare," Pastor Tyler said, referring to him and Deni, "but God often works in a vacuum. He allows difficult situations to come about into our lives so that He can demonstrate His power. That is what He did for Deni and me. It was a miracle that we came out of that virus. One minute we were near death. The next we were ready to run a marathon."

"Well, speak for yourself, Pastor," Deni replied. "I was ready to go home and get a good night's sleep. It had been a long day that day, and I was ready to slow down from all of the drama."

"Drama indeed," Pastor Tyler affirmed. "By the way, Cam, has anyone caught that weird guy who kidnapped Cody?" Scott asked.

"Ah, no, they haven't."

"Well, have the police given you any possible leads?"

Pastor Tyler chimed in. "Cameron didn't go to the police. He was afraid that it might put Cody at risk. Praise God that Cameron was able to find Cody and bring him back home safe."

Cameron listened to Scott and Pastor go back and forth about the events of that night. He could only think about the fact that he had to tell Pastor about Ser Pentino, and now Jepson.

"Deni, you know what I want to order. Pastor, can I talk to you outside for just a minute?"

"Sure, Cam, but can't it wait until we eat?" Pastor Tyler said.

"Not really, sir."

"Well, what could be more important than Sunday lunch?" Cody was used to his dad taking life pretty seriously. And lately he had a lot to take seriously. He knew this was about Ser Pentino. His dad had not told him everything because he didn't want Cody to worry. Remarkably, Cody saw how God was changing his dad from just a dad to a great man—his hero. He knew that everything would be okay because his dad was Cameron Kale. And Cameron Kale's God was Jesus.

Cameron and Pastor Kit walked outside so that Cameron could share what was on his heart with the pastor.

"Pastor, I am sorry for pulling you away from the dinner table like this, but I have to tell you something. It's Jepson!"

"Oh, Jepson. Well, why didn't you say so?"

"I am trying, sir."

"Well, go on."

"Jepson is involved in something very bad."

"Well, that's news. I have been trying to tell you that. Remember I told you to watch your back. He has been trying to get me to resign for a while now. What have you found out?"

"Some of this you will have a hard time believing."

"If you tell me something, I am going to believe you, son."

"Okay. Remember the weird man that kidnapped Cody? Well, he is Ser Pentino."

"You know him, Cam?"

"Well, I have met him before, and he is the epitome of evil, sir."

"Well, anyone who would kidnap someone's child is definitely evil in my book. Who is this Ser Pentino?"

"This is the part you may have trouble believing. He's the devil, sir."

"I met a few of those in my time, Cameron."

"No, sir, he *is* the devil. He is God's enemy himself."

"You are pretty shaken up, but what does this have to do with Jepson? I know that he has been involved in something shady, but you're not making any sense, Cam. Spit it out."

"Ser Pentino is a man who has been taunting me in my dreams for several years now. He has continuously accused me of not being the man God has called me to be. I have shared these dreams with Deni and Cody, but they always thought I was—well, to be honest, sir—crazy. But then the Sunday that you asked me to share and many came forward to be saved, Deni saw him sitting in a church pew. Cody saw him too. He was the one who took Cody, and I saw him talking with Jepson in the deacon's office."

"Cameron, I thought I would never have the chance to tell you this. In fact, I never thought that I would tell anyone, but I believe I have met this same man in my dreams—but he was not a man. He was a tormentor named Drawg, a spirit of the outer-world."

Cameron gulped and shook his head. "That is him. He is also known as Drawg."

"It was these dreams that I had that I also heard the Lord tell me that someday Cameron Kale would be a leader in this church and community and show many the way of salvation. I didn't want to tell you about these dreams because I thought you would go along with Jepson and the others and think that I am just a senile old man and ready to be put out of the church to pasture."

"I understand now more fully why Ser Pentino has battled me. He has tried to get me to give up my calling to Mariah City Community Church. He threatened me with taking Cody and then with the virus you and Deni contracted."

"That was the doing of Ser Pentino?"

"None other."

"I suspected as much. Praise God for His miraculous power. Let's get back to the meal. We don't want to unnecessarily alarm the others, but you and I need to talk further, pray, and seek the Lord as to how to deal with Jepson and this Ser Pentino."

"Yes, sir."

—◦∅◦—

As Cameron, Cody, and Deni were driving home, Deni asked Cameron about his conversation with Pastor Tyler.

"Cam, what did Pastor Tyler say about Sir Pentino?"

"He knows him."

Deni raised her voice several decibels. "He knows him? You don't mean they are friends?"

Cody, taking his earplugs out of his ears from his iPhone, overheard their conversation and interjected. "Mom, Pastor Tyler probably has the same dreams Dad does."

"Well, Code, it's something like that. Pastor Tyler did have a dream like mine where he saw Drawg, the spirit of the outer-world. In the same dream, God told Pastor Kit that He desired to use me to bring the evangel to Mariah City."

"Dad, what's the evangel?"

"It means *good news*, Cody. It is what God wants us to share with others who don't know Christ. The good news is that Jesus died for our sins and we can become part of God's family by turning from our sins and accepting Jesus as our Lord and Savior."

"God told Pastor Tyler that you were supposed to bring the evangel to Mariah City? That's cool, Dad. You are sort of a superhero."

"I am glad you see it that way, Cody. But any of us can be superheroes with God's strength."

<hr />

The Kales pulled into their drive and entered their home just as the phone was ringing. Cody picked up the phone and said, "Kale's residence."

"This is Scott Benson. Cody, can I talk with your dad for a minute?"

"Sure. Dad, Mr. Benson is on the phone for you."

"Thanks, Cody."

"Scott, we must have arrived home at the same time. Great lunch, huh?"

"It sure was. I need to talk to you and feel that you are the only person I can talk to. Can we get together?"

"When?"

"How about now? Can I come over there?"

"Sure, Scott. Come on over. We can talk in my den. See you in a few minutes."

Scott Benson arrived minutes later, and both men entered Cameron's study and shut the door.

Chapter Nine

NEW REVELATIONS

"Scott, what's going on? You really sound troubled."

"You know that I usually take things to the Lord, and I am praying about this, but we are also supposed to seek counsel."

"How can I help?"

"The police called me as soon as I got home. They told me that they are certain now that Amy's death was—" Scott choked on his words.

"What?"

"Amy's death was murder."

Cameron rubbed the back of his neck and stared into Scott's eyes. "How do they know? What evidence do they have—how—why would someone want to kill Amy?"

"I have asked all of those same questions over the past half hour. I don't know. They said that the brake lines had been severed on the Tracker, but they didn't see it at first because of how damaged the vehicle was."

"I can't imagine Amy having any enemies."

"That is what I wanted to talk to you about. I never made much of this before, but it makes more sense to me now. I don't want to accuse anyone, and this is very awkward. There is a reason I am talking to you about this and not Pastor Tyler. Jepson LaPlant was in our home several weeks ago. Amy wanted to invite different deacons for a meal to show our hospitality to those who are serving at church.

"She was, well, *we* were shocked when Jepson spent most of his visit telling us why Pastor Tyler needed to resign from the church. Pastor Tyler had been Amy's pastor since she was in youth group. She couldn't imagine any reason why anyone would feel that Pastor Tyler would need to resign his position as pastor. Jepson said that it was hard for him too, but I didn't feel he was sincere. He said the pastor had become senile and was saying things and doing things that didn't make sense. He accused him of neglecting the church and not having any focus for its future. He also said that he and several others were going to bring this before the church and make it official. He said that they had evidence and that the church would have no choice but to get rid of Pastor Tyler.

"Amy was really upset, Cameron. She said if Jepson thought he was going to seriously carry out his threats, he should know that she had a lot of influence in Mariah City and would see to it that his plan was thwarted. Jepson laughed and said, 'I wish it was as easy as that to stop this.' He thanked us for the meal and left before dessert was served.

"Jepson is well liked by many in the church. They believe he is doing a great job as a deacon. No one would believe that he could do such a thing. I cannot even believe that he could kill Amy because of what she said."

Cameron was listening and shaking his head. Every word that Scott spoke further confirmed to him that there were forces of darkness at work to keep the church and the community from hearing the evangel. He knew now that he needed to let Scott know about what he and Pastor Kit knew about Jepson.

"Scott, I don't know how to tell you this, but Jepson is not who you think he is. He is not your friend or mine. He is God's enemy."

"You don't mean…?"

"No, but he is a friend to the enemy of God."

Scott sat speechless as he took in what Cameron was telling him. He trusted Cameron and knew that he would never say things without having a solid basis for truth.

"How?"

"It's a long story. Deni and I can fill you in tomorrow. Why don't you stop in after work and join us for supper."

"That sounds good. What do I tell the police?"

"For starters, tell them about the conversation Jepson had with you and Amy last week. He does have a motive."

"What about the church? Jepson told me to keep silent about what the deacons are planning concerning Pastor Tyler. They said we are to keep things confidential."

"How convenient for Jepson. No, Scott. I think all of this needs to come out in the open."

"Pray with me that God will expose the darkness," Scott pleaded. "We can deal with things that are exposed so much better than when things are hidden. Amen."

"I will pray with you."

Cameron and Scott joined hands and bowed their heads. Cameron led the prayer.

"Gracious God, You are almighty and see what has happened. We know You desire to expose darkness. Lord, if Jepson is involved in this situation, please reveal this to us. I also pray that You will lift up my dear brother Scott. Give him your peace that surpasses knowledge, Lord. Help him through this difficult trial. We know that You have heard us. We pray it in the name of Jesus. Amen."

"See you tomorrow."

"Blessings, dear brother."

"Blessings to you also."

Just after dawn the next morning, Pastor Tyler was out power walking in his neighborhood and as usual spent most of the time in prayer.

"Lord, I give praise to You, and know that You are a Sovereign God. You are in control. I know that You tell us not to worry because You will take care of us, Lord. I am sensing danger to come to me and the church because of Your enemies. Lord, You know whom I am speaking of. I ask You, dear Lord, to stop Jepson from his selfish and evil plotting. Lord, give Cameron and me wisdom. We can't allow Jepson to destroy *Your* church. I am not sure what connection he has to Your enemy, oh Lord, but Cameron has seen him with this one who calls himself Ser Pentino and reveals himself as an outer-worldly demon.

"Oh God, intervene and protect Cameron, his family, the godly leaders of Mariah City Community church, and the believers there. We ask in the wonderful name of Jesus to help us. Give us Your wisdom and strength, dear Lord. Show us the way."

Just as Pastor Tyler was finishing his prayer, his cell phone rang.

"Pastor Tyler? This is Jepson. I just wanted to let you know that I am calling a meeting for Tuesday night. I have e-mailed and called many of the members to be ready to talk about the path forward for Mariah City Community Church."

"Jepson, you can't do this," Pastor Tyler said boldly.

"I can, and I am doing it. Your time will be short, Kit. Count on it. You will not have your way."

Just as Cameron was finishing up with a patient, his secretary told him that Pastor Tyler was on the phone.

"Cameron, we have to get together as quickly as possible."

"How quickly? What is this about?"

"It is Jepson. He has called a meeting for Wednesday night."

"Can he do that?"

"He believes he can, and it seems that many others believe he can as well. We have to stop him."

"Come over tonight for dinner. Scott will be there. I think what Scott has to share will help us with the answer."

"I'll be there. Meanwhile, be in prayer, Cam. The devil is on the prowl."

"I believe he has been, sir."

"Yes, Amen to that."

"See you tonight."

Chapter Ten

GREATER IS HE THAT IS IN YOU

Cameron left the office early Monday so that he could help Deni get ready for dinner with Scott and Pastor Tyler. He also felt that he needed to spend some time with her. Taking on new responsibilities with the church made greater demands on his time. He always believed that his family was his first ministry, so he wanted to guard that responsibility.

"What are you fixing tonight, Deni?"

"Don't worry. I made your favorite."

"Beef Stroganoff?"

"You got it!"

"Fantastic!

"So Scott thinks Jepson is responsible for Amy's death?"

"Scary, isn't it?"

"Yes. Cam, do you realize what this scandal will do in the church?"

"There is already a scandal in the church. Jepson and his mobsters are planning to run the pastor out of the church."

"I hate this kind of stuff."

"Tell me about it."

"Wouldn't church be wonderful without the warfare?"

Cameron responded like a teacher. "Sure, but that isn't the real world, is it?"

"No, it isn't."

"Remember that we wrestle against principalities and powers and the rulers of spiritual darkness of this world."

"Very true."

"We need to pray that God will give us wisdom. People like Jepson can make others believe that he is God's gift to the church, but underneath he has his own agenda. Now that we know he has contact with Ser Pentino, we know that his agenda is bigger than himself. It is Satan's agenda for our church and this community."

"Let's pray before Scott and Pastor get here."

Cameron agreed. "Oh God, You are amazing and awesome. We know that You are in control of all things. You desire that we call out to You and seek Your face. We need wisdom, Lord, on how to deal with Jepson and Your enemies. Lord, keep us humble and free from sin. May we have Your heart and do only what is right in Your sight. Guide us tonight in our discussion that what we will say pleases You. Direct us, Lord, to know how to address this meeting that has been planned for Wednesday night. In Jesus's precious name. Amen."

After some great conversation and Cameron spending a few minutes playing with Cody on his Xbox 360, Scott and Pastor Tyler knocked on the door.

"Come on in, fellows. Did you two come together?"

"No, we just have impeccable timing," Pastor Kit said with a smile.

"Well, dinner is about ready. Come on in the den, and we'll serve some coffee."

"None for me, Cam," Pastor Kit said. "I have to watch my health these days. Too much coffee slows down my morning exercise."

"Okay, no coffee for Pastor Kit."

"I could use a cup," Scott said.

"You got it, Scott. Comin' up!"

As the Kales, Scott Benson, and Pastor Tyler sat around the table, they began to discuss the meeting that was being called by Jepson. Scott asked if Cody should be listening to their conversation.

Pastor Tyler interrupted. "Cam, I hope you don't mind if I interject here, but Cody probably knows how to deal with the devil better than any of us, having tangled up with Ser Pentino himself. He's a pretty bright boy and is anointed of God. I, for one, think it is okay for Cody to listen in."

"Who is Sir Pentino?" Scott asked.

Over a course of an hour, Cameron, Deni, Pastor Tyler, and even Cody explained to Scott about their experience in dealing with the small man with the pinstriped business suit who transformed into a lion-man beast called Drawg. While some of the accounts seemed too unbelievable to be real, the spirit of God in him witnessed that what they were saying was true.

Both Pastor Tyler and Cameron believed that it was very possible that Jepson could be the one connected to Amy's murder. Now they realized that the church was in grave danger too.

Cameron, Scott, and Pastor Tyler agreed to go to the police the next morning and report what they knew about Jepson. They believe it had to happen before the meeting at the church. Jepson had to be stopped.

———◦◊◦———

As the three men walked through the doors of the Mariah City police station, a recognizable voice came from within.

"Thanks, Chief Bormand. I will have that donation for the police fund this week. Let's get together and play some golf."

The voice was Jepson.

"Cameron, Scott, Pastor Tyler, what are you fellows doing here? Are you trying to sell raffle tickets to our church picnic, or are you here on business?"

Jepson reeked with overconfidence and self-absorption. It was sickening to Cameron and angered Scott to think that this man could take his life partner away from him. Even though he knew Amy was ready to meet her Lord and it was the Lord's time for her, it angered him to think that this man could be so evil but claim to be a follower of Jesus.

"How can I help you fellas?" Chief Bormand said.

"We have a matter we would like to discuss with you if you have a few minutes," Cameron began.

"Come in. Want some coffee? I think you can stand a spoon up in it, but it isn't too bad."

"No, thanks," Cameron replied. "It's about Jepson."

"What about him? Good fellow. The church must be happy to have him, huh, Pastor?"

"Chief, we believe that Jepson may have had something to do with Amy Benson's death."

The chief cocked his neck and slowly glanced over at the three men. "Those are some pretty heavy charges, Pastor Tyler. What do you have to back that up?"

Scott spoke up. "Jepson was in our home the week before Amy's crash. All he could do was complain about the pastor and the direction the church was going under the pastor. Amy was not happy with Jepson and told him that she knew a lot of people in Mariah City and would never allow Jepson to run the pastor out of the church."

"Well, that sounds like some thin grounds to accuse a man of murder."

Cameron chimed in. "Jepson has plans to run the pastor out of the church and has called a meeting for tomorrow night. He wants Pastor Tyler out. I believe he will not stop at anything to get rid of him."

"Even if that were so, it still doesn't give grounds for murder. Jepson is a good guy. I just don't see it. You have to have a lot more evidence than what you have, which is really nothing at this point."

Cameron, Scott, and Pastor Tyler left the police station bewildered as to what to do. It was clear that Jepson and the chief have some kind of relationship that was making the chief protect him. These were not powers of God but powers from God's enemy at work.

Driving back across town toward the church, Pastor Tyler asked, "Men, what are we going to do? The law will not help us. The church will listen to Jepson and is certainly not ready spiritually to hear anything about outer-worldly beings. I am not sure my congregation even believes there is a devil. What are we going to do, fellas?"

"I have an idea." Cameron said.

"Come with me."

The three men went to the church and walked to the front. Cameron asked if they would kneel or get on their face with him before God and seek Him about what to do.

"I knew you were the right man to lead this church forward," Pastor Tyler said. "Why didn't I think of turning to the Lord? He is our answer."

Cameron smiled. "You're right, Pastor. Let's all get before God."

For several hours the three men prayed deeply from their hearts that God would give them wisdom and understanding. They prayed that Jepson would not be able to lead the church to do something that was not God's plan. They prayed for Pastor's, Cameron's, and Scott's protection. They prayed that God's will would be done for Mariah City Community Church and Mariah City. They also prayed that God would bring to light whoever murdered Amy Benson.

———

Chief Bormand and his deputy, Clem Mager, walked into the Missy's Café to have some lunch.

"What can I get you guys?" Nancy Dawson, the owner of the café, asked.

Nancy was a single mom whose husband went to prison five years earlier for selling drugs. She was raising two beautiful daughters—Kim, five, and Karen, eleven—on her own. Nancy often said that she would have never made it a few years before had it not been for Deni and the help she gave her at the Mariah City Family Center, a local pregnancy center that helped men and women who were in crisis from unplanned pregnancies. When she sold her home, she bought the diner, which in earlier years was just called "The Diner," but since so many often called her "Missy," she changed the name to "Missy's Café." Clem and Chief Bormand ordered their usual—a gourmet hamburger and fries.

"Clem, you won't believe who I talked to today," said Chief Bormand. "Your pastor."

"Pastor Tyler?"

"Actually, both of your pastors, Pastor Tyler and Cameron Kale. Scott Benson was with them."

"Why did they come to the station?"

Chief Bormand shook his head. "They think Jepson LaPlant had something to do with Amy Benson's death. Isn't that ridiculous?"

Clem swallowed a gulp of coffee too quickly, jolted by what he was hearing. Chief Bormand pressed the issue.

"Well, isn't it ridiculous? Those guys don't have a bit of evidence. From a lawman's perspective, they have nothing to go on but some speculations."

Clem was listening. "What did they say about Jepson?"

"Scott Benson seems to think that Jepson was threatened by his wife, Amy, because she was going to stop him from making the pastor resign his post."

Clem flew back into his seat as though he was a cowboy getting his rope and balance ready to ride a bull. "Chief! Jepson is trying to get the pastor to resign? Now you have to keep this all confidential, of course."

"I know you have been attending that church."

"Okay, he wants the pastor to resign. I could see how that would upset Amy. What else do you know?"

"I guess Pastor Tyler was her youth pastor. She knew him most of her life. But come on, Clem. You can't think Jepson would do something like that. He is practically a saint at that church."

"I am a pretty new Christian, but one thing I have learned is that everyone doesn't always show on the outside what they are on the inside."

"How profound, Deputy. Come on, the burgers are here. Let's eat up."

—◦◦◦—

As Pastor Tyler, Cameron, and Scott got off their knees, it was clear that they had to take some necessary action to stop the meeting that Jepson was planning for the next day. On their knees, they prayed for wisdom, and just as the Bible declares, "He will give it liberally," He did just that.

"Fellas, we have to be obedient to the Scriptures—God's Word," Cameron said. "He will not honor anything else. Secondly, in doing so, we cannot fear this man. Jepson is not our Lord. We also have to let Caesar handle the things that are Caesar's. The police must handle Jepson. People need to see who Jepson really is."

"I agree," Scott said, "but he has fooled so many people to believe that he is a saint."

"There is a precedent set for this same behavior in the Bible," Cameron said. "Remember Absalom, David's son? He wanted the kingdom that was rightfully David's. So he spent a lot of time counseling the people and changing their hearts toward him. At precise timing, he decided to take the kingdom for himself and claimed himself to be the king. That is what Jepson is trying to do here. We have to obey God."

"Cameron, I agree too, of course, but how are we going to get the police involved? You heard Bormand today. I don't think he will be much help to us," Scott replied.

"No, but maybe Deputy Mager will. He is a Christian and sees things a little differently than Bormand."

"Isn't Bormand a Christian?" Scott asked. "He claims to be, and I am not his judge, but there doesn't seem to be much fruit."

"Since I am the reason Jepson has called this meeting, I need you to take the lead on this one," Pastor Tyler said. "Just tell me what you need me to do. I hate to put you in this position, son, but I have no choice."

"Don't worry. We are laborers together and brothers. I would do anything to help you, and Scott too. *We have to remember that the evangel is at stake!*"

Though Cameron's words were not inspired, they were certainly words of wisdom. God spoke these words to Cameron's heart—words that motivated these three men to be obedient to God. Cameron believed that Jesus wants nothing to stop His evangel from being preached to all nations.

"Scott, I have to ask you a difficult question." Cameron said.

"Fire away."

"Would you be willing to press charges on Jepson because he made threats in your home?"

"I know that Bormand will not go for it, but he respects Clem, and if Clem pushes them to make an arrest, we have a chance," Pastor Tyler said. "Should we make this a matter before the public?"

"Pastor, with all due respect, it is a matter before the public," Cameron said. "If Jepson was involved in Amy's death, and the three of us have good enough reason to believe it is very possible, we have to rely on our civil authorities. You taught us that they are ministers of righteousness."

"I did indeed. Well then, you and Scott better get going and talking with Mr. Mager. Our time is running short."

Chapter Eleven

THE MEETING

It was Wednesday, 6:30 p.m., and Deni was getting ready to leave for the meeting that Jepson had arranged at the church. Even though Deni and Cameron were not contacted about the meeting, they were prepared to go. Cody stayed with a friend from school. This was not the type of meeting any Christian parent wanted to subject their children to. Church meetings should be the happiest meetings anywhere in the world, but in truth, they are oftentimes some of the worst. It is also true that church meetings where people, principles, and policies are debated are often more greatly attended than church services. There is something inside of man that makes him want to fight. Man is not at peace as much as he is at war. This was the case tonight in Mariah City. The stability of this small, peaceful rural city was at stake and the opportunity of God bringing in His harvest of souls in His time. The stakes were high, and the players were earthly and outer-worldly.

There was no mistake. Something historical would take place at this church tonight, either for good or for evil. Nevertheless, God is seated on His throne.

At 6:45 p.m., Cameron and Deni turned into the church parking lot. As Cameron entered the building, he ushered Deni to go into the auditorium and sit down where she usually sat. He met with Scott and Pastor Tyler in his office. They again prayed for God to intervene.

There was an unholy rumbling among the people and an eerie sense of oppression in the place. Even still, Cameron, Scott, and

Pastor Tyler sensed the power of God's spirit in the room where they prayed. They were ready for whatever God was going to do.

It was 6:50 p.m. and near time for Jepson to go to the podium and address the congregation. As usual, Jepson was in his office preparing his notes and began to gather them and walk out into the hallway that led to the auditorium. The halls were quiet and only lit with backlight in the ceiling soffits. Only in the distance could you hear an echo of the crowd that had gathered in the main auditorium.

As Jepson walked from his office into the outer hallway, he was greeted by what looked like an ambush. Cameron, Scott Benson, Pastor Tyler, Chief Bormand, Deputy Mager, and other uniformed officers met Jepson head-on fifty feet from the auditorium doors.

"Jepson LaPlant, you are under arrest for the murder of Amy Benson."

"Are you crazy?" Jepson blurted out.

"Please, sir, keep your voice down—we do not want this to become a scene here in the church. You have the right to remain silent. Anything you say may be used against you in a court of law." Deputy Mager finished giving Jepson his rights.

The officers muscled Jepson out of the building, cuffed him, and put into the cruiser. It was a question of how long they could hold Jepson on these charges, but Scott was able to convince Clem Mager and at least put a seed of doubt in Chief Bormand's mind that Jepson was something different than what others had perceived. While Jepson could have remained a suspect for Amy Benson's murder, he could not be arrested unless there was a greater motive or threat. Scott told them that Jepson spoke these words to Amy: "You will regret this if you try to stop me." That was enough to make the arrest.

With Jepson out of the building, the atmosphere seemed like a mighty rushing wind sweeping away the darkness and ushering in beautiful rays of sunshine. There was an unexplainable peace in that hall as Cameron, Pastor Tyler, and Scott emerged into the auditorium and headed for the platform.

"Ladies and gentlemen, I need to make a very important announcement."

Cameron waited a moment for the sound to die down and for God's spirit to speak to his heart.

"I know you were told this was going to be a meeting called by Jepson LaPlant, but he was unavoidably detained tonight and could not be at this meeting. We do not have all of the details and do not know what is going to happen, but we must tell you that Jepson was arrested tonight by the Mariah City Police Department, as he may have had something to do with the death of Amy Benson."

As gasps and voices rose in varied decibel levels, Scott Benson took the microphone and began to speak.

"No one here wants to believe something like this could be true of someone like Jepson. I don't want to believe it. None of us do. But, folks, I have reason to believe, and our city police have reason to believe, that Jepson was involved somehow. We do not know. We are here, though, to encourage you and quiet your hearts. This is not easy for any of us."

Tom Tharston spoke out from the congregation. "We were told that Jepson had some things to tell us about Pastor Tyler that warranted our being here and listening to what he had to say. Is this some kind of cover up, Scott?"

Cameron could sense the oppressive spirit in the room and the confusion on the faces of many of the church members gathered. Cameron whispered a prayer.

"Lord, by Your Spirit, anoint my words and let me speak only what *You* want me to say. Amen."

Cameron took the microphone and began to speak.

"Dear hearts. I am a new pastor among you, even though we have been friends and co-laborers for a long time. I am coming to you with the purest of heart and purest of intentions. Most of you know that I have helped out here at the church whenever and wherever I can. Some of you are my students from various classes and Bible studies I have taught. Some of you have been with me on some of the teams Pastor Tyler has put together to minister to our community. And there are many of you who are my patients. You know that I have helped many of you, not charging some of you for services because you were in pain and needed the help. You know my love for you. I have never given any of you any reason to disbelieve me about anything. If so, I do not deserve to stand here and speak to you tonight. But I am not asking you to listen to what I have to say because of how you feel about me but because of how you feel about Jesus, your Savior.

"Does anyone here really know what is happening in our world, our community, and here in our church? God's enemy— yes, the devil, who wears many masks—is trying to keep us off guard from what Jesus wants us to do.

"There are some of you who came here tonight to do what you believe sincerely is the work of God. I don't doubt your sincerity. This room is packed with sincere people. But do you believe we would be giving God the greatest glory to have a public meeting to humiliate a man who has labored with us for the past twenty years? He has married some of you and held your hands as you buried many of your family members. He has prayed for you and wept with you. He has stayed up late hours counseling with you. He has given this church his service and his life. For the past ten years, he has done this without his precious wife, Belinda, who went home to be with the Lord some years ago. If we plan tonight to meet to talk about hearsay, gossip, and trumped-up charges of the pastor mishandling this ministry and direction, we do this church a great disservice to Christ and this lost community.

"Folks, please listen to this. It is not my words but God's very own breathed-out words. How shall men know that you are my disciples? Jesus said, 'It is by the love that you have for one another.' How will Mariah City know that we love Jesus if we don't love our own? Love covers a multitude of sins. If the pastor was or is guilty of any errors, sins, or any incompetency, is this how we treat a man who is like our father, friend, and brother? If we love him, we want to understand.

"Jepson has been loved by many of you. If he is love, then shouldn't he follow the same rule as all of us and love Pastor?

"You are asking, *What is this about? What has the pastor done? Why are some questioning him?* I have learned in the few short years that God has been leading me into ministry that oftentimes it only takes one person to blow a horn and blow it loud enough and it will seem like an army. Too often a person will speak as representing a group that shares his or her sentiments when it is only that one person who has the concerns.

"If you must know, here is what I have heard. Some have mentioned it is time for Pastor to resign. Some have questioned his ability to lead and give new direction. I have heard nothing else. I have seen nothing else. I stand with our pastor and believe him to be a man of God. I would not be here tonight calling us to focus on our number one priority, to spread the evangel, the good news of Jesus Christ to our community, if it were not for this man. It was through his prayers and God speaking to Him that I came on board with a new vision to carry the evangel to this community and win men and women to Jesus Christ. Pastor has led a faithful charge. He has encouraged me to use the gifts that God has given me, and now I am beginning to grow in my faith as I am being obedient to God and sharing with all of you.

"How many tonight are with me? We need to rally together like we never have before because the days are evil. The time of redemption is very near. We need to live upright and redeem the time. We need to make every moment count for Christ in these days. Christ is coming soon. Are we ready? Are we winning souls? Are we gleaning the harvest? Are we doing what we should? Folks, we are so busy fighting each other in our churches today that we do not have time to care for each other. We are killing our own. Let's band together and be unified in the Spirit and let God win this for us."

A voice rang out, "I agree with Cameron. He's right!"

Several others chimed in. Heads began to nod, and faces were more relaxed. God was touching the hearts of His people.

"Let's pray," Cameron said. "Let's pray now. Above all, let's have God's heart about things, folks. Worry, fear, doubt, and anger only stops what God wants to do. We have to trust each other and love each other."

Another cried out, "What about Jepson?"

"Fair question. We will love him too. He, above all people right now, needs our prayers and our love. We need to also ask that God will reveal the truth and that God will do what He desires for Jepson. If Jepson is guilty of anything, we will pray that God will change his heart."

For over an hour, people prayed all over the auditorium. Some met in small groups and prayed. Others prayed out loud one after another. There was an unexplainable unity in the room. It was the presence of the spirit of God.

As the hour was coming to a close, several began to sing familiar choruses, and many joined in and sang together. Dozens came to the platform and asked Cameron to pray for them, as they did not believe they were truly saved, while others came to repent of sin and offenses toward others. There was weeping and light laughter expressing the joy of the Spirit in the room.

It was an outbreak of revival in a night that was called for the purpose of stopping God from carrying out His perfect will. So true is the scripture "Greater is He that is in us, than he that is in the world" (1 John 4:4, KJV).

Chapter Twelve

SPIRITUAL WARFARE

"Cameron! Cameron! The phone is ringing."

"What? Who is it at this time of the morning?" Cameron picked up the phone. "Hello?"

"Hello, is this Cameron Kale?"

"Yes."

"A Reverend Tyler was brought to the hospital by ambulance, and he is asking for you, sir."

"W-W-What is wrong?"

"If you can come to the hospital, we will explain further. You should do your best to hurry, sir."

"Yes, I will. Thank you."

Deni looked concerned. "Cam, who was it?"

"It was the hospital. Pastor Kit is at the hospital and asked me to come. It sounds urgent. I better get dressed."

"I will pray. All of this stuff at the church has been too much stress on him."

"Yeah, it has. I will call you as soon as I hear something."

Cameron prayed as he drove to Mariah City Hospital.

"Lord, it is not up to me to question You. You are God. I know You have a reason, but why Pastor Kit now? He has been through so much and has given You his best. Strengthen him, Lord. Be present with him in a powerful way. Let him know that You are present and give him Your peace, which is greater than our understanding. And, Lord, protect him. Protect all of us. Give us discernment in these times, as Your enemy desires to match everything that you accomplish for good with evil. We give You glory in the name of Jesus. Amen."

As Cameron approached the hospital elevators, he came face-to-face with Jepson LaPlant.

"Jepson! What? How? What are you doing here?"

Jepson stared at Cameron like a mountain lion ready to pounce on his prey. "You thought you had me, didn't you, Dr. Kale? Well, I told you they couldn't keep me with no evidence to the charges. I heard you pirated my meeting last night."

"No, Jepson, it was a meeting to get people to focus on truth."

"Truth? What do you know about truth? You think just because you have been made an assistant pastor that you possess all knowledge, don't you? You think you are better than everyone else. Well, I have been around, Cameron Kale, and I know a thing or two myself."

"All that I know is that you have been making some serious errors in judgment and leading the church with your agenda. It is keeping people from the more important matters of the church."

"What, building you a better office as you try to take over Tyler's job? I will see to it that they get rid of you along with Tyler. Neither of you are fit for the ministry." Jepson began to enter the elevator as the doors opened.

"Where are you going?"

"I am here to see our friend Tyler, of course. I heard he was ill. What a shame. Too much commotion, I guess."

Cameron straightened his back and shook his index finger at Jepson. "I can't stop you from going up there, but I swear if you say one thing that makes Pastor Kit upset, I will drag you out of that room myself!"

Jepson crimped his brow and shook his head. "Don't worry, my friend. There will be other days for warfare. Today we will just agree to be enemies."

As Jepson entered the elevator, Cameron decided to take the stairs, striding several steps up at a time. He tried to get to the third floor before Jepson could get there.

Cameron approached the nurse's desk and asked to see Pastor Kit Tyler as Jepson walked up behind him.

"Can I help you, sir?" the attending nurse asked Cameron.

Though the nurse was speaking to Cameron, Jepson, standing behind him, answered, "Oh, I'm with him."

Cameron whirled around and gave Jepson a look like a laser that could burn through steel.

"Mr. Tyler is in room three-zero-nine," the nurse answered.

Cameron mustered up a little smile through his stern and frustrated expressions. "Thank you."

As both men walked down the broad corridors filled with blood pressure machines, gurneys, and food carts, they came to Pastor Tyler's room. Stopping short just outside Pastor Tyler's room, Cameron turned to Jepson, pointing his index finger in his face again.

"I mean it. Not one word to upset him."

Jepson grinned. "You've got my word. I'm a kitten."

It was odd, but Cameron noticed Jepson taking on some of the characteristics of Ser Pentino. While inwardly evil and not to be trusted, he could come across as compliant and pliable. His art of deception seemed to be increasing, and Cameron knew a spiritual battle of unprecedented proportions was ahead.

A voice welcomed the men as they entered the room. "Good morning, gentlemen."

"What are you doing here?" Cameron blurted.

It was Ser Pentino. Pastor Tyler was lying on the hospital bed, hooked up to an IV and heart monitor.

"Pastor Tyler, are you okay?"

Ser Pentino was sitting in the guest chair near the hospital bed. "I believe we have all met. I thought a little meeting might be in order, and this was the best place to do this."

Cameron noticed there were no doctors or nurses or sounds of anyone in the hall. The lights were dim, and the room seemed closed in. Pastor Tyler lay back on his white hospital bed with an oxygen mask around his face. His eyes were half closed, and it did not seem that he was lucid.

Now Cameron felt surrounded by two very evil persons. There was an obvious presence of evil in the room, and he was feeling oppressed by it all. Cameron felt dizzy and drowsy and sensed this was just another one of his nightmares. Both Ser Pentino and Jepson looked alike. Both were wearing pinstriped suits and had that sheepish, rather devilish grin on their faces. They spoke in unison that this was Pastor Tyler's last hour.

"It is over, Cameron Kale. Your day is next. You cannot win this battle. You are only a man—a mortal. You will fail."

As Jepson stared Cameron down, his teeth looked like that of a lion. His face was powder-white, like the face of a ghoul. Drawg began to cry out and roar that this was the final hour. Cameron bent over and was feeling nauseated. His head began to ache, and it felt as though he had been drugged. Cameron's trancelike state slowly started to disappear, as he could only hear the steady hum of the flat line from Pastor Tyler's heart monitor. His heart had stopped. Jepson was right. This was Pastor Tyler's final hour. It was over. Or so it seemed.

He saw a pale light that was growing brighter and brighter. It almost appeared as though the sky opened up from the enclosed room, and a brilliance that he had never seen filled the room. It had to be a vision. It was unlike anything he had ever witnessed before but seemed like something he read about in the New Testament. He saw a man who was brilliant like the sun. He was wearing white and sat on a white horse. He kept saying to Cameron again and again, "It is not over. It is not over. I am the resurrection and the life. He that believes in me even though he was dead, yet he will live, and whoever lives and believes on me shall never die."

I got it, Cameron said to himself. *This is a dream, a vision from the Lord. He wants me to know that even if Pastor Kit has left this life, he is not dead but is alive with the Lord.*

Ser Pentino and Jepson were lying. It was not over. They had not won the victory. There was still work to be done for the kingdom of God.

"Thank you, Jesus," he whispered. "I praise you."

In seconds, the room was clear, and everything seemed like it was back to normal. Deni was lying next to Cameron. The sun was shining into the bedroom. Cameron realized that everything had been a dream. *Jepson must still be in the jail, and Pastor Tyler must be okay*, he thought. What was important was that the dream convinced Cameron that no matter what, it is not over—Jesus has won the final victory.

Chapter Thirteen

A NEW CHARGE

As Cameron was shaving, Deni came in and put her arms around him.

"Cameron, I'm sorry, but I just got a call from Mariah City Hospital. Pastor Tyler was brought into the hospital by ambulance last night. It was his heart. There was nothing they could do."

She put her hand to her mouth and couldn't say any more. She sobbed in Cameron's arms as he stared into the mirror, trying to put this all together. *It was just a dream,* he thought. *No, it happened, just like I dreamed. God was preparing me. Now I will be needed more than ever.*

Cameron turned and faced Deni. "I'm sorry, Deni. It must have been God's time for him. I wish I could have been there."

"Yes, I wish I could have been there for him too."

Cameron excused himself and found a quiet place on the patio in his backyard. Deni knew he needed some time alone. Cameron always struggled with expressing his emotions but knew that even Jesus cried at the funeral of his close friend Lazarus. He looked up in the sky, as he would typically do when he was alone out of doors praying. Although he knew that this was God's plan, sorrow welled up deep within him.

"Oh God, I cannot describe the pain of my loss of my dear friend Pastor Kit. He has become so close to me, and I thank You that we had the chance to know one another in time and eternity. I praise You for him because without him, I would not have been given the message of Your call to me. But I deeply sorrow, Lord."

Cameron began to weep and sob deeply and continued his prayer when his sobs subsided.

"Lord, I don't know how I am going to do this alone. I am weak. What You are asking me to do seems beyond my ability. Lord, help me. Give me your strength. Help me through this struggle. Help me, Lord. Help me."

Cameron's prayer reached God's heavenly throne. Within minutes Cameron felt as though a fresh spring-like breeze brushed past him. He looked up and sensed a tremendous peace. It was unquestionably the "peace with surpasses knowledge" that Paul wrote about in his letter to the Philippian church in the Scriptures.

"Thank You, Lord. You are awesome."

Pastor Tyler's brother, Kraig, flew in from Houston, Texas, to attend the funeral. Cameron came to meet him at the airport and expressed his condolences.

"It is good to meet you, Kraig, although it would be better under different circumstances."

Kraig answered in his big Texan way. "Well, I'll tell ya. He's with the King! He is happy, so I am happy. I will miss that man. He has always been a blessing to his big brother, but God must have needed him there. I have heard Kit say many wonderful things about you, Cameron. He believed that you would replace him and be the one God would use to reach Mariah City with the gospel."

Cameron grinned. "It is kind of you to say so. I am very thankful to have known your brother and to have shared the ministry with him for the time that I was able to."

Kraig put his arm around Cameron. "I want you to bring the message at Kit's funeral. I know that is what he would have wanted. Are you up for it?"

"I would be honored, Kraig."

Kraig nodded his head and put his hands together. "Good, then it is settled. Oh, and I appreciated your offer to stay in your home to save some money, but I have always stayed in a hotel. I just like being fussed over. Is that a problem?"

"No problem, Kraig. Let's go there, and we will get you settled in."

The days ahead would be difficult for Cameron and the many who loved Kit Tyler. There would be rejoicing because everyone knew Kit was with the Lord, but they would greatly miss their dear friend and mentor.

Cameron could not help but wonder how much of the troubles that Jepson brought into Pastor Kit's life were part of his ultimate demise. However, he didn't want to think about that because he knew God uses every circumstance in our lives to bring about His purposes for us and for the kingdom. He also knew that God had given him a keener sense of his calling and mission and that it had been God's plan all along for Cameron to be there when the church's leader went home to glory. Tempted to feel incapable of handling such a huge responsibility, he was also keenly aware of God's hand upon him through the past few weeks of miraculous interludes with the spirit of God in the battle of the ages.

Pastor Tyler had planned his own funeral arrangements long before his hour of home going. He wanted it to be a day of celebration because he would be with the Lord. He understood that people would grieve and miss him but hoped people would come together to rejoice, because death for the Christian is just going home to be with Jesus.

Just hours before the funeral service, Tom Tharston called Cameron Kale.

"Cameron, I talked with a few of the other deacons, and they feel that Jepson LaPlant should bring the message for Pastor Tyler's funeral."

Cameron had to hold his breath for a second or two to keep from saying something he shouldn't. Even so, he was a little bolder in his confrontation than usual. "What? Are you kidding, Tom?

Even if it was the right thing for Jepson to bring the sermon, how is that possible? He is in jail."

"Well, that's just it, Cameron. He is not in jail. They said they could not hold him in jail on the charges that were brought with the little evidence they have."

Cameron rubbed his face hard with his hand and whispered a prayer. "Lord, You will have to figure out this one." Emboldened to speak frankly, Cameron took charge as if someone higher and greater than he was guiding him, and He was. "Tom, listen. I don't care what Jepson thinks. One day he is ready to force the pastor to resign, and the next he wants to share his sermon? Besides, Jepson is a suspect in a murder investigation, and the church does not need more things to gossip about and bring slander upon it. You know, it is not really about the church but about Pastor Tyler and what his family wants. His brother, Kraig, is here and asked me to bring the sermon. He said this would be Kit's wishes. So at this point, it doesn't matter what the deacons think. It matters what is right and what is decent and orderly. This is not going to be another political move by Jepson."

Tom was surprised by Cameron's boldness and strength in giving pastoral direction. Everything he said made sense. "I don't disagree with anything you have said. It seems lately that Jepson has been trying to push his agenda. That hasn't seemed right to me. I will tell the other deacons, and we will let Jepson know."

"Just so you know, I am going to make sure that Jepson does not create any problems, so I will have Deputy Mager standing by."

"That is good, Cameron. We don't need any drama at our pastor's funeral, for goodness sake."

"No, we don't, Tom. I will see you at the funeral."

As people flooded in to take their seats at Mariah City Community Church, many greeted one another. Some were cheering up grieving members shocked by the sudden loss of Pastor Tyler. Many others came who first learned of Christ at Amy Benson's memorial. Still others were there who came to know Christ on the Sunday Cameron had shared with the congregation. Some crowds came who had heard about Cameron Kale and believed that he might become the new pastor of Mariah City Community Church. The church was packed with mourners— standing room only.

Jepson was met at the doors to the auditorium and faced off with Cameron, who was flanked by Deacon Tom Tharston, Scott Benson, and Deputy Mager.

"You have not heard the last of this," he muttered in a low growl in Cameron's direction.

The men surrounding Cameron reassured him that Jepson's spirit was not the Lord's. They encouraged him to ignore it and let God use him that day when so many were in attendance to this important service.

⎯⎯⎯✺✺✺⎯⎯

The service began. Several women from church sang solos and shared testimonies of God's goodness and the pastor's faithfulness that lifted up many in the room.

While Cameron, Deni, and Cody Kale sat with Scott Benson and Pastor Kit's brother, Kraig, worshiping and giving praise for the life and example the pastor lived, a little elderly lady came up quietly to speak to Cameron. He had seen her and knew she was a member of the church but did not know her well.

She bent over and whispered quietly in Cameron's ear. "Pastor Cameron, I am Mrs. Dressler. I was told to give you this."

She handed a DVD to Cameron that had a phrase on it scrawled in somewhat legible print with a permanent marker. It read "Cameron, you must show this at my home going, Pastor Kit."

He wondered why Pastor Kit had not mentioned this to him. "Where did you get this?"

"Pastor Kit told me to hang on to this and give it to you if anything were ever to happen to him. I tried to get it to you, but truthfully, I almost forgot. At my age is it is hard to remember anything."

"Thank you!" Cameron whispered.

He rushed back to the AV booth and handed the DVD to the men running the booth and instructed them to play it once the preliminary participants were finished, just before it was his time to bring the sermon.

The screen lowered as many across the crowded auditorium wondered what they were going to see and hear. Cameron himself was more curious than anyone. No one, not even Jepson, knew about the DVD that Pastor Tyler had prepared for his funeral. Cameron knew that God had given his pastor much wisdom, vision, and direction and knew that this DVD might answer some questions for many folks.

The lights dimmed, and a video that Pastor Tyler had made of himself appeared before the massive crowd. With his opening words, a pin drop could be heard in that room of several thousand.

"Dear friends, my long-time and short-time co-laborers at Mariah City Community Church. I hope this does not shock you. Yes, I am actually not here but with our wonderful Lord. I prepared this so that your transition would be easier but more importantly your direction would come from the Lord. I cannot tell you what to do. You will have to act according to your conscience, heart, and protocols, but I want to be sure to share some things with you that will help you and keep you safe and from harm.

"Some months ago, I had a dream. It seems that it was the only way God could get my attention. God showed me some things about the needed direction for Mariah City Community Church. He showed me that the church, our city, state, and nation were going to begin to go through tough times. You didn't need this DVD to tell you that we are going to see times of economic hardship, hard times in our families, increases in poverty and crime, not to mention spiritual oppression, as well as times like the church has not seen for ages. What is not so unreasonable about the message of this dream is that it is simply Jesus's focus for us—to love each other and tell others about their need for Jesus. There is no greater focus for the church today than this.

"But we are not heeding it. The harvest of souls is ready, but there are not enough laborers in God's harvest field to bring them in. We must turn to God and obey Him and bring in His harvest. I have taken this seriously."

"Folks, you have heard about Pastor Kit getting senile and unsure of the direction of the church. Well, just consider that the person who would tell you that is wet behind the ears and hasn't learned much."

Jepson was twisting in his seat again. He looked at people all over the congregation who knew him and his agenda and wondered what they were thinking.

"So, here it is, folks. The direction for the church is Jesus's direction. We need to get serious about winning the lost for Christ. We have heard this but have not heeded it. We know it but do not do it.

"In my dream, God told me there was a man among us that He would use to bring the evangel to Mariah City—and God confirmed this to me, but He has already confirmed it to you. His name is Cameron Kale."

There was an unexpected burst of applause and praise in the auditorium. Pastor Tyler's words paused as if he anticipated knowing how the congregation would respond.

"Folks, Cameron is your evangelist, but he is also your pastor. Let him lead you. He is a good, decent, and honest man. He will also tell you the truth and has God's anointing on him. He will have enemies and those who will try to stop him. Personally, Cameron, I believe you will not only help Mariah City Community Church, but also you will become a leader and blessing to this community. I see you not only as an evangelist but also a man given the gift of prophecy as well."

Cameron understood that some men, and typically pastors, are also given the gift of prophecy and the ability to use the prophetic Word of God to declare God's truth for the day in a bold and emphatic way. Cameron pondered this thought in his heart, as he never thought about God having given him the gift of prophecy.

The DVD of Pastor Kit continued. "Cameron, I hope I didn't steal any of your thunder. Do what you do with the gifts God has clearly given you. Dear hearts, I give you Cameron Kale."

The screen faded out, and the clip ended. The screen was retracted, and it was time for Cameron's sermon. Cameron stepped up to the podium and paused with what seemed a minute of silence before he spoke. In a very human moment, Cameron deeply sensed his need for God's spirit to help him speak.

"The last thing a speaker wants to say is 'I am not sure what to say.'" Everyone laughed. "I have known Pastor Tyler for a number of years. Like many of you, I knew him as a congregation member. Like some of you, I knew him working on ministry teams. But I never knew him like I have in just the past month of my life. It is difficult to become close to someone and lose them early in your relationship with them. Some of you can relate to that. I will miss him. Pastor would not want me to talk about him. If I did I could tell you that he was a man of faith, fortitude, and family. He loved his church. He loved the lost. I know he spent hours in prayer for the lost of Mariah City. He also spent hours in prayer for many of us—his congregation. He loved us. Thank you, Pastor Tyler, for giving us the privilege to be loved so much by someone like you. You showed us the love of the Lord Jesus.

"I did not know about this DVD. In fact, it wasn't until Mrs. Dressler came up and told me about it moments ago that I knew it existed. In fact, I think Pastor only told Mrs. Dressler to remember to show it. No one else knew that this DVD existed. I am glad that it was shown, but if I had known some of what Pastor shared, I may have debated about his showing it. I am glad, however, that he shared what he did, because there is no doubt in my mind that he was directed by God.

"Pastor spoke like I was some sort of man of the hour. I am humbled by what I heard. I know my weaknesses and sins but desire to be fully obedient to God. I want to share with you that we are all men and women of the hour when we focus to do exactly what God has called us to do." Some *amens* were heard all over the auditorium. "If I share nothing else today, it is that Pastor would want me to emphasize the importance of the gospel, the good news, the evangel that Jesus told us to carry and share with others. There is no greater priority in this life for believers than to share Jesus with others. If we are the light for the city but we do not shine that light, how is the city lighted? It isn't."

Cameron shared his heart concerning Jesus's words from Matthew chapter five of being a light on a hill. He continued to plead with those there to recognize the need to believe the truth that Jesus died on the cross for their sins, that He was buried, but that He also rose again. He mentioned that we must trust Jesus and follow Him and then tell others about the change that God has made in us. That is carrying the evangel. He said that we don't have to be evangelists to carry the evangel. We can all share the good news.

At the end of the service, Cameron called many to come to trust Jesus for the first time and for others to dedicate their lives to Christ to share what God has done in their lives. As Cameron asked hands to be lifted up, they were raised all over the auditorium, both for salvation and rededication to Christ. Now tears were not for grief of their lost friend and associate but for a renewal that was happening in their hearts that day.

As Cameron gave opportunity for people to make their decision public, he asked them to come to the altar and the group would be prayed for. Out of 2,500 people attending the service, over 800 men, women, and children made their way to the front of Mariah City Community Church either to give their lives to Jesus for the first time or to rededicate their lives to serve Him.

Cameron's eyes were filled with tears as he saw police officers, city officials, community leaders, and others accept Christ that day. Bill Hanson, the mayor of Mariah City, came forward saying that he had made some profession to know Jesus as a boy but that Jesus had been what was missing most of his life. He gave his life to Christ. Tim Borden and Teresa Savage, both city council persons, gave their lives to Christ. Steve Merson, one of the leading firemen of the city, also gave his life to Christ. Cameron remembered many occasions being on the receiving end of some hilarious pranks Steve would pull. He never knew a guy, though, who was more caring and helpful to people than Steve.

Kraig Tyler and Scott Benson were sharing with each other how amazing it was that God was miraculously working in the service. There was no doubt that revival was beginning to break out in Mariah City.

—◦◦◦—

Soon after the sermon, Cameron had a chance to greet and talk with many of those who came. Tom Tharston and several other deacons came to Cameron with some special news.

"Cameron, can we take just a minute of your time? Thank you for that powerful message. We have talked briefly and want you to know that the committee is recommending to the church for you to succeed Pastor Tyler as our pastor. Take some time to think about it and pray about it."

"Thank you, Tom. I will."

As Cameron left the auditorium, he brought Deni and Cody into his office, and they kneeled together to pray.

"God, thank You for Your love for our dear brother and friend, Pastor Tyler. Your ways are definitely not our ways. You used Pastor Tyler to prepare the way for the Kale family to serve here at Mariah City Community Church and to be used today to reach many leaders in our city. Thank You for clarity about my new charge, Lord. It is wonderful to know and hear Your voice and to know our calling.

"Bless the Kale family. Protect my wonderful wife and son, Deni and Cody. Keep them safe, and may this calling be their calling too. May their lives be blessed through the ministry here."

When Cameron finished praying, he said, "Let's go have some dinner. Your pick, Code. How about Fire and Ice again?"

"Sounds like a winner, Dad."

"Let's go!"

Chapter Fourteen

JEPSON'S JEALOUSY

Victory brings joy, and obedience to God brings blessings. While there was some sadness, there was also joy with the Kales this night. Cody wanted Kraig Tyler and Scott Benson to join the family, so everyone went out to the Fire and Ice restaurant. Cody loved the lights dimmed and every table dressed with white linen tablecloths and candles. There was nothing like good service, great atmosphere, and good food.

"Cam, great service. Kit would have been proud," Kraig said.

Cameron smiled. "Thank you, Kraig. God showed up!"

"He sure did," Scott Benson concurred. "We are beginning to see revival, Cameron."

Cameron turned to look at Scott. "I believe we are."

Deni touched Cody's arm. "What are you ordering?"

"I want lobster."

Deni reacted in a louder response than she intended. "Lobster? Are you paying for it?"

Kraig Tyler piped in. "Let him have it, Deni. This meal is on me."

"No, Kraig, you don't have to do that," Deni said.

"Nonsense! I can afford it. While Kit was preaching, I was making money. Honestly, of course. I created a business learning nonprofit work and began consulting others how to start nonprofits. I have made millions doing that. Have your lobster, son. You too, Cameron—whatever you want." Kraig leaned over and whispered in Cameron's ear. "By the way, Cameron, if you ever need anything for the church—and I mean *anything*—you let me know, and I will take care of it."

"Thank you, sir. I don't know what else to say."

"Don't worry. You said it all today. Bless you, son."

As everyone was enjoying their meal, there seemed to be a commotion at the entrance of the restaurant. The Kales, Scott Benson, and Mr. Tyler were stretching their necks to see what it was all about. It seemed that someone was arguing with the host at the door. The sound died down, and everyone went back to eating and sharing. Cameron and Cody were chatting away about a new game he wanted for his Xbox 360, and Cameron noticed his coffee cup was near empty. Raising his cup to his mouth for the last drop, a waitress came up and asked if he would like a refill on his coffee. As she was filling his cup, a man came running in toward the Kales' table in what seemed like slow motion.

"Cameron Kale, I told you that you had not heard the last of me," the man yelled out, raising a gun from his side.

The man was Jepson. Enraged with jealousy and hatred of Kale, he followed them to the restaurant with the intent to end Cameron Kale's life. Shots rang out with the people crowded in the restaurant falling to the floor as glass mirrors shattered above them. Cody whirled around to get behind a booth, but his arm caught the hot cup of coffee the waitress just poured. Like a catapult, the coffee whirled toward Jepson's chest. His gun dropped to the floor, and his soaked shirt revealed a tattoo on his chest that he had kept concealed. It was the form of a serpent. The tattoo was very appropriate for a man who would attack a man of God like the enemy of God himself.

Fortunately, Chief Bormand and Deputy Mager were passing by the Fire and Ice and heard the shots that rang out and some windows shatter. Running into the restaurant, they saw Jepson on the floor and a pearl-handled, nickel-plated, snub-nose pistol lying on the floor near his hand. They grabbed him, raised him to his feet, and cuffed him. Police back up soon arrived and ushered

Jepson to a patrol car parked in the oval drive in front of the restaurant. Paramedics arrived on the scene to assess the situation and bandage the wounds of people who were caught under the shattered glass. It seemed like a miracle that no one had sustained any serious wounds or death.

Deputy Mager rushed over to Cameron's side as he was trying to get off the floor. He had been shot.

Cody ran over to his dad, crying. "Dad, are you going to be okay?"

Cameron, grasping his shoulder, managed to grunt, "I'm fine, son. We can all be thankful God kept his eye over all of us."

Deni was by his side, trying to reassure Cameron that he would be all right. It only looked like a flesh wound, but no one wanted to take any chances.

Deputy Mager called the paramedics over to look at Cameron. "Cam, let the paramedics help you. I'll come back in a moment to check on you. I have to deal with Jepson."

As Deputy Mager stepped outside through the restaurant doors, several uniformed officers were pushing Jepson's head down and seating him in the back of the patrol car. One of the officers radioed the dispatcher that they would be bringing in the shooter and that he was cuffed and in the car.

The other uniformed officer walked toward Deputy Mager to report that everything was secure and that they would be taking Jepson in. Deputy Mager told him to make sure everything was done by the book. He did not want any mistakes on intake. As the uniformed officer replied, "Will do," the patrol car Jepson had been seated in blew up in a huge explosion. Everyone ducked and hit the ground or sought cover as glass and metal flew everywhere like shrapnel behind enemy lines.

Paramedics and firefighters were on the scene and ran with extinguishers to the car to put the fire out. Bormand and Mager were watching from a distance and could see that the fire was out, and the firemen were trying to see what was left of the body inside. Cameron looked on with curiosity as he was escorted to a waiting ambulance on a gurney.

Steve Merson was the head fireman on the scene and shouted back to Chief Bormand, "Chief, there is nothing left. That flame was so intense. It burned bone and all. Nothing left, sir, but ashes."

"Impossible, Steve!" Bormand shouted. "It takes three hours to completely burn a body under intense heat!"

Cameron wondered, *Could it be? Could Jepson have been incinerated? Is it possible that he survived it? There is no way he could have survived that explosion. Certainly life in Mariah City will be better off without him. But no one should have to experience such a tragedy in their life.*

Jepson had no family that lived locally. His grandparents had adopted him since his parents were killed in a car accident when he was only seven years old. His grandparents were no longer living. A cousin who knew Jepson contacted the church and expressed their wishes to not hold a memorial. They would handle things their own way.

In light of the circumstances, a memorial for Jepson at Mariah City Community Church did not seem like a good idea. It was a very sad story.

Jepson was a jealous man who wanted what did not belong to him—he had wanted Cameron's position. He wanted people in the church to recognize him as their leader and pastor. This was not the place God had given to him. Jealousy can bring about tragic ends. This was a tragedy that came from jealousy. But it expressed in real life what happens when men choose evil over good. Perhaps now there would be some peace at Mariah City Community Church and in the city of Mariah itself.

PART II

Times of Refreshing

Chapter Fifteen

A TIME OF PEACE

Aside from a visit from Chief Bormand, today seemed like a normal day at the Kale home. Cameron Kale was at home on bed rest, ordered by his doctor from the flesh wound on his shoulder by Jepson's bullet. Deni had taken some time off from the pregnancy center so that she could help Cameron and make sure he rested.

"How are you feeling, Cameron?" Chief Bormand asked.

"I am doing better today. I should be back on the job tomorrow."

"Hey, take a break. What you have been through has been pretty traumatic. Get all the rest you can."

Deni spoke up. "I don't think I have *ever* seen Cameron rest like he should. He always has a project or several projects going at the same time. Good luck, Chief. He'll be back to work tomorrow."

"Cameron, I still don't get it."

"What, Chief?"

"Jepson. I can understand he was pretty upset about Scott Benson pressing charges and you and the fellas from the church upsetting his plans to remove Tyler from the church, but attempted murder?"

"There is a lot more to the story."

Chief Bormand squinted his eyes and crinkled his brow. "You are not withholding evidence are you?"

"No, that's not what I mean. The leaders of the church have seen a different side to Jepson. He was a true case of a wolf in sheep's clothing."

"Well, I have to say he did a good job covering all this up."

"Chief, what about the investigation into Amy Benson's accident?"

Bormand scratched his head. "We are still working on it. It is more difficult now with Jepson not around to answer our questions."

"Yes, but I think many things will be less difficult with Jepson not being around."

Chief Bormand turned to leave the Kales' home. "Okay, well, heal up, Doc, and don't work too hard."

"Thanks, Chief. I won't."

The phone rang, and Deni informed Cameron that the call was for him. "You know that you are not going to get any rest today."

"I know. It's just that so much has been going on." He picked up the phone. "Hello, Cameron here."

"Cameron, it's Tom Tharston. We would like to set up a meeting with you later this week to get things rolling about your taking over Pastor Tyler's place. We plan to have a dinner on Sunday in your honor."

"Sounds good, Tom. When do you want to meet?"

"Let's meet at seven p.m. Friday."

"I'll be there."

"Hope you are feeling better, Cameron. We are all praying for you."

"Thanks, Tom, I appreciate it. God's blessings. Bye now"

As Cameron hung up the phone, Deni came over and gave him a hug. "Are you really ready for all of the things you will have to do?"

Cameron smiled and looked into her eyes. "Yes, of course I am. I just have to take it a day at a time. I know God is going to bless Mariah City Community Church, this community, and us too. We can't deny what we have seen God already do here. He has big plans, and we have to trust Him day to day. It won't be easy, but it will be a time of blessing."

"Okay. I just needed to hear you say it."

"With Jepson out of the way, we will see a greater time of refreshing and getting busy with the work God has called us to do. It will be great to preach and teach and be involved in positive ministry instead of constantly putting out fires."

"Yes, you are right about that."

"Hey, Dad!" Cody came in from school and asked how his dad was feeling.

"I am feeling pretty good, Code. How about you?"

"I'm not the one who was shot."

"No, but you are the one who saved my life. Just a few inches closer to my heart, and I would not be here today. You are my hero, son." Cameron pulled Cody down affectionately and tucked his head into his chest.

"Thanks, Dad, but everyone knows that you are the hero."

"Well, let's say that Jesus is our hero. We can all be heroes if we trust and obey the Lord."

"I know that, Dad, but I am not sure many people do."

"Why do you say that?"

"So many people believed Jepson and followed him. There was a time that they were willing to follow him instead of the pastor that God called to the church. They didn't want to believe you either, even though God used you to lead many to Christ. Everyone knows God has given you gifts and is using you in the ministry, but people don't easily see it."

"That's a pretty wise observation, Cody. You're right. People can be easily deceived. They tend to see what they want to see. Jepson made friends, but he did it with the intention of leading them astray. He tricked people to believe bad things about Pastor Tyler because they assumed Jepson had an inside scoop. Praise God that Jesus sees all of this, and He intervened and helped us through this ordeal."

"He sure did, Dad. He *is* our hero."

⟋◦◦◦⟍

Deni fixed the boys dinner but had to go out to the pregnancy center for an evening clinic. Several women who were thinking about having an abortion would be getting an ultrasound, and she had counseled both of these girls. Though they were different, their stories were similar. Both of them came from a home where they had little support of the parents. They were afraid to talk to their parents and knew that their parents would coerce them to terminate the baby's life. They thought it would be an easier road to just choose an abortion and keep the information from their parents.

Deni knew they just needed to know that they had support. Many women choose to not keep their babies even though they want to keep them because they do not believe they have the support they need. Deni had been a proxy mother to these two girls and knew they needed a lot of love and attention during this difficult time of decision-making.

Cameron and Cody decided to watch a movie and enjoy some time together. Cody could cook up a mean bowl of popcorn in the microwave, and Cameron could put it away pretty fast too.

As Deni walked back into the house from her brief trip to the pregnancy center, the phone rang. "Cameron, it's Kraig Tyler."

Cameron gave Deni a welcome back kiss and took the phone. "Cameron."

"Cameron, this is Kraig Tyler. I wanted to check up on you and see how you are doing. That was some dinner the other night."

"Well, it was quite an ordeal, sir, but God is good. We are all okay, and I am healing up."

"Wonderful! There is another reason I called. I wanted to let you know that I was serious about helping you and the church in any way I can. I know these are difficult times financially and no church really has the funding it needs to grow its ministries. I want to help with that."

"Kraig, I don't know what to say other than thank you. It is very much appreciated."

Kraig wanted to be sure Cameron understood how much he wanted to help him and the church. "I believe God has a purpose for your being there at Mariah City Community Church and that God uses money in His work."

Cameron laughed. "Yes, He does, sir."

"So instead of putting the burden on you to come up with how the money can be used, I want you to open up a bank account and let the church know that you will have the ability to use the money. If you believe it's a project that God is for, let me know, and we will release the funds for the project."

"That's...wonderful, sir!"

"I will put fifteen million dollars in this account first thing tomorrow."

"Fifteen million? Did I hear you right, sir?"

"Yes, you did. That's just to get us started. Cameron, the church is going to grow. You are starting to max out your facility, which only seats fifteen hundred people—you are going to need to build, son. Now you can. Just don't want you to have any barriers as to what God can and will do."

"I don't know what to say."

"You have already said it. Take care. I will keep in touch. Tell your church board as soon as you can about our discussion. It should be a major encouragement to them."

"It will be, sir. Thank you again."

"You're very welcome, Cameron. Talk to you soon."

Cameron walked into the family room, where Deni had joined Cody in watching the end of the movie Cameron and Cody began to watch. His face was glowing, and his mouth was open.

"Cam, what was that all about?"

"You won't believe it."

"What?" Deni asked, raising her hands.

"Come here," Cameron said, directing her into the kitchen. "I don't want to say it too loudly."

"I know, Dad. It's not for my ears!" Cody said.

Deni and Cameron laughed.

"Cam, what is it?" Deni asked after they walked into the kitchen.

"Kraig Tyler is going to help us with the church."

"What do you mean?"

"Financially."

Deni already knew this but was wondering why Cameron looked like a kid on Christmas Day. "Good! What is he going to do?"

"He is going to open up an account for us to use to help with expanding church ministries and the facility."

"Cameron, that is fantastic!"

"You haven't heard all of it. It's fifteen million dollars."

"I heard that!" Cody said, overhearing them from their excitement.

"Oh gosh, Cam, that is crazy!" Deni said.

"Yes, but not when God is in it!"

Both of them hugged each other and whispered praises to God. They knew God was going to provide for the church to become what He wanted it to become in the days ahead.

Cameron woke up the next day to the sun shining through his window. With the window slightly opened, a fresh morning breeze came into the bedroom. Cameron said his usual first prayer of the day before he got out of the covers.

"Lord, this is Your day. May You do as *You* please and lead me to be obedient to You in everything. And help us, Lord, as we are all going to miss our good friend Pastor Kit. Amen."

Despite his joy, his shoulder was still sore from the bullet grazing. Cameron jumped onto his feet and headed to shower and dress.

It was a beautiful day, and it seemed as though many days following were as fresh and invigorating as this one. It was indeed a time of refreshing. Cameron had not realized how difficult the battle had been and the depth of spiritual battle that existed with Jepson fighting him, Pastor Tyler, the church, and Jesus Christ.

Praise God for times to rest. Cameron was thankful for the break from all of the drama.

———◦⁄◦⁄◦———

Friday came, and Cameron showed up to the church boardroom to meet with the church officers. Tom Tharston headed up the meeting and welcomed Cameron.

"Cameron, would you open up our meeting in prayer?"

"Certainly. Heavenly Father, I thank You for the fact that You are a God who is in charge of all things and that You are the God of provision and direction. Lead us, Lord, here at Mariah City Community Church. May what we do be what You want us to do—guide our meeting that every word and action may honor You. We pray in Your wonderful, precious name. Amen."

Tom Tharston began the meeting. "Thank you, Cameron. We want to let you know we have discussed your stepping up to fill Pastor Tyler's position and will have the church vote on Sunday." The other men sitting at the table were nodding their heads. Tom continued. "It will be an official vote, although it will be a formality. We are certain the church will love to have you on board with us and be our spiritual leader. Of course, this is all depending on what you believe God wants you to do."

"I have no doubt in my mind that God wants me to fill the gap and help the church in Pastor Tyler's place," Cameron said. "I am willing to come as a servant. I am sure, though, you know I am an evangelist. It is my major gifting."

While Tom did not say it, and Cameron was not thinking about it, he remembered Pastor Kit telling the congregation through his DVD that he believed Cameron also had the gift of prophecy. This would be a helpful gift for Mariah City Community Church.

"Yes, we have all discussed that," Tom responded. "It is evident that your major gift is evangelism. But we need an evangelist. We need someone to teach us what we should focus on. We also know you are a gifted teacher too and know the Word of God.

Pastor Tyler trusted you, and therefore, we trust you too. Will you accept this position?"

Cameron sat up straight at the table and smiled. "Yes, gentlemen. I am certain this is the direction God is leading me."

"Wonderful!" Tom replied. "Is Deni supportive of this too?"

"Absolutely. She is a great helpmeet and believes God is working in and through both of us. While she is passionate about her work with the pregnancy center, she is also focused on the work of the church."

Tom Tharston smiled. "We are planning to vote after the morning service and hold a dinner in the fellowship hall welcoming you and your family to the church as pastor. Is there anything else, Cameron?"

"Yes. Most of you know that we have been growing quite rapidly in just a few short weeks. Many have accepted Christ and intend on joining this church. We are already at maximum capacity with our facility and need to expand."

Tom looked at the other men, concerned. "Well, Cameron, we just don't have the money to do something like that right now. Perhaps after some months of better tithes and offerings we can take a look at that."

Cameron smiled. "Gentlemen, I am here to tell you that God has already given me the money."

Tom squinted, wanting to understand. "Cameron, we are talking five hundred thousand dollars or more to make that kind of expansion."

"No problem, Tom."

"No problem?" Tom came back. "You have five hundred thousand?"

"Yes, sir, I have *fifteen million* dollars."

The men sat back in their seats grinning at each other and looking at Cameron with their mouths open wide.

"How is that possible? Where—?"

Cameron interrupted and told them that Kraig Tyler had taken a liking to him. He shared with the men that Kraig had told Cameron he wanted to help the church accommodate the growth that is going to happen and that he opened an account and put Cameron in charge of it. With Kraig's permission, he would approve any dollar needs up to the amount needed for the church to grow. They were amazed.

Tom spoke up. "Well, this is just another confirmation that God is in this. Praise God! Cameron, these are going to be some exciting times!"

"I agree! They are going to be times of refreshing."

They all said, "Amen." Tom closed in prayer, and the meeting was adjourned.

———

Sunday had come and gone, and now Cameron Kale was officially the pastor of Mariah City Community Church. Though everyone recognized him as pastor, they also declared that he was also the church's resident evangelist. No one could deny that this was one of his God-given gifts.

These were exciting times. Numbers were added to the church, and more and more folks were attending the services. Now the new pastor would raise up a building committee, begin plans for expansion of the current auditorium, add classrooms and offices, and expand the fellowship hall as well. Kraig Tyler was excited that the church was expanding and that he was able to help.

In Cameron's first several months as the pastor of MCCC, he focused his sermon series on the need for every Christian to actively share their faith. He called the church to see it as the Christian's priority until Jesus returned. During this time, Cameron worked with some of the city councilmen, the mayor, and Christian leaders in the community to set up a series of evangelistic campaigns that would reach larger numbers in the city for Christ. These campaign meetings were called "Harvest Gatherings." Leaders from MCCC taught teams how to invite friends, family, and associates who were unsaved to these Harvest

Gatherings. These meetings were led with exciting worship music and testimonies but centered on evangelistic preaching.

Harvest Gathering teams were established, and members proudly wore Harvest Gathering T-shirts and committed themselves to market the importance of these meetings and to coordinate local churches in participating. Months of preparation went into launching the Harvest Gathering events.

Night after night the downtown coliseum was filled with thousands of attendees. Many came out of curiosity from the advertisements in the newspapers, on the radio, and on television. Kraig Tyler had advanced dollars specifically to pay for the advertisements needed to reach the crowds that needed to hear the gospel message at the gatherings.

Cameron boldly preached how the times indicated that it was near the time Christ predicted He would come back for His church. He told them that we could not know the exact day or hour but that we could know the seasons. He shared that many needed to forsake secularism and begin to believe that truth is beyond the empirical formula and the five senses. He called people to have faith and believe what is beyond what we see.

Thousands came to know Christ in the meetings. Television cameras were recording the events. Reporters were interviewing attendees and hearing testimonies of those whose lives were changed through the Harvest Gatherings.

Mariah City quickly became known as the city with the fastest conversion rate to Christianity anywhere in the United States. NBC and CBS sent reporters to talk with Cameron Kale and find out what made the Harvest Gatherings unique. What was the secret of so many people turning to Christianity?

It was difficult for Cameron to accept invitations to *The Today Show*, *Good Morning America*, and other such programs. He was not comfortable with interviews since he believed the media was always looking for some angle, some underlying motive for change in people. Would they simply accept that God desires for men and women to come into a living relationship with Him and that the time was ripe for a harvest of souls?

Matt Lauer of *The Today Show* asked Cameron why he thought the Harvests Gatherings were a new phenomenon. He replied, truthfully, it is not new but a phenomenon that has been going on for several thousands of years. He explained that at some periods of time there were greater seasons of revival than others but that when God is moving and people are looking for something real, Christianity happens.

"But we have heard this before," Matt Lauer responded.

"Then we agree—it's not a new phenomenon!" Cameron said humorously.

Matt Lauer just smiled. "Thank you." Looking into the camera, Matt Lauer said, "Cameron Kale, pastor of Mariah City Community Church in Mariah City, Nevada, now dubbed by many as the 'Evangel of Mariah City.' Thank you for coming on the show."

"It's been a privilege to be here, Matt."

With phone calls, dinner engagements, interviews, and trips to several cities for radio and television spots, Cameron needed to draw the line so that he could fulfill his primary duties as pastor of MCCC and of caring for his own family.

Deni and Cody went with Cameron to New York City for his interview with *The Today Show*. Cody wanted to visit the Empire State Building and Ground Zero, where the Twin Towers had fallen due to terrorist attacks. Deni wanted to visit the largest pregnancy center in the city and see some of the shops and stores there too. Cameron, Deni, and Cody had a wonderful time seeing the sites of the Big Apple, which was quite a big change from their small Nevada community.

The Kales' lives had been truly blessed over the months that followed, as well as the life of Mariah City Community Church and the neighboring community. No one could believe all the changes that were happening in the city. The church had completed the expanded sanctuary that would now seat ten thousand. The new fellowship hall, classes, and offices were completed. Over the course of six months, the church had grown from 1,500 to 6,000. Many of that number were new believers in Christ but also included laborers that the church had prayed God would send to the harvest field. With capable teachers and church leaders, classrooms were utilized to develop a Bible institute offering numerous biblical courses. MCCC was becoming a Christian learning center and training men and women how to be servants of God. Several properties were acquired around the church property to expand parking and consider new phases of building as the church needed. Kraig Tyler gave money to purchase the properties the church needed for expansion.

In addition to God blessing the church, He used its ministry to bless the community. Many dollars were given to help area nonprofits, including the pregnancy center that was a frontline ministry to reduce the numbers of abortions in the community. Many young couples were given a new lease on life, and they learned the value of keeping their babies and building a family. The church, which reached many young people, funded a coffee house. The coffee house featured Christian musicians and offered coffee, lattes, and cappuccinos and amazing french fries with cheese on Thursday and Friday nights. Someone always shared their testimony about how Christ had changed their lives. One of the most phenomenal changes in Mariah City was that many bar owners came to know Christ and reduced the number of bars in the city. Mariah City was becoming like the old Chicago in the days when Billy Sunday preached and dried up the city.

Community leaders were beginning their meetings with prayer and hiring chaplains to work with their businesses. Sundays were becoming more sacred, and businesses were honoring it by closing their businesses during church hours.

The talk on the street was that these were new days, unlike anything anyone had seen for years. People were moving to Mariah City because they heard how good the school system was.

Many teachers and school board members, principals, and school personnel had accepted Christ through the Harvest Gathering campaigns. There was no doubt that God had used the ministry of the Kales and Kraig Tyler's funding to bring new life to Mariah City. These were indeed times of refreshing.

—⦅⦆—

Meanwhile, Cameron Kale, Scott Benson, and Clem Mager became close co-laborers in the work of the ministry. Only one year had gone by since Amy's accident and death, but God was faithful to provide a special lady friend for Scott, Kim Carson. Her husband had passed away from cancer several years earlier. In many ways, she was like Amy. She was passionate about ministry and was well liked by many women in the church and community. She loved to speak out about things she believed in. She was a local anchorperson for Mariah City Channel 5 and was everyone's favorite reporter. Scott was thankful for her friendship but was not ready yet to make any deep commitments to her. Amy was still fresh on his mind, and it seemed too soon to get too involved in another relationship. Nevertheless, Scott could not deny that God brought Kim into his life and that she was just what he needed. Cameron; Deni; Clem; his wife, Magee; Scott; and Kim became very close friends and spent much time serving together on various ministry teams. Mariah City Community Church was blessed to have this special team of committed ministers of the gospel.

Numerous ministry teams and cell groups had developed as the people of MCCC were being discipled and reaching out more into the community. The more ministry teams and cell groups added, the more people came to know Christ and grew in Christ so that MCCC had now grown to nearly 10,000 within one year.

It had also been one year since Cameron had turned over his chiropractic business to one of his former classmates and associates. It was necessary for him to give himself fully to the ministry of MCCC. He had always wanted to continue his practice because he thought Cody would some day take over his business. He had often talked about being a chiropractor, but since Cody had grown in his personal faith over the past year, he was talking about being a pastor or a criminologist or both. He thought a lot like a thirteen-year-old.

Cameron felt blessed to see his wife and son living a productive and joyful Christian life. He often thought how difficult it would be to serve without them both. He loved them deeply and wanted to make a good life for them. His hope for both of them was that they would reap the greatest benefits of living solely for Christ and doing exactly what God had called each of them to do. He knew that God had called Deni to be by his side and be the helpmeet he needed in life and ministry, but he also knew that God had some special ministry for her as well. He had no doubt it was the pregnancy center work. He had seen how passionate and full of life she was as she talked about the need to reach these young women and men. She loved every girl who came in with the love of Christ and spent many hours listening to them and giving them direction, support, and hope.

Cameron knew how important this ministry was. He knew God is the God of life and that we must uphold the sanctity of life. He knew that the little ones were gifts from God (Psalm 127:3) and that they were our future society. As Christians, we should do all that we can to help these innocent ones who have no voice. We must be their voice. Cameron oftentimes shared with the congregation at MCCC how important the ministry of the pregnancy center was and that abortion was one of the great sins of our modern day. With Cameron's openness about abortion and the sanctity of life, he gained enemies as well as friends. With abortion being such a hot-bed issue in the nation, as he was becoming better-known by people across the country, his position on pro-life was becoming known as well. This being true, Cameron was given numerous opportunities to speak out publicly about his views.

Chapter Sixteen

Being God's Voice on Social Injustices

C ameron Kale was focusing much of his evangelistic meetings in the city and surrounding cities leveled at exposing social injustices in our society, such as abortion-on-demand, euthanasia, human trafficking, gay marriage, and poverty.

Through Cameron's preaching, people in high places became Christians, but he made some enemies too.

Cameron was invited to a forum to speak along with many others that the city set up for university professors, teachers, pastors, and lawmakers and civil servants to discuss a variety of social topics and how the city could improve by addressing these topics. Each speaker was given fifteen minutes and then ten minutes as a follow-up. The moderator introduced questions that were raised by citizens about the issues that concerned them the most. The large town hall meeting room seemed to be filled with chatter while the speakers gave their opinions. The height of the ornately carved ceiling created an echo of voices and made it difficult to hear with any clarity.

When Cameron approached the podium, there was a serenity that had not possessed the room that night. Everyone was quiet and seemed as if they were really interested to hear what Cameron Kale had to say.

Cameron knew God had provided this occasion to be a leader to city leaders. They were the movers and shakers of Mariah City.

Most knew that Cameron Kale had made a difference for their community, but they also knew that he was a Christian preacher and would put his Christian slant on everything. Nevertheless, he had the respect of the audience, and they listened with anticipation of every word.

"Dear friends, thank you for the opportunity to share my thoughts on the questions placed before us as a community. There are no easy answers. There are clearly different sides on some of these issues. If we are to be a successful community and work for the betterment of everyone here, we have to be unified. You have heard that a nation divided against itself cannot stand. There is no room for values clarification here—there is absolute truth. Both reason and experience tells us that this is true. How can we unify on these issues and what should we be unified on?

"Most of you know that I am not a politician. Yes, I am a pastor. But I know many pastors who are politicians." There was some laughter. "I am not a politician but firmly believe in representing those who hold to healthy and necessary values.

"My time is limited, so let me be brief and to the point. We often think of our communities being run on dollars." There were many nods in agreement. "We need money to run a city, don't we? But money doesn't make up the community. People do. So what is our priority, money or people?"

Everyone waited in anticipation to see where Cameron was going with this before they began their chanting as they did with the other speakers.

"Listen, folks. If we focus on the value of people and their needs, we won't be as concerned about the dollar bill. Many of us support abortion, not because we believe it is best for the girl who is in crisis with her unexpected pregnancy, but because we have fears about what this will do to the community if she keeps it. We fear unwanted babies with no one to care for them, child-abuse cases, families that can't afford to raise the children so they will need community benefits to help. So we decide to terminate the unborn infants. Has anyone stopped to think what it costs the community to terminate these pregnancies and then pay for the problems that ensue following the abortion? Many of these women don't stop becoming pregnant, so these terminations continue several times for many women. Then, as we raise the bar and eliminate enough children, we have eliminated a future society. How will we pay for the future? We can't because we have eliminated many of our finest taxpayers." Many nodded affirmatively and whispered to others nearby.

"We want to help our society handle the massive need of elderly care, so we decide to end their lives early. Does it save society money? Perhaps it does, but it eliminates much of the wisdom, knowledge, and value that grandmothers, grandfathers, great uncles or aunts, etc., bring to our younger generation. What are they learning about family? How is removing the glue that holds the family together helping us to remain strong as a community?

"Let's help each other discover the best in life as we reach out to help those who don't have a voice or who are less fortunate instead of buying into policies and legislation that just tries to make our life easier. No one said building a community and maintaining it was easy. It should be. But the effort will be well worth it. Thank you."

Instead of the typical noise of people hurling their opinions and shouting out of turn as they did with previous speakers, the entire meeting hall rang out with applause. God had given Cameron wisdom to speak the truth, and it touched the massive audience that night.

Cameron came home around 8 p.m. that night. "Hey, everyone. I brought some pizza."

Cody ran through the house, shouting, "Yeah! Let's watch a late movie."

"Sounds good," Deni responded. "How was the meeting?"

"All I can say is God showed up!"

She hugged and kissed him. "I knew you would have a good report. You are always so positive."

Cameron got excited. "No, really. It was amazing. People were actually listening and responding proactively. Don't be surprised if you get some interested volunteers—maybe even some donations."

"That would be great! Let's have some of that pizza."

As the Kale's sat down to eat and enjoy a late movie, the phone rang. Cameron got up to answer the phone.

"Dr. Kale?"

"Yes?"

"I'm sorry to call you so late. This is Donna Travers, one of your previous patients. I was watching television and thought you may want to turn your television to channel five for the news. There is something you may want to see."

"Okay, thanks, Donna. By the way, how have you been doing? I haven't seen you in quite some time."

"We are doing well. You were a great help getting our family physically better."

"Come by and visit the church sometime. We would love to have you."

"We would like that. Thanks for the invitation. Dr. Kale?

"Yes?"

"Channel five."

"Oh yes. I will check it out right now. Take care."

"Bye now."

"Cody, change the channel quickly over to channel five."

"It's Mayor Hanson and several councilmen. They are talking about your speech tonight, Cam," Deni said.

"We just want to say that we are supportive of everything that Cameron Kale shared at the forum tonight. He was eloquent about what we must do to make this a growing, caring community. We need to form a task force and will ask Cameron to head this up to begin to make a positive difference in our community. We may need to meet with some nonprofits and talk about new approaches to handling old hot topic issues like abortion and euthanasia. It won't be easy, but if anyone can do it, it is Cameron Kale."

"Wow, Dad. You are a hero again."

"I am glad you see it that way, Code, but like I said before. Any of us can be heroes when we are obedient to speak up for the truth God has given us to share. We have to be bold and openly share the truth."

"Your right, hon," Deni replied. "Thank you, Lord."

The Kales uttered a brief prayer standing between their kitchen and family room in praise to God for His goodness.

Deni smiled and rallied everyone back to their family get-together. "What do you say we get back to the movie?"

"Sounds good," Cameron bellowed. "So does some more pizza."

The next morning at breakfast, Cameron received another call, but this time it was the mayor of Mariah City, Bill Hanson.

"Cameron?"

"Yes, sir, what can I do for you? You sound upset."

"Well, I don't know if you caught the news last night, but Councilman Tim Borden and Councilwoman Teresa Savage and I were singing your praises and raised the idea of starting a task force to help the city work out some of these social issues."

"Yes, I did see that. I would be happy and honored to do what I can."

"I knew I could count on you, but there is a problem."

"What is it?"

"Do you remember Dr. Joan Canthrop?"

"Yes, vaguely."

"She is a professor at Mariah U and, well, quite honestly, a bigmouth. I am serious, Cameron. She took everything you said last night and trashed you before some anxious young reporters who just wanted to get a quick story. I just want you to know that you have made some enemies. The good news is that you have a lot of friends here in the city too. I think we can make a difference together, but you will have to watch your back with this Dr. Canthrop. She likes witch hunts."

"Thanks for the warning, Mayor."

"You're welcome. Let's get together and set up some meetings to get this task force going, Kale!"

"You got it!"

Deni and Cameron focused much of their energies on the church and gained more roles with the community. Deni also gave a lot of her time to directing the local pregnancy center, helping others to see the value of life. What they both needed and worked hard to guard was their quiet time. Typically, each morning before breakfast, Cameron and Deni would spend some personal time in prayer and reading their Bibles. Sometimes they would share some of their concerns and burdens of the church and challenge each other to find God's answers to those questions. Often they would share with each other their personal struggles and need to grow in their faith in Christ.

Cameron's greatest struggle was to be everything he knew God wanted him to be. So often Cody would call him a hero, and he would remind Cody that all of us are heroes when we obey Christ. He would often tell Cody that we can be like those heroes of faith written in Hebrews chapter eleven. Though he knew this, at times his faith would wane, and he would have this nagging feeling of his inadequacy.

He couldn't help thinking about the fact that he had not had vivid dreams or any encounters with Ser Pentino for over a year. He knew God had given him strength and victory over the enemy and had blessed his life, but he was not foolish enough to think there would be no more spiritual battles. He wanted to be prepared.

Deni was as busy with the pregnancy center as Cameron was with the church. Seeing the need to share truth with the community, Deni attended the local community collaborative. Many nonprofit and education directors gathered to discuss the agendas for their programs and provide information for other shareholders of their corporations. Deni knew many of these leaders were pro-choice and did not appreciate the work she did through the pregnancy center. Nevertheless, it was her duty to share the work.

At one of these meetings, Deni felt particularly blessed by the positive response to many of the directors who attended the community collaborative to her discussion on the nonpolitical nature of her work. She declared that it did not matter whether her clients were pro-choice or pro-life—she helped all of them. She emphasized that her job was to help them in their time of crisis. She shared how these women needed care and compassion regardless of their situation. She said this was a pro-woman position. Some women even applauded, but one loudly objected.

"Ms. Kale, you may have heard of me. I am Dr. Joan Canthrop. I am a professor at Mariah U. You surprise me. I am not sure you are telling these women the truth. I have heard about your fake clinic where women are coerced to believe they will be damned if they give up their babies. You show them terrible videos of babies being aborted and make them feel condemned if they don't buy into your pro-life views."

Deni was doing her best to keep from snarling at Dr. Canthrop. "I assure you that you are completely wrong about—"

"Wrong, you say?" Dr. Canthrop interrupted. "No, I am not wrong. It is just that I see completely through you and your pastor husband, Cameron Kale. You are all about imposing your religion and are trying to dupe the people of Mariah City into your cult."

The moderator of the collaborative spoke out. "Joan, I don't think we need to make accusations. Deni is just sharing her program with us."

"Oh, I don't have to make accusations. Some of you will see in due time what the Kales are trying to do. You will all see. Trust me."

Deni came home somewhat exasperated, telling her husband about her day. "Cam, my gosh. It was horrible. I was sharing with the directors at the collaborative about the heart and soul of pregnancy center work and its nonpolitical nature. I even received some applause, and then the shark lady spoke up."

"Shark lady? Who was that?"

"Dr. Joan Canthrop."

"Oh, Dr. Canthrop. Bill Hanson warned me about her. He said she has a thing against us and for us to be careful around her. Evidently, she wants to stir up some trouble."

Deni put her hands on her hips. "She seems to have a hatred for what we do."

"Yeah, you're right. She may have had some bad experience with the church or something in her past. I know it's not always easy to pray for those who are on the attack. But that is what Jesus wants us to do. Let's pray for her. God can change her heart toward us."

"You're right. Besides, I would rather have her as a friend than an enemy. Good suggestion."

Cam nodded. "Go ahead, Deni, *you* pray."

"Dear, God, we have been so blessed by You. We know that You are working. We pray for Dr. Canthrop. We don't know why she is so against Your Word and us. But we know You do. We pray You will save her, Lord. She needs You. She would be such a go-getter for You if she accepted You as Lord and Savior. Protect us also, Lord. Help us so that we can accomplish the work You want us to do and not be hindered by this very angry lady. Amen."

"Amen. I have some news for you, Deni."

"Well, I hope your news is better than mine."

"It is." Cameron paused as what seemed like several minutes as he stared at Deni with a grin.

"Okay, give it to me."

"Mike Hanson came over to the church today and talked to me about a task force the city wants me to head up to address social issues in our city."

"Cam, that's great!"

"Here is the good part. They want the pregnancy center to be an example to the community of how to help those who hurt."

"But what about Planned Parenthood? We will have some debates from them for sure."

"Well, they are not denying Planned Parenthood any rights or opportunities. They are just going to allow the center some opportunities that it has been denied."

"That is amazing news, Cam. Wait until Dr. Canthrop hears about this."

"I think she has. She is on several boards and committees at Mariah U, and some of the people on those committees are on Bill's staff."

"Sounds like we are in for a ride."

"You bet! Hang on, though, it's gonna be a fast one."

"Kind of like your Camaro?"

"You got it!"

Deni laughed.

It seemed as though months were rolling by as the Kales were involved with both the church and the pregnancy center. Interested and gifted members of the church body developed new ministry teams. Body life was growing as more cell groups were raised in the community. The membership was growing too. Within less than two years, Mariah City Community Church had grown to 11,000 members. Cameron added a number of young pastors to his pastoral team and a number of Bible Institute teachers. The first board that only consisted of six deacons and one pastor had now grown to five pastors, twelve deacons, and ten trustees.

Church members had learned to discover their gifts through a series of biblical studies and then were surveyed to assess those gifts. The pastors aided in assisting members to find ministries where they could use their gifts. Mobilizing gifted members to ministry became a necessary strategy in helping MCCC grow and accomplish God's plan for the church.

Scott Benson and Clem Mager had become two of the teaching deacons of the church. Cameron often said that these guys were strong links in his pastoral team. Though they were not seminary-trained pastors, both men were spiritual men and gifted leaders. Tom Tharston continued to support Cameron and even more so when his wife passed away the second year Cameron was pastor at MCCC. Tom's wife, Dawn, was one of the ladies who had had the Jezebel spirit before Cameron came to be pastor. However, God's spirit had touched her heart, renewed her spirit, and made her an on-fire Christian. She would be greatly missed.

Both Scott and Clem were sidekicks to Cameron in the city task force for social justice. Both advocates for the sanctity of life, as well as grace and respect given to the elderly, they helped Cameron find ways to convince the community of its need to help the innocent who do not have a voice.

Kraig Tyler gave several million dollars to Cameron to help his task force make some significant differences to help those who didn't have a voice.

One million was designated to the Mariah Family Center, the pregnancy center that Deni ran, to help it with operations, education, and outreach. Another million dollars was given to help a local assisted living home improve services for the elderly.

Cameron Kale found his days filled with activities inside and outside of the local church. His community work with the mayor and councilmen was providing tremendous services for the community. Cameron and Deni worked together to get radio ads and small, local television ads out to make the community aware of services to help young women in crisis pregnancies. Donations flooded the center to provide baby clothes, diapers, and formula for those who needed it. Volunteers were coming out of the woodwork to help at the center. Both Cameron and

Deni had opportunities to speak in the community and stressed the nonpolitical nature of what they were doing. They explained that while they believed in the sanctity of life, their desire was to help all women regardless of their choice. They explained that they were the true pro-choice. They were pro-woman. Many in Mariah City were discussing the local pregnancy center as a place where good Samaritans help others in need.

While there were many positive responses to the work the Kales and the task force were doing, there was also opposition. Dr. Canthrop seemed to attend every meeting that Cameron and Deni were to speak at. She always seemed to put in a word or two, desiring to raise suspicions with the public about the Kales' work.

On one occasion, Dr. Canthrop talked to a local news reporter, encouraging him to call Deni Kale and try to get an interview with her. She mentioned to the reporter that it was not right that a local group donated money for a parenting education curriculum the pregnancy center wanted to purchase. It was her contention that the local group was positioning themselves with pro-lifers and that this was not right.

Deni received a call from the *Nevada Sun.*

"Hello, is this Deni Kale?"

"Yes, it is."

"My name is Todd Canton, and I'm with the *Nevada Sun.* We would like to do an article on you folks."

Deni's first response was a smile. It had been a blessing to have so many folks recognize the positive work the center was doing for the community. The reporter told her that he had received word from a source that some people in the community were concerned about the money donated to the center from the local women's group since the center was pro-life. Deni was ready for a fight.

"Sir, I want to invite you to our center and explain to you why no one should be concerned about our donations. Shame on whoever made those complaints."

Todd Canton kept his appointment, and Deni was anxious to share with him the purpose of the pregnancy center. She took Todd on a tour and then finished the tour with an interview for the *Nevada Sun*. Todd asked questions that led Deni to believe that he was also of the opinion that the pregnancy center slanted everything in a pro-life direction. Deni tried to convince him that they truly reached out to all women and avoided any coercion or brainwashing to convince women to keep their babies. Todd left and thanked Deni for the tour.

The newspaper article came out a few days later in the *Nevada Sun*. Several of her board members apprised her of the article and its negative slant against the center. Deni was upset that Todd Canton did not share any of Deni's perspective on the center but rather promoted his own bias against the center and pro-life positions. She felt that he was far from fair and balanced in his reporting. She called him immediately and expressed her disappointment in his reporting and not sharing some of the important points she had discussed with him.

Within hours of the article being printed, Deni received several calls from donors and folks in the community. They were upset with Todd Canton as well. It was obvious to them that Todd was liberal in his views and himself a pro-choicer.

Deni called the chairman of the woman's group that had donated the money for their parenting curriculum. Deni felt badly that this was negative press for the group and was concerned for their organization. The chairwoman was thankful for Deni's call and told her that she expected as much from Todd Canton. Out of this situation, many came to support the center because of their stand and concern for women.

Deni learned a lesson about sharing information with liberal reporters who were simply looking for an opportunity to promote their liberal viewpoints. She wondered if the person who encouraged the reporter to call was Dr. Canthrop. Deni prayed that God would stop this woman for creating such havoc for the center but thanked Him that her attempt to hurt the center ended up bringing more donors to help out.

Cameron would take time to share truth about the sanctity of life each year on a Sunday in January near the date of *Roe v. Wade*. Thousands of churches participate in what is called "Sanctity of Life Sunday." Pastor Cameron would share how believers needed to get involved in helping others see the value of life. He would always bring the congregation to be aware that since the Supreme Court declared abortion on demand to be the law of the land in 1973, 55 million American babies had been killed—over 1.4 million per year, 4,000 every day.

Pastor Cameron called for believers to be the arms of Christ and reach out to these women, not callously call them murderers. He shared how mercy, love, and grace could change the heart of these men and women and cause them to change their views about life too.

As Pastor Cameron shared these views, women who had previously aborted their children felt encouraged to come forward and ask God for forgiveness and also desire for help. Deni's post-abortion classes were filled with both women and men who wanted healing from their abortion experiences. God was blessing the work of the Kales in the community, and social injustices were being made right.

Cameron was also involved with the assisted living program at a nearby elderly home. With the dollars Kraig Tyler had given to the task force to invest in this home, Cameron, Mayor Bill Hanson, and the councilpersons were able to help the home with new equipment, new personnel, facility improvements, and new programs that would assist the center in educating clients on the ills of euthanasia.

Cameron was becoming an avid speaker against what he felt was another one of our nation's social injustices: euthanasia. While the Bible does not specifically mention euthanasia, the

Bible does address the principle of valuing life. Since Christians believe the Bible to support the sanctity of human life, we are to respect Bible truth. The Bible does say "Thou shall not kill" in the Ten Commandments, and Christians, therefore, believe that life is precious and that only God can take life away. Pope John Paul said, "We should not kill those whose suffering we cannot bear." These are a few of the many reasons Christians believe euthanasia is wrong.

Cameron loved to quote Francis Schaeffer, the great theologian of the twentieth century, noted for his position on the decline of modern society. One of Cameron's favorite quotes was from Schaeffer's book *Whatever Happened to the Human Race*. He would often share this in his lectures.

"At one time, blacks were not recognized as human beings. This was the rationale behind the slave trade that brought black Africans to the United States. They were transported in slave ships that held them confined in the same manner that livestock is confined when shipped to the slaughter houses. In Nazi Germany, only the Aryan race was considered human, and we know the consequences of that thinking. The treatment of Jews and other non-Aryans was similar to that of animals. And the Nazi genetic experiments remain a source for horror stories even today. Will a society, which has assumed the right to kill infants in the womb—because they are unwanted, imperfect, or merely inconvenient—have difficulty in assuming the right to kill other human beings, especially older adults who are judged unwanted, deemed imperfect physically or mentally, or considered a possible social nuisance?

"The next candidates for arbitrary reclassification as non-persons are the elderly. This will become increasingly so as the proportion of the old and weak in relation to the young and strong becomes abnormally large due to the growing antifamily sentiment, the abortion rate, and medicine's contribution to the lengthening of the normal life span. The imbalance will cause many of the young to perceive the old as a cramping nuisance in the hedonistic lifestyle they claim as their right. As the demand for affluence continues and the economic crunch gets greater, the amount of compassion that the legislatures and the courts will have for the old does not seem likely to be significant considering the precedent of the non-protection given to the unborn and the newborn."

The mayor of Mariah City set up a dinner funded by the task force and asked Cameron to speak to city leaders and the city's medical community on assisted suicide. The local news reporters were there with their cameras to capture the story. There was no question that this was another hot topic not only in Mariah City but also in the entire nation.

Over 500 community leaders attended and enjoyed their entrée of wood-broiled salmon, almond green beans, small red potatoes, salad, rolls, New York cheesecake for dessert, and coffee or tea. Mayor Hanson was the master of ceremonies for the occasion. A nationally known musician, a comedian, and recognition of many dedicated leaders in the city for various meritorious services performed highlighted the evening. There was laughter, shared sentiments, and a few serious moments, but nothing in this evening would be as serious as the topic of the evening's guest speaker, Cameron Kale.

Mayor Hanson came up to the podium again and addressed the city leaders. "Dear friends, it is my privilege to allow one many of us have come to know as our friend, counselor, and pastor, Cameron Kale. I often kid him that he should not have left his day job as a chiropractor. But I only say that because my back has never been the same since Doc Kale left the business. With all kidding aside, I do not know a man that is more sincere but also sincerely knowledgeable about the ills of our day and the solutions to social injustices. I hope you will give him your full attention and appreciation for his willingness to come and address this group tonight. Cameron Kale."

Every one in the room stood from their tables and gave applause that broke out like thunder claps in the high ceilinged foyer of the Community Center at Mariah University.

"Good evening and thank you for your generous applause. Don't let Mayor Hanson fool any of you. He always had trouble with his back because he didn't take the doc's advice and change that terrible golf swing he has!" Laughter ran out through the room. "Thank you, Mayor Hanson, for the invitation to speak tonight, and thank you community leaders for attending and for all of the support many of you have given to our task force and the dollars and time you have given to make this a better community." Again, many members of the community stood to their feet and kept applause going for what seemed to be minutes.

Cameron nodded with a smile. "Thank you, thank you. I appreciate that."

When the applause ceased and everyone was seated again, Cameron looked down at his notes and then at the crowd. He did not speak a word. His pause seemed appropriate and not rehearsed. It was clear that what he was about to say next was something deep from within him. He was about to address something that deeply troubled his soul. What his listeners did not know was that Cameron was also praying silently for God to give him the evening in convincing men and women of their need to stand with him against the evil of euthanasia.

"Dear friends. What I want to speak to you about tonight is something that weighs deeply on my heart. It does so because I uphold the rights of those who do not have a voice to have the opportunity for life that I do."

The look of the crowd was serious, and every eye was on Cameron Kale. It was evident that Cameron came to speak his heart, not just his head. He had the ear of most of the community's leaders, at least for this moment.

"I am thankful that many medical societies across our land have opted to vote against support of assisted suicides. However, many of you are aware that the states have the power to make laws in favor of this practice.

"I am not here tonight to presume upon our medical leaders to tell you how to run your practice but to appeal to you concerning humanity. I know that I do not have to convince many of you medical doctors and medical administrators here tonight of the value of life. You have dedicated your lives to saving lives. Some of you wrestle because there are not always easy answers to dealing with pain, suffering, and death. When you know that you have done all that you can and you see your patients writhing in pain and you know that there will be an ultimate demise for them, you are tempted to side with those who say it is compassionate to help these folks to reach their end comfortably. It seems like the humane thing to do. It seems like it speaks compassion for those who hurt. But here is my deep struggle with the topic of assisted suicide, euthanasia. We do not have the authority to end life. Even in the short time I have been a pastor, I have had the experience of spending times in the homes of terminal patients. Hospice provided attending nurses to make them as comfortable as possible. Family and friends would come by and be by the patient's side. I have seen firsthand families singing songs to their loved one, playing their favorite hymns on the piano and singing, or just sitting by their side, stroking their heads and whispering prayers of encouragement to them in their final hours.

"It brought the best out of those who have experienced the dying and death of their loved ones in this way. As difficult as transition from this world to the next is, is it possible that the love of those who attend these bedsides are God-ordained moments for family in their appointed times to leave this world? Shouldn't something be said for those survivors and how these experiences strengthen them for life and death? Many of us remember the death of Terri Schindler Schiavo. In my opinion, Schiavo's death was a huge violation of human rights. The whole nation watched her family as they tried to save her life, but the courts and proponents of euthanasia ended Terri Schiavo's life. While some of us may not identify with the greater grief Schiavo's family experienced by her letting her die, there are elderly homes and terminal care providers in homes of the dying who are assisting people in suicide all across this nation. It has become a social ill that has become pandemic in our nation."

Cameron shared some stories of some document cases of assisted suicide. His conclusion was to applaud the state of Nevada for its position on euthanasia. He shared how a medical director of a Northern Nevada Medical Organization, members of the Nevada State Medical Association, and the American Medical Association opposed physician-assisted suicides. Cameron shared that while most people support the right of a person to refuse treatment or artificial life support, he shared how a current Senate bill was a measure to prevent an act that would cause the death of a person prematurely who would not have otherwise died of natural causes at that time. He further shared how this bill was to prevent unwanted assisted suicide of elderly persons where someone in authority could decide a person's care costs too much or their quality of life comes into question.

"Dear friends, I respect one's personal decision to end their own life because they do not want to live in pain or become a vegetable. However, the decision to end life is not that simple. I am thankful that many Nevada leaders are acting on good medical advice, suggesting a person could make a decision to die just because they received bad advice from a doctor. I am talking about a doctor who just doesn't know how to treat pain. The truth is, in most cases where people get good care, they want to live. Let's do what we can in our community to educate others on the issues of euthanasia, assisted suicides. Let's do what we can to promote life and rest the moral questions with the one who governs them, God Himself. Thank you."

The room had remained virtually silent while the attending crowd was attentive to their speaker. Table by table, community leaders stood to their feet and applauded. This time the applause was deafening and continued.

Cameron raised his head and looked to the ceiling and whispered, "Thank You again, Lord. They listened. I believe they really heard what I had to say."

Mayor Hanson came to the podium and shook Cameron's hand and put his arm around his shoulder. He reached for the microphone. "Folks, thank you for attending and supporting the task force on social issues. Thank you, Cameron, for your moving speech. We all have a lot to think about. I personally can say that I was moved by your honesty and your passion and the information that you brought tonight." The audience applauded again. "Thank you, everyone. Good night."

As Cameron left the podium, several medical leaders in the community approached him. One of Mariah City's Medical Clinic's surgeons said, "Dr. Kale. Excellent presentation!" A chief surgeon of a neighboring hospital attended the dinner and said, "Dr. Kale. We need men like you in our community. Keep up the good work. You give doctors a good name."

Dr. Canthrop was one of the people waiting in line to speak to Dr. Kale. "Mr. Kale, interesting speech! I wonder if you have ever had someone in your family who was dying and an assisted suicide might have relieved their suffering. If so, did your preaching help them?"

Bill Hanson was standing near Cameron and heard her comment. "Joan, don't you ever stay home when Cameron Kale comes out to speak?"

"No, I don't want to miss the circus!

Cameron was quick-witted and didn't want to miss this one. "Joan, you missed the circus you were supposed to be at. It must be down the road somewhere. This event was not for clowns but for committed community leaders. You need to get on board with the community instead of being an outsider." Cameron's bold and pointed words were like carefully aimed arrows at this enemy of the gospel.

With glaring eyes toward Cameron Kale, she quickly turned herself in the other direction like a whitetail deer that sensed danger. Dr. Canthrop bolted for the door with nothing more to say.

Mayor Hanson commended Cameron for speaking the truth to her. "That is the first time I have seen Dr. Canthrop without anything to say. If you can do that, you *are* a miracle man!"

They both laughed, but Cameron would have rather won her over to his way of thinking than to stir up her anger and antagonism.

On his way home, he prayed and asked the Lord to forgive him for his sharp tongue and speaking too quickly to Dr. Canthrop. He was concerned that if he had a chance to win her to the Lord, it may not happen now that he had directly challenged and offended her. He knew there would be future confrontations by this person who strongly disliked him, his family, and their cause.

As Cameron approached the street near his home, he noticed a fanfare of vehicles and people on his lawn. His front door was open, and Deni and Cody were standing on the porch.

Cameron pulled into his driveway, opened his car door, and shouted, "Hey, what is going on here?"

It seemed as though half the block was crowded around his home. Several police cars were at the curb, and four uniformed officers were talking with Deni and Cody. As Cameron approached his wife and son, he hugged them sensing that they may have been in danger.

"What is going on?"

"Dr. Kale," one of the officers responded. "Some of your neighbors reported hearing a car screeching outside your home and some shouting. Your wife called because whoever it was threw a rock through your front window. We are glad that your wife or son was not near that window. The rock could have easily killed them."

Cameron turned toward Deni and Cody. "Are you guys okay?"

"Dad, Mom was in good hands," Cody said.

"I know that, Code." Cameron was relieved but troubled about the event that had just taken place. "Praise God that you're all right!"

The officer spoke again. "Sir, one of the neighbors believes she saw the person who was driving the car. She described her as a thin lady. She said she seemed very tall even though she was seated in the car. Her head nearly touched the ceiling of the vehicle. She said she was wearing a blue dress jacket."

"I can't believe it," Cameron said.

"Well, it appears the neighbor is telling the truth," the officer said.

Cameron, furrowing his brow, shook his head. "No, that's not what I mean. I left a meeting tonight and confronted a lady who was very angry about my presentation."

"Can you tell us who she is and how we might find her?"

"She is Dr. Canthrop."

"Dr. Canthrop, the professor from Mariah University?"

"The very same."

"Okay, Dr. Kale. We will check this out. We will tell your neighbors to go home. Appreciate the information. We will let you know what we find out. Meanwhile, stay inside. Keep your doors locked. And if anyone else comes by to harass you folks, call us."

Cameron shook the officers' hands. "Thank you, officers. We appreciate it."

The neighbors had gone home and the Kales were all together inside.

"Looks like another time we need to pray, huh?" Deni asked.

"Yes, it is. I just can't believe it. The neighbor told one of the officers that the driver was tall and thin and was wearing a blue dress jacket. That's what Dr. Canthrop was wearing at the meeting tonight. If this was Dr. Canthrop, what would make her resort to threats and assault?"

"You know that people on both sides of the issue of abortion, euthanasia, and a number of other social issues don't always deal with their beliefs with decorum. There are some crazy people out there who will do anything to prove their point."

"You're right. I don't ever want to justify my beliefs by behavior that is unjustifiable."

Deni smiled. "Well said, husband."

"We ought to pray."

"Let's do it."

Cameron, Deni, and Cody kneeled by their living room couch, which was their custom when they prayed as a family. Cameron led the prayer.

"Father God, thank You for your protection of Deni and Cody tonight. I praise You. Thank You for our neighbors, who were concerned enough that they were willing to contact the police. Thank You for our police force that came in a timely fashion. Thank You for the neighbor who was able to see the person in the car who threatened our family. Lord, I find it hard to believe it could be Dr. Canthrop. I pray for her tonight, Lord. I pray that what I said did not push her over the edge that she would go so far as to assault my family. I ask that You bring to light why this happened. I pray the police will be able to find the person who did this. Keep watch over us, Lord. We know that we are under the attack of Your enemy because we are standing for righteousness. We praise You tonight, Lord, for the ministry You have called us to. Thank You for your protection and love for us. Praise You, Lord. In Jesus's name we pray and give thanks. Amen."

———

The next morning, the Kale family was getting ready for work. Cody had already left for school.

Cameron kissed Deni. "Have a great day, hon. It is going to be busy at the church today. We have a lot of meetings."

"You have a great day today too. Let me know if you hear from the police today."

Just as Cameron opened the door, the phone rang. Cameron answered it to hear Bill Hanson's voice.

"Cameron?"

"Yes, Bill, what's up?"

"I suppose you haven't heard."

"Heard what?"

"Dr. Canthrop has been admitted to the psych ward at Mariah Community Hospital."

"How did you hear about this?"

"Everyone at town hall is talking about it. Evidently one of the docs out there called our office and told someone that she was admitted. Of course, it is supposed to be confidential. Supposedly she checked herself in. We also heard the local police were at the hospital and questioning her about something. I didn't hear what it was about."

"Thanks for calling me, Bill. I will pray for her. When I get a chance, I would like to talk to you more about this."

"I gotta say, you really pushed her over the edge, my friend."

Cameron wondered if Bill really meant what he said or if was teasing him, as was his custom. "Bill, is that what you think?"

"I am just having some fun with you. The old battle-axe had it coming! She has been a pain in the neck at just about every community and collaborative meeting this city has had over several years. The way I see it is that she drove herself to where she is at—literally and figuratively."

"Well, I feel somewhat responsible."

"No, don't do that. I was only kidding you. She was in your face, and you told her the truth. Sometimes the truth can kick you in the seat of the pants. Anyway, don't let this trouble you too much. It'll all make sense someday, my friend."

"Thanks, Bill. I think you have the gift of encouragement."

"Yeah, I think I do."

"Take care." Cameron hung up the phone and ran his fingers through his hair.

"What's wrong?" Deni asked. "What did he say?"

"Dr. Canthrop checked herself into the psych ward.

"You were right—it was Dr. Canthrop."

"Yes. We need to pray for her. She must be a person in a lot of pain and grief right now."

Deni responded, "I understand that even though she tried to kill Cody and me."

Cameron blurted, "Even though she tried to hurt us, I cannot help but have a burden to share the gospel with her."

"You are the evangelist," Deni said with a smile.

Cameron smiled too. "Yes, I am."

Cameron knew he would use this situation to help Dr. Canthrop come to know the Lord. He knew sometimes God allows people to find some misery in their lives so they will turn to the Lord for help. He could not shake his need to talk to Dr. Canthrop about the Lord. He determined that he would do so at the first opportunity.

———✺———

Later that day, Bill Hanson called Cameron at the church. "Cameron, I have some good news for you."

"This doesn't have anything to do with Dr. Canthrop, does it?"

"No, I got a call from a couple of senators in D.C., and they want you and me to fly to Washington to talk about an opportunity for you."

"What kind of opportunity?"

"Well, they heard about our task force and the kind of work you have been doing. They have seen some of the television spots and news programs and want you to come to D.C. to work with the Surgeon General and help spearhead a national task force on social and health issues. Can you believe it, Cam? This is big stuff, buddy."

"Yes, it is, but what about the church and my responsibilities there?"

"Don't worry. They know that your church is a priority for you, so they want you to do some of the work here and come to Washington only when they need you."

"Thanks for the call. I will talk to Deni, and I will get back to you."

"Take a few days. They are not expecting an answer until the end of the week. God has some big plans for you, Cameron. Just remember, this whole nation needs the evangel."

"You are right about that, Bill. Thanks again. I will get back to you."

"You got it!"

It was a long day of meetings, and Cameron had a lot on his mind. Two things seemed to stick out in his mind the most. First was the lady who threatened his family and now was in the psychiatric ward of the hospital. He could not get it out of his mind that he needed to share Christ with a lady who hated everything Cameron stood for, and that included his faith in Christ. He could also not get it out of his mind what Bill had shared with him about an offer to come to Washington to lead a task force on social issues. He knew God wanted to use him in a big way, and for all practical purposes, he had done that in Mariah City. He could never have imagined being used on a national scale as Bill had described.

Cameron arrived home at the end of the day and bear-hugged Cody standing at the fridge. Cody ate food like it was going to disappear forever. He was now nearly fifteen years old, and he could not eat enough food to fill him up. Deni came in the door and kissed Cameron on the cheek.

"Hey, what happened to a kiss on the lips?"

"If you want that, come and get it!"

Cameron liked it when Deni was in this teasing mood. He knew it meant that she had a good day at work or was just content to be who she was in the Lord. "Well, I think I will take you up on that!" Cameron grabbed Deni like he was about to dance with her and gave her a kiss on the lips.

"Okay, guys, get a room!" Cody said.

"Mr. Cody!" snapped Deni. "I beg your pardon. I can kiss my man whenever I want to."

"Yuck! Whatever you think, Mom!"

Cameron and Deni knew Cody liked it when they were loving to each other. It was securing to him that his mom and dad were close. He was like many teenage boys who think parents who are kissing is just about as bad as kissing a girl with braces or maybe just kissing a girl. It just didn't seem right! But, nevertheless, it provided a security that Mom and Dad were a secure relationship in a time when many marriage relationships are breaking up.

The Kale family was inquiring about what was for dinner, and consensus was going out to eat. Cody liked to stay home and enjoyed playing his Xbox in his room and getting a plate of hot and delicious food while he played his games. Deni loved to have someone serve her a meal instead of fixing it, especially after a long day at the office. Cameron was willing to do whatever made Deni happy. They all went out for dinner to Cody's favorite place, Fire and Ice.

The Kales arrived at the Fire and Ice and were seated at a table that was nowhere near the booths that had mirrors above them. These were the mirrors that shattered from Jepson's bullets some time ago. Even though the restaurant was a reminder of what could have ended in a tragedy, they enjoyed the atmosphere, the help, and, of course, the food. Cameron had some news to share with Deni and Cody too but had not made any decision. He wanted to share what Bill told him earlier that day but didn't know how Deni would respond. Cameron was excited about the opportunity and the possibilities of being used of God on a national scale. But he believed his first responsibility was his family, and Deni would have to believe this was God's will for them for Cameron to take the position.

Chapter Seventeen

THE CHURCH MEETING NEEDS AND HAVING NEEDS MET

Mariah City Community Church was continuing to grow both numerically and spiritually. Cell groups had grown to over 200, and there were over seventy ministry teams. Pastor Kale had appointed more pastors to head up key ministries and still more people were coming who had never visited the church before. Pastor Kale was as much of a pastor-teacher as he was an evangelist. Not only had Mariah City Community Church benefited from many new converts to Christianity, but also they were benefiting from his no-nonsense teaching of the Bible.

Scott Benson and Clem Mager had become excellent teachers of the Word. Both of them helped Pastor Kale head up the ministries that were geared to meet the social needs of the community.

—◦◦◦—

Sunday morning Tom Tharston came to the platform before Pastor Kale came to preach. Cameron was not sure what Tom was planning to say.

"Ladies and gentlemen, we know that we have been blessed with our pastor. God has given us a true gift in him." The congregation gave applause. "Pastor Kale did not know that I was going to do this, but I would like the deacons to come forward. Pastor, we have something to give to you."

The deacons and Tom Tharston stood around their pastor as he came to the platform. Each man had a sparkle in their eyes with their lips pressed together expressing that this was a proud moment for them. The deacons passed a plaque to Tom Tharston, who read what had been inscribed on it.

"Pastor, I would like to read this. 'To Pastor Cameron Kale, the evangelist and our brother, friend, and pastor. We are proud to call you pastor, as you have taught us so much, ministered to our needs, and have sincerely reached our community for Christ.' And Pastor, we know that you will hear this when you meet our Lord and Savior, but we had it printed here, 'Well done, good and faithful servant.'"

Pastor Kale wiped away tears as the appreciation for him deeply moved him. "Thank you, Tom, deacons, church. I don't know what to say other than thank you for being the church that you are. I am fortunate to have a church family like you. Thank you."

Pastor Kale came to the podium to bring his message, but Tom stayed beside him a few moments longer. Pastor Kale turned toward Tom.

"Tom is there something else?" The congregation laughed.

"You aren't getting rid of me that easily, Pastor. I wanted to share a rumor with everyone. Folks, good sources tell me that our pastor has been offered an opportunity at the capitol of our nation."

Pastor Kale bowed his head. He knew what Tom was going to share.

"No, he's not leaving us as pastor, thank goodness, but he is going to be going to Washington on assignment for our government from time to time to work with our nation's Surgeon General and head up a task force in D.C. on social and health issues. We have a lot to be proud of today, Pastor Kale. Thank you for what you have done for Mariah City and what you will do for our nation."

As Pastor Kale stepped sideways to shake Tom's hand and hug him, the congregation stood to their feet again and began to applaud.

"Folks, give applause to Jesus. He is the one that deserves our praise and applause."

As the congregation quieted down, Pastor Kale was gathering his thoughts and preparing to bring the message.

"Dear church, I want to share with you the importance of meeting needs in the community. The Bible is full of passages about the importance of meeting needs, but, as most of you know, I like to focus on one particular passage. But before I do that, I want to give you some historical perspective. I don't believe we have anyone here who lived during the turn of the century, but during that time there were already many colleges and universities in this country that were raised up for the purposes of training ministers of the gospel. Many of the Ivy League schools like Princeton, Yale, and Harvard were such schools. But at the same time, ministers who had been trained in Germany came to this country did not believe in the authenticity of the Bible, the trinity, virgin birth, the necessity of the new birth, and the second coming of Christ. This liberalism changed many of the universities, as they had hired these men to teach in their universities. Pastors were trained with new theology and went into the local churches across our country.

"Many of you were born before or during the 1950s. Liberal theology developed during this time period and was called "modernism" by most conservative Bible-believing Christians. Battles raged in our country as those who fought modernists, called "fundamentalists," sought to defend the faith "once for all delivered to the saints" (Jude 1:3, KJV). A set of books, called the "Fundamentals," was given out to every preacher of the gospel to provide fundamental, Bible-believing truth as a defense of the gospel.

"Many throughout the twentieth century believed in the social gospel. This was the ideology of the liberal modernist. They thought the social gospel was meeting needs of the community and that these good works would give you salvation. Fundamentalists reacted to this teaching and declared that the gospel was the death, burial, and resurrection of Jesus and repentance and faith in Him and His work would bring a change of heart within, converting the soul and making one a Christian. Of course, they were right. But here is the problem. They forgot that while we are saved through Christ, when we become truly saved, we need to meet the social needs of people. That is how we show them the love of Christ."

Cameron led the congregation to look at James chapter two about faith and works and explained that a person with true faith in Jesus will also have works to meet the needs of others. He also shared the Good Samaritan story and told the saints at MCCC that we were to be Good Samaritans and show the love of Christ toward the sinner.

While Pastor Cameron was always foremost an excellent gifted evangelist, he was becoming a powerful teacher of God's Word. The sermon concluded, and many came both for salvation and also to grow in their commitment as believers to meet the needs of others.

Scott Benson was healing from the tragic death of his wife, Amy. It had been three years since her accident, and Scott had not been ready for any companionship. Scott and Kim Carson from Channel 5 News had been spending time together in a purely plutonic relationship. Scott could not deny that God had provided her in this season of his life as a helpmeet. It seemed as time went on that a romance was beginning to brew. At least that is what Cameron and Deni and probably most of the Mariah City Community Church congregation thought.

Just after the Sunday morning service, Scott Benson leaned over to Kim, who sat beside him every Sunday, and whispered in her ear, "Can I take you out for a special lunch?"

"My, Scott Benson, what do you have on your mind?"

Scott grinned. "I have the pastor's message on my mind."

Kim winked at Scott. "I am sure you do," she whispered back. "Yes, I would love to go for a *special* lunch."

As Scott and Kim pulled out of the church drive, Deni turned to Cameron and Clem Mager, who were standing next to her. "Something's going on with those two. I just know it."

"Pastor, I think your wife is playing cupid," Clem said.

"Think? I *know* she is!"

Scott and Kim arrived at the Fire and Ice Restaurant. Scott asked the host if they could have a nice private spot. Kim overheard his request and knew that Scott was up to something, but what?

The host smiled and led them to a corner table in a somewhat secluded spot of the restaurant. The white linen reflected the candlelight, and the nice chinaware mirrored glistening light from the chandeliers. Scott pulled Kim's chair out until she was seated and then took his seat.

"Thank you. You are a gentleman." Kim blushed.

"What else could I be in the presence of such a lady as yourself?"

Kim was getting wise and was not afraid to speak her mind. She was a lot like Amy in that way. "Okay, what's up, Mr. Benson? I am not sure I have seen you exactly like this."

Scott smiled but had a serious look in his eye. "Well, I have been doing a lot of thinking and praying."

"And that is making you romantic?"

Scott chuckled. "I love your quick wit. It is one of the things I love about you." Scott said, "May I?" and began to lean over to give Kim a soft kiss.

She could not resist. Kim blushed more this time. "Okay, now I know you're up to something!"

Scott pulled a ring box out of his jacket pocket, opened it, and slipped down on one knee. Several customers looked over to Scott and Kim's table as they noticed the proposal beginning to commence.

"Will you?" Scott asked.

"Will I what?" Kim replied, beaming with a smile and a slight turn of her head.

He held the ring closer. "Will you marry me, my sweet Kimmy?"

"Are you ready, Scott? Really ready?"

"Without a doubt. I want you to be my wife."

Her arms stretched out to pull Scott toward her chest. "Then my answer is yes. Yes, I will marry you, Scott Benson!"

As they both kissed, a small crowd gathered just a few tables away, and the group began to applaud, whistle, and shout congratulations.

Pastor Kale, Deni, and Cody left church and went to the Mariah City Hospital before they went to lunch. Cameron wanted to stop in to see how Dr. Canthrop was doing since she checked herself in to the psych ward of the hospital.

"Cameron, I'll stay with Cody. We'll wait here for you. I will say a prayer."

"Thanks, I'm not sure how welcomed I will be."

Cameron got off the elevator on the fourth floor and went to the window and pushed a buzzer that told the nurse someone was at the window. The nurse came to the window.

"Can I help you?"

"Hello, I am Pastor Cameron Kale. I am here to see Dr. Canthrop."

"Yes, sir, let me see if she wants to see a visitor."

While Cameron waited, he ushered a prayer before the heavenly Father. "Father, give me words that will reach Dr. Canthrop. I pray that she will be open to me today and know that I truly care about her."

The nurse returned to the window and spoke through the squawk box. "I will let you in."

A buzzer buzzed as the metal door with heavy wired glass opened. The nurse led Cameron Kale to a visitor's room a short way down the hallway.

"Have a seat, Pastor. She should be with you in a moment."

"Thank you."

A minute or two passed, and Dr. Canthrop came through another door into the visitor's room. She made no expression and walked over near the table Cameron was sitting at with folded arms and her hands grasping her shoulders. She was somewhat unkempt and appeared very depressed.

"Hello, Dr. Canthrop."

After a pause, Dr. Canthrop responded. "Dr. Kale. I—I am surprised to see you here." She paused again, looking down at the floor and not making much eye contact. "I have not been one of your favorite fans."

Cameron smiled. "I have not been one of yours."

Dr. Canthrop broke a little smile. Cameron's honesty and humor were refreshing to her. Cameron spoke from his heart.

"Dr. Canthrop, I am not really sure why the Kales have been such a negative experience for you. We are not really that bad of people. You might even get to like us."

Dr. Canthop made another effort to smile. "Well, I don't know about that." She began to open up to Cameron. "Do you know about the incident at your home?"

"Yes, I do."

"Then why would you want to come here? I could have injured your family."

"Yes, but I am sure that that wasn't you, Dr. Canthrop. Something made you act in a way that you would not normally act. I can't believe you would hurt anyone. I know you are a professor at Mariah, and despite the fact that some of your philosophies and worldviews are different from mine, I know you're a good teacher."

This time Dr. Canthrop made a big smile.

Cameron smiled and revealed more of his humor. "That's three."

"Three what?"

"Smiles. You smiled three times."

"That has to be some kind of record lately." She paused again, looking down at the floor, but smiling. "Thank you for your kind words."

"You're welcome. I just came by to tell you that it's okay. I forgive you for what happened. If I can be of any help to you, Doctor, let me know. And really, I am not such a bad guy."

Dr. Canthrop gave a look of self-confidence for the first time during Cameron's visit. "You'd be a lot better if you would ease up on some of the God talk."

"I would be really boring if I didn't use God talk."

Dr. Canthrop smiled again. "Thanks for coming, Dr. Kale."

"Call me Cameron. You're welcome. Let me know, and I would be glad to come back. Here's my card. Call me anytime."

"Call me Joan."

"Thank you, Joan."

The nurse let Cameron back through the locked door of the psychiatric ward, and he headed back down the elevator to the lobby floor.

"Lord, thank You for helping me make a connection with Dr. Canthrop. I know You will give me an opportunity to tell her about You. Thank You."

"How did it go?" Deni asked as Cameron got back into the car. "You were up there for twenty minutes. Wait! Don't tell me. God showed up."

"You got it!"

"I thought so." Deni grinned and touched Cameron's shoulder. "Praise God, Cameron."

The Kales reached their home, and Scott Benson and Kim Carson were waiting for Pastor Cameron.

"Sorry to bother you on your Sunday afternoon, but we have something to tell you."

Deni grinned with her hand over her mouth, anticipating their words.

"We're getting married, and we want you to marry us!"

Cameron hugged both of them. "Yes, but when is the big day?"

Kim spoke up. "Well, we need a few months to get everything ready, but we don't want to wait any longer."

"Wonderful!" Cameron exclaimed. "We will look forward to the celebration. You know we will have to meet a few times for premarital counseling. I have to make sure the two of you are compatible."

Scott laughed, knowing Cameron's sense of humor. "Yes, we will enjoy the counseling and your humor too!"

Two months went by rapidly, and Scott and Kim were married at the Mariah City Community Church. It was one of the largest weddings ever held at the church. Scott and Kim had ten groomsmen and ten bridesmaids. As Kim's dad, Jeffry Carson, walked her down the aisle in her beautiful, traditional wedding dress, complete with a train five feet long, the congregation stood at attention with nods, smiles, and, of course, tears.

Scott and Kim gazed into each other's eyes as though they had been absent from one another for many days. They had only been apart for one day, since it was tradition for the groom to not see the bride before the wedding.

Pastor Kale began to share about the biblical meaning of marriage—how it is that God began the institution of marriage. He went on to explain that a marriage without God is like a team of oxen without a yoke. He mentioned that he was pretty sure there was some Nevada rancher that understood the purpose of a yoke. It keeps the oxen working like a team. He said that this is what God does with a couple. He keeps them together to focus on raising a godly generation and to fulfill God's purposes for that family while they live.

Scott and Kim repeated their vows, kissed each other, and were pronounced man and wife. The congregation rose to their feet with applause and cheers for the happy new couple.

Soon after the reception in the fellowship hall of the church, the Bensons were on their way to their honeymoon, unannounced to anyone as to their whereabouts. They wanted assurance that they would be alone and uninterrupted.

As Scott's rented limo arrived, he chivalrously picked his bride up and put her into the vehicle. Waving good-bye to the crowd, they whisked their way off to their honeymoon destination.

"Well, preacher, we're next!" Clem and Magee said to Pastor Kale.

Pastor Kale squinted at Clem. "You guys are already married."

"Yes, but we want to be married like that!" Magee said.

Pastor laughed.

"No, seriously, Pastor, we want to renew our vows, and we can't think of anyone we would want to officiate than you," Clem said.

"Thanks, Clem, Magee, that is very kind. When do you want to do this?

"Well, give us a few years so we can think about it." Clem grinned, trying to use some of Cameron's humor.

"I get it, Clem. I am glad that I know that you and Magee are close to each other."

"Yes, sir, and thankful. God has really blessed our marriage and given us wonderful kids, sons, and daughters-in-law and grandkids. We are very happy."

As the crowd dissipated, the Kales left for home.

The Kales spent several days at a local lake, camping, swimming, and enjoying some rest and relaxation. Cameron knew he and his family needed some time away together since the first of the next week he would be flying to the nation's capital to meet with government leaders about the new task force for social justice.

Cameron and Cody loved to pass the football, as well as play Frisbee and baseball outdoors.

"Code, run for a pass!"

Cody ran a straight line and then swerved to the left with his arms open. "Here, Dad!"

Cody made the catch like a pro. "Good catch!"

Cameron enjoyed playing ball with Cody and talking to him about spiritual things. He could see that God's anointing was on his son and that He had a special plan for Cody's life. With the busy schedule that Cameron and Deni kept, they knew how important it was for them to give quality time to their son, God's gift to them. Things like picnics, outings, and just spending time talking with each other was important.

Everyone enjoyed dogs and burgers on the grill and Deni's famous homemade potato salad. Cameron thought no one could make a potato salad like Deni.

Cody went down by the beach to look for different kinds of rocks, which gave Cameron and Deni some time to talk alone. This was not a rare occasion, as both would make time to share with each other their thoughts and burdens from time to time.

As Cameron and Deni sat in their camping chairs facing the lake, watching Cody run back and forth by the water, they shared some intimate thoughts about their recent experiences, trials, blessings, value of family, and their walk with God.

"Deni, I am really enjoying it out here. I needed this."

Deni turned her face from the beach to look at Cameron. "I know what you mean. I needed this too. You look like you have a lot on your mind."

"I do. I know a lot is expected of me by so many people, the church, the community task force, the community, now the folks in Washington, not to mention you and Cody."

Deni was hearing Cameron from her heart. She was concerned for her husband, who tended to take on the world since he committed his life to serve Christ in ministry. "I know you have your hands full, but I want you to know that I am in your corner and here to support you in anyway I can. Cody loves the time and attention you give him. You're a good dad, pastor, evangelist, and leader in the community. Soon you will be a good leader in our nation."

Cameron furrowed his brow. "Do I sound weak to say I'm afraid?"

"No, Cam, you're human."

Cameron took her hand and put his head down so that his chin was touching his chest. Unexpectedly, he became emotional. Cameron tried to speak, but it was broken.

"I—I'm trying to do what is right, but I feel weak. Some treat me like a celebrity or someone on a pedestal that cannot fall. Deni, I am not God. I am just a man with fears, doubts, hurts, and struggles. Besides all of that, I am wrestling with being who Jesus wants me to be. It must be less of me and more of Him!"

"Well, don't worry, Cam. I am proud of you, because you *are* a man, but I see you putting your trust in the Lord and you believe in His power. You know that He can overcome your fears. Don't forget, I have lived with you for many years now. I know the old Cameron who didn't put his full trust in the Lord. It'll be all right. Isn't that what you tell me when I am afraid or worried?"

Cameron smiled at Deni and wiped his tears away with a napkin from their picnic. "You're right. What is to fear when God is with us? He won't fail us!"

"Dad, Mom! Come down to the beach! It's fun!"

"We're coming, Cody!" Deni yelled back.

Cameron and Deni held each other's hands and walked down to the beach to spend some special time with one of God's great blessings to them: Cody.

———✦———

It was early Monday morning, and Cameron left the house saying good-bye to Deni and Cody before he headed for the airport to fly to Washington, D.C.

"Love you, Deni. I will call you when I get to D.C. Help your mom, son."

"I will. Have a good trip!"

Cameron pulled Cody's head toward his chest and kissed him on the head. After kissing Deni, he headed for the cab waiting by the curb. Sticking his head out the window, Cameron said, "Cody, take care of Old Blue for me, huh?"

Cameron's cab sped off to the airport. Cameron took a good look at his family waving as if it could be the last time he would ever see them. He believed that we should never miss a day loving our family because it could be our last.

Cameron met Bill Hanson, mayor of Mariah City, at the airport. They would be flying to Washington together. Bill would be introducing Cameron to the Health Task Force and bringing a report to them of Cameron's work on the Mariah City Social Issues Task Force that had gained so much local and national attention.

On the plane, Cameron has an uneasy feeling that he could not describe. He sensed a presence that he had felt before during his encounters in the dreams. This Superman now felt like there was a lethal dose of Kryptonite near him.

As Cameron looked over his shoulder, he noticed with great dismay Ser Pentino sitting on the plane. Ser Pentino made eye contact with Cameron, smiled, and nodded his head up and down. As he did this, Cameron was grimacing as one who looked like he may throw up. Suddenly, without warning, the huge Boeing 757 dropped from the sky like a roller coaster speeding to the bottom of the tracks in a matter of seconds. The airline attendants were doing their best to tell screaming passengers to brace for a possible crash landing as the plane dropped thousands of feet to a dangerously low altitude.

Cameron cried out to God. "Lord, watch over my Deni and Cody—give them your peace!"

Just as quickly as the plane rapidly descended, it leveled off, and things quieted down. As Cameron lifted his head from his hands and lap, he looked over his shoulder and noticed that Ser Pentino was gone. He knew he did not imagine this evil one's presence, and he certainly did not imagine the near-fatal crash of the plane. It was just another reminder that Satan was alive and well on planet Earth.

Bill, nearly out of breath, leaned over to Cameron. "We almost didn't have someone to clean up the mess in Washington, Cam!"

Cameron forced a partial grin. "The emergency crews below almost had a mess to clean up!"

Bill laughed at Cameron's typical humor. "Cameron, you are all right. You are all right!"

"I am glad to hear that, Bill. You have no idea how glad I am to hear that!"

When the plane landed, a limo was waiting, and the Surgeon General and several staff aides emerged from the vehicle to welcome Bill and Cameron to Washington. Soon they sped off to the Capitol for lunch and a rather long afternoon meeting.

While Cameron was busy in Washington, Scott and Clem shared ministry opportunities at MCCC. Scott and Kim returned from their honeymoon in Aruba and didn't miss a beat coming back and getting involved again in ministry. Scott and Kim started some cell groups to help grow the many new believers that had come to Mariah City Community Church. There were so many that Clem and Magee helped to run one of the groups.

It was a blessing to see many couples, young and old, come and become familiar with the fundamentals of being a Christian and also learning about what is involved in being a member of a local church. Each week the couples were finding the intimacy of the cell group experience, helping them to mature and become closer to other believers in the church. Many were discovering that they had spiritual gifts and how these gifts could be used in various ministries of the church. Cameron had taught his leaders how to recognize spiritual gifting and how to mobilize them into ministries in the church. Pastor Cameron had always said that this was really a special gifting that some pastors have, but that it could be learned. While there are blessings in the ministry of the local church, there are oftentimes testing and trials that come with those blessings. This was the case at MCCC.

While the four pastoral associates and Scott and Clem were overseers of now over 400 cell groups, they saw their share of troubles that arose when people work together. Leaders were appointed over the various cell groups, and the four associate pastors and Scott and Clem handled any difficulties that needed serious attention.

As older believers joined in to some of the new believers' classes, they wanted to be sure that the new believers understood the church the way they did. Clashes in music styles—traditional styles that used hymns and just piano and organ versus more contemporary styles that appealed to the younger members that incorporated praise bands and more recently composed songs— became a dividing issue, among others. How the young people dressed, piercings, tattoos, and choices of movies became topics for discussions that were usually promoted by the older members.

Instead of these being fruitful discussions for learning, they became ways for the coexisting generations to be critical of the other. Some of the younger new couples had left MCCC, and others were thinking about leaving the church. The Pastoral Team knew they had to meet and figure out how they could resolve the problem. They decided to get the group together for a luncheon and talk about how the differing members could work together in the body of Christ. Scott met with the leaders of the cell groups and shared some practical advice with them on how to have unity in the body. He preached from 1 Corinthians 12 how that each group was a unique part of the body, like the hands, feet, and the mouth, etc. He shared how that the church could continue to have a variety of different approaches and yet remain as one. He told the leaders of the cell groups that it was okay to love the kind of music that you were accustomed to and to have differences, but he shared how much of a blessing it would be if services combined the variety of styles appreciated by different groups knowing that it was practicing body ministry.

As the leaders heard Scott's passion, they were excited to go back into their small groups and teach them how to stay unified with other groups and enjoy the variety that God had allowed to be present in the church. Soon the different small groups were meeting as a larger group to talk about their roles in the church and the importance of unity. Unity was catching on, and while there was some measurable success, there were still some stick-in-the-mud people who just couldn't change.

Meanwhile, at the Kale home, Cody was getting to the age where he needed money to pay for the high price of technological gadgets that interested him. He wanted to keep up with the newest game systems, as well as keep up with the newest phones.

Clem called Cody one evening, asking him if he would like to make some bucks working for Jeff Grant, a local mechanic. "Cody, do you remember Jeff Grant from church?"

"Yes, I know him," Cody replied. "Didn't Jeff come to the church, and doesn't he work on Mariah City's police cars?"

"Yes, that's him. He needs a young man to help in the garage. You could learn a lot about mechanics and bodywork and make some money doing it. Of course, that is if your mother will let you do this in your spare time after school and Saturdays."

"I think she will. I'll ask, but I think that would be great! I'll let you know, Deputy Mager."

Deni gave Cody permission to work at the garage as long as he kept up with his homework and kept his grades up too.

Cody started working in the shop after school and was learning a lot from Jeff Grant, the owner of the garage and head mechanic.

"Cody, I want to show you something."

"What is it?"

Jeff pointed to the back of the garage to what appeared to be a vehicle that was covered over with a tarp. "Come over here. I want to show you something under that tarp. Give me a hand with this."

Both tugged on the canvas tarp and revealed the treasure buried beneath it. It was a blue Camaro very much like Old Blue that Cody's dad had. Cody stood in statue-like form as he gazed at this beautiful car. Jeff broke Cody's silence and stare.

"Cody, do you think you and I could fix this baby up in our spare time?"

Cody was speechless but nodded.

"Good. If you work hard and do a good job for me, the car is yours."

"Thanks, Jeff. I don't know what to say!"

"Don't say anything, Code man. It won't be very long, and you are going to need a good car. This one will be a great one to start with."

Jeff spent weeks and months teaching Cody about mechanics and bodywork and helped Cody get the car in shape.

Chapter Eighteen

Developments with Cameron Kale in Washington

After a great lunch at the Capitol, Cameron and Bill Hanson met with Virginia Bassman, the Surgeon General, who was appointed by President Barabas Othama, the current Democratic Party president, soon developing into the Democratic League. Surgeon General Virginia Bassman introduced Cameron and Bill Hanson to the background of this task force.

"Gentlemen, typically the Surgeon General heads up task forces that deal with medical and health issues in the nation. Since Dr. Kale has done a lot of work in the area of abortion-on-demand and euthanasia, we went on your recommendation, Mr. Hanson, and the reports we read and heard on his work that you, Dr. Kale, be consulting in these areas. It didn't hurt that you are a chiropractic doctor but more importantly a very smart chiropractor."

Both Cameron and Bill looked at each other and smiled. Surgeon General Bassman continued.

"While the American Medical Association may call into question some holistic practices, you, Dr. Kale, have spent additional years studying anatomy and have pursued much of the education that a medical doctor would pursue."

Cameron Kale always believed there needed to be a balance between holistic healing and medicine or surgery.

"We have learned that you are respected by the Medical Community and are a credit to the chiropractic community."

Cameron replied, "Surgeon General Bassman—"

"Call me Virginia, Dr. Kale."

"You may call me Cameron."

"Fair enough," she said.

"I am a Republican, but I have worked well with both Republicans and Democrats in my own city, Mariah City, Nevada."

"We are well aware of your political positions, but your mayor and friend, Bill Hanson, is a Democrat."

Cameron laughed. "I see. He will be keeping an eye on me?"

Bill Hanson smiled at the Surgeon General. "Madam, may I?"

"Of course."

"Cameron, when I reported to Virginia what you have done at Mariah City and how you have worked on both sides of the aisle, she was impressed. You have been able to get a lot done in our city and have won the support of city leaders and state legislators who are both Republican and Democrats."

Bill Hanson was like the older Democrats and believed many of the views of current Republicans. Bill did not believe that abortion-on-demand was something that should be legislated, and he believed in the sanctity of life for all life, including the unborn child. He remained a Democrat because he believed in the party.

Cameron returned home after four days of meetings in Washington, DC. That same evening, Deni came home from the pregnancy center and noticed that the garage door had been opened and Old Blue was gone. Old Blue had been stolen. The local police found the car an hour later over a nearby embankment, but it was wrecked and totaled beyond recognition. As Deni picked Cameron up at the airport, she broke the news about what happened to his car. It was a very trying time for Cameron, having shared with her the near tragedy on the plane and that he saw Ser Pentino again on the plane that nearly claimed his life.

Even through all of this, Deni and Cameron were happy to be alive and to live for the King of kings.

Cody and Dad hugged and talked about throwing the ball around and about his new job with Jeff Grant. Cody did not tell his dad about the car that was just like Old Blue. He thought he would keep it a secret for now as he planned to restore the car in Jeff's shop and give the new Old Blue to his dad on his birthday.

The next day, Clem called Cameron to welcome him back. "Glad your back, Pastor."

"I am glad, very glad, to be back."

Clem told him that he was sorry to see him lose Old Blue. "It was a shame what that guy did to your car."

"Did you say, guy? Do you know who did this?"

"Well, we only have one witness, but he said that he was walking a dog past your home when he saw a man drive your car out of your driveway. He was pretty sure he had seen you and others in your family outdoors when he walked his dog before, but the man driving the car did not look like anyone in your family to him."

"Did he give a description?"

"He said all he could tell was that it was a small man wearing a pinstriped business suit."

Cameron sighed and shook his head, muttering to himself, "God's enemy is hot on the prowl."

Clem overheard him. "You can say that again, Pastor!"

"How have things been going at the church? Scott has called and filled me in some. Sounds like blessings and some bombshells."

"Yes, Pastor, it seems they go hand in hand, as you have taught us."

"How did the meetings go that you, Scott, and the associate pastors were leading?"

Clem smiled. "They went really well, and I think we made some progress in getting the older and younger members to work out their differences, but we have some who just don't like change."

"Clem, you are learning fast!"

"Let's get together with Scott and talk about this further."

Cameron enjoyed some quality time with his family for several days. Scott and Clem were still leading the midweek cell groups, and Cameron did not have to check into the church until Sunday. The Kales spent some evenings at home watching old movies, eating more pizza, and driving to the coast for some beach time.

On Saturday, Cameron and the Kale family were back home. Cameron received a call from the hospital that Joan Canthrop had been asking for him and wanted him to visit.

Dr. Canthrop was sitting at a table in the visitation room with a few other patients sitting at other tables visiting with friends and family. Cameron knocked on the door and then entered the visitation room.

"Joan!"

Dr. Canthrop was happy that Cameron remembered to call her by her first name. "Hello, Cameron."

Cameron smiled. "That sounds so much better than "Dr. Kale." Joan nodded in agreement.

Cameron sat down across the table from Joan and held out his hand to shake her hand. She took his hand and shook it with a smile.

"I heard that you wanted me to come."

"Yes, I have been doing a lot of thinking and feel that I need to tell you some things so that you might understand why I have been so angry with you, your wife, and your ministry."

"Sure, Joan, be free to share whatever you would like."

Joan began to explain. "Dr. Cameron, I know about the gospel. I heard it as a child. My grandmother used to talk to me about Jesus and the Bible. As a child it gave me comfort to hear her share stories from the Bible. I used to look up in the sky and believe that God was looking down and listening to me and that He cared about me. But to tell you the truth, Cameron, I had some bad experiences as a young woman. In my last year of high school, I was dating a fellow, and we became too intimate. I found out that I was pregnant. My boyfriend pressured me to get an abortion. I didn't know what else to do. So I went to an abortion clinic that was confidential and had the abortion. It was the worst experience of my life. I knew that that baby was a human—my baby—but I was confused, alone, and afraid. I was going to church and felt that I needed to share with the pastor about an abortion experience that I was so ashamed of. The church ridiculed me and shunned me and treated me as a murderer. I never heard of forgiveness nor saw the compassion that I needed to see. I became very hardened toward the church and Christianity. It was the reason I was so vehemently opposed to your ministry. I was further hardened as you spoke about the abortion industry. I figured anyone who was a Christian had no right to speak about such private issues because they did not understand it in my estimation."

Cameron, listening intently, looked at Joan with compassion. "What has changed? Your perspective seems to have changed."

"Well, some of the things you shared with me sounded like the things my grandmother used to say. I asked Jesus to come into my heart and save me just this past week, and He did! He has changed my perspective."

Cameron was excited to see how God had changed this lady from a very bitter, angry woman to a delightful and graceful person. "Praise God, Joan! I have been praying for you. I am thankful that God has changed you. I can see and hear the change in you. You do know that all the angels in heaven are throwing a party because you have come into the kingdom as a child of God?"

"Yes, my grandmother used to say that. No one has ever thrown a party for me before. It feels good. I should be getting out of here soon. I think the doctors here will notice the change too. Thank you, again, for all of your help."

Cameron stood to his feet. "You are welcome, Joan."

Joan rose to her feet and made an expression of remembering something she wanted to say. "Oh, Dr. Kale—I mean, Cameron. Could you talk to Deni? I would love to help her with the center if she thinks I could be some help there."

"I will do that. Blessings to you."

Deni had been praying for Dr. Canthrop and was excited about the news that she had accepted Christ. Cameron told Deni how Joan asked specifically if she would want her to help at the center. This made Deni even more excited about what was happening in Joan Canthrop's life. Soon, Dr. Canthrop joined Deni in an effort to get Deni on the campus and other universities to speak about the truth about the work of pregnancy centers.

Dr. Canthrop had been a long-time advocate of NARAL, which originally stood for National Abortion rights and Reproductive Rights Action League but was changed to NARAL Pro-Choice America. Dr. Canthrop spent time at the center with Deni and shadowed some of the counseling sessions. It didn't take long for her to discover that many of the things that NARAL and Planned Parenthood said about pregnancy centers were false. NARAL proudly speaks against pregnancy centers because of their belief in the sanctity of life. They slander pregnancy centers, claiming that they are fake clinics in existence only to promote their pro-life views and frighten young women with false information. Dr. Canthrop had many discussions with Deni and staff at the center, telling them how different the pregnancy center was from NARAL's views. She knew that NARAL and Planned Parenthood had an abortion agenda. She shared how these organizations encouraged women to consider abortion as the answer to their stress. She also shared that abortion centers would not allow women to see their baby on an ultrasound because it might change their minds. Dr. Canthrop was deeply moved by her experience at the pregnancy center as she saw counselors give young women and men all of the information but allowed these women to make their own choice. She saw that they did not coerce clients as NARAL and Planned Parenthood would claim was true about pregnancy centers.

Joan Canthrop assisted Deni on numerous occasions to speak at Mariah University, as well as other universities. They worked together to plan a counter message to college students revealing the false statements made by NARAL and Planned Parenthood about pregnancy centers. State senators and local leaders of the city were challenged to come to the pregnancy center, take a tour, and learn firsthand what pregnancy centers are all about. As these leaders came to Mariah Family Center, they saw that much of what they were hearing from NARAL and Planned Parenthood was not true about pregnancy centers at all.

Chapter Nineteen

KALE'S IMPACT IN WASHINGTON

Cameron was back in Washington after several months and asked to give the morning prayer before a breakfast with many members of Congress and Washington movers and shakers. He knew he would have an opportunity to work with the Surgeon General and some Washington politicians, but he never dreamed that God would give him a voice, be it a small voice in Washington.

As Dr. Kale entered a prestigious hall billowing with the noise of Washington insiders, he walked through a maze of handshakes and "welcome to Washington" greetings. Cameron was led to a podium and microphone and introduced by the US chaplain.

"Ladies and gentlemen, it is my deepest pleasure to introduce to you a man who is new to Washington but not new to getting things done—something we all like to believe, anyway, that we do here in the Capitol!" Everyone laughed. "Lead us in prayer this morning, Dr. Kale."

Everyone in the room applauded as Cameron Kale stood for a moment, taking it all in how God had extended the borders of his ministry to reaching leaders of the nation.

Cameron silently whispered a "Thank you, Lord. This is *your* doing."

He began to pray.

"Father in heaven, we address You this morning in prayer, and we do so humbly as we are only privileged to do so as Your Son, Jesus Christ, has given us access before Your throne through the blood that He shed on the cross."

Several members in the chamber began to look at each other and were thinking how different Cameron's prayer was from many who stood in that spot leading their morning prayers. This was not something written down or scripted, but it came from the heart.

Cameron continued. "Father, I am blessed today to stand here among some of the most powerful men and women in our nation. They are our elected leaders and representatives. I stand here before You and them, asking You to intervene in their lives and give them favor and wisdom as they seek to do what is best for this nation, as well as giving honor to You."

Some members swallowed hard, while others brought their heads from their hands and looked up at Cameron while he prayed. They had never heard someone pray for them like Cameron was praying for them at that moment.

"And Lord, remember these men and women. They are people for whom You made great sacrifice so that they could have life. I pray that as they are men and women who sacrifice for their states and constituencies, they are doing so because they want to give them the best life they can in this country. So Father, cause them to know Your love for them and Your desire for them to know You and serve You and believe that You are ordained to lead men and women in life. You are our representative from heaven. May we look to You in all that we do and remember to give You all of the glory, praise, and honor, and not in ourselves. Amen."

As Cameron vocalized the "Amen," everyone in the chamber stood, saying, "Amen," and gave applause. Some of the men and women who were believers in this body that gathered whispered, "He's an evangelist. He is speaking boldly for God like we have never heard in this chamber!" While there was a list of great preachers and evangelists that had prayed before Washington's leaders there, no one present thought they had ever heard a prayer like Cameron Kale's.

Shortly after breakfast, a small group of both men and women, all leaders of some of the biggest states in the nation, came up to

Dr. Kale and asked him if we would be willing to meet with them and share more about him, his ministry, and about government and God. Several asked Christ into their hearts as Cameron was praying and shared this with him in the chamber before they left.

God was, no doubt, up to something big. God was using His evangel to reach men and women that could make important changes in the laws of our land.

———⟆⟆⟆———

Later, Cameron, Virginia Bassman, and several others began working on a project to start a national AD campaign that would target changing public opinion about American values that support life. Virginia was a Christian and didn't mind ads that had a strong Christian emphasis to them. She did not believe, like some of her colleagues, that separation of church and state meant that Christianity had no place in government. She knew that, historically, separation of church and state was *not* in the constitution or in any laws of the land. It came from a letter written by Jefferson to the Danbury Baptist Association in 1802 to answer a letter they wrote to him in October 1801. Their state was inhibiting their rights by saying that their religious freedoms were favors granted by the state legislature. Jefferson said in response that there was to be "a wall of separation between church and state." In that letter, Jefferson said quite the opposite of what modern interpreters say separation of church and state means. Jefferson did not want the United States to become like it was in England. In England, the government told you where you had to go to church—the Church of England. Jefferson did not want to see government control one's freedom to worship as he or she pleases but according to one's conscience. Separation of church and state never meant that we should keep religion at bay and never find its presence in the practice of government. Surgeon General Bassman did not believe like her colleagues, who believe it is wrong to say anything about God when you work in government. She often wondered what they thought the concept of representatives of the people meant. Certainly, many more Americans are religious and/or are Christians than those who are not. She felt that if government were truly representing America, it would speak about God much more often.

Cameron came up with the idea of running some billboard and television ads with the slogan "*Some say life is what you make it, but it's God who makes life.*" They felt that this AD would embrace a right-to-life concept, as well as one that embraces the value of life for the elderly. President Othama did not like the AD because people would say it was promoting a special Christian brand of religion. Others said it did not say whose God it was. Many who were in the chambers as Dr. Kale prayed said, "If Cameron Kale is for it, so are we. It will only have a positive impact on the nation."

Soon, the ads were running across the country on billboards in every major city. Television commercials were running using well-known celebrities who believed in the sanctity of life to speak the slogan "*Some say life is what you make it, but it's God who makes life!*"

God was providing many opportunities for Cameron in Washington to make a national impact on the nation. He was making friends and influencing them as God was bringing favor into Cameron's life and touching others through his life as well.

Many in Washington, DC, grew to love Cameron Kale, and those who didn't love him at least respected him. They could see that he was a man who could get things done in Washington. Some even said, "Who knows? Maybe he is a future presidential candidate." When Cameron heard this, his body language would make it clear he had no intentions to become the president of the United States. He would grin, shake his head no, and wave his hands back and forth rather quickly.

What Cameron did not know is that God's plans for his life would be to use him to affect many in the nation while he himself would not become a politician. Though Cameron had no idea of God's plan, this was a plan that would sit well with Cameron Kale.

—◦◦◦—

While Cameron enjoyed a season working with proactive pro-lifers not so unique to the Democratic Party but were unique to the kingdom of God, there were movements within the party to orchestrate something new in Washington. The far left of the party was always leaning left. There were growing tremors of movement toward some extreme policy changes, indicating an epic earthquake of leftist ideas coming soon with seismic strength.

What was developing in Washington was an historic change to the Democratic Party to become what was known as the "Democratic League." This party would fancy a horrific platform that would change the face of America. Its leaders planned to build into its policies the ends to what abortion and euthanasia can go, as well as throwing the idea of family values out the door. Absolutes would disappear, and the nation would no longer make any reference to God. This new party would imbibe an entirely secular humanism as its philosophical base.

The Democratic League would do away with capitalism and buy completely into socialism. Their plans are to build into this model of government taking away privacy, free speech, and the right to bear arms. Pregnancy centers across the nation would have to put signage in their lobbies saying that they couldn't advertise to abortion-minded women, even though they offer free goods and services and have the right to free speech under the Constitution's First Amendment. This amendment would allow pregnancy centers to offer services to whomever they chose.

Cameron knew states were already legislating that pregnancy centers put signage in their windows that they do not offer services to these women but that other courts were overthrowing compliance to these laws, declaring it unconstitutional. It is the pregnancy center's reason for their existence to minister to these women. Many of these women are confused and often coerced by Planned Parenthood to consider abortion.

When the woman wants to keep her baby, many workers in Planned Parenthood organizations across the country would tell them that they couldn't help them. It is unfortunate that these Planned Parenthood organizations do not have to put signs in their windows and lobbies saying "We really don't encourage *parenthood.*"

As Cameron was learning bits and pieces about this new party, he, as well as others he worked with in Washington, both Democrats and Republicans, were concerned about the direction government was taking the United States of America. He wondered how long he would be able to have the freedom to affect change in Washington with these leftist politicians who want nothing more than to change the United States of America into something it was never intended to be by her forefathers.

Chapter Twenty

SURPRISES AT HOME

Upon Cameron's return to Mariah City, he was met by his family at the airport. They were acting rather suspiciously.

"What's goin' on gang?" Cameron asked Deni and Cody as they gave him hugs and kisses but were giggling like they were hiding something.

"Oh, you'll see, Dad. You'll see!"

It was Cameron's thirty-ninth birthday in just a few days, and he hoped they had not prepared some kind of birthday party, but he suspected that this is what they were up to.

Cameron put his bags into the back of their Chevy minivan and began to drive out of the airport. Cody chuckled and put his hand to his mouth to control himself, as he was about to stir the pot of suspicion with his dad.

"Hey, Dad, you kind of look cool driving a minivan!"

Cameron smiled and looked in his rearview mirror at Cody sitting in the backseat. "Oh, that was a low blow, son! Nothing is cooler than driving Old Blue! You had to remind me, didn't you?"

Deni looked back at Cody and grinned, and Cody grinned back. "Sorry, Dad. I didn't mean to get you depressed or anything. I was just joking."

"It's okay, son. Nothing could get me depressed tonight. God is doing amazing things in our lives, and I am home with those I love the most."

Cody snapped his back upward. "Cool. Glad you're home, Dad. We missed you too."

Making sure that they would arrive at the destination planned by Deni and Cody, Deni asked Cameron if they could stop in at the church on their way home. She said she needed to get something for the pregnancy center that she left there.

"Sure, we can stop there. What did you forget?"

"I left some posters there and need them for the pregnancy center."

———

Soon they had reached the church driveway, and the parking lot was filled with vehicles. Cameron stopped the minivan and asked Deni and Cody what was going on.

"Is this a church meeting we are supposed to attend?"

Cody piped up, thinking it was safe to let the cat out of the bag. "Sure, Dad, like you didn't know we would cook something up for your birthday!"

"So that's what this is about? You got the whole church out here for my birthday?"

Deni replied, "Well, we didn't get the whole church, but we did get several hundred of them."

"Wonderful. Sounds good, but no practical jokes or pin the tail on the donkey!"

"No, none of those things, dear!" Deni said.

As the Kales walked into the fellowship hall, Tom Tharston; Clem Mager; and Scott Benson, along with his new bride, Kim, came to meet him. Several of the associate pastors; their wives; Bill Hanson, the mayor; and Steve Merson, the fireman, greeted Cameron as he entered the room.

Leading a chorus of "Happy Birthday," the rest of the crowd moved toward the entrance of the fellowship hall, where Cameron, Deni, and Cody were standing. A huge cake with the number *39* stood in the middle of the cake surrounded by giant frosted roses.

Cameron blew out the candles and thanked everyone for the surprise. He shared with them how much it meant to him to have such a loving and thoughtful congregation.

Everyone ate finger foods and talked with each other and the Kales until the presentation. The presentation was another surprise for Cameron.

Clem got up and asked everyone to gather around because they wanted to make a birthday presentation to Cameron.

Cameron put his hands to his face and shouted out, "You have to stop presenting me with things!"

Everyone was smiling and just ignored their pastor's ranting. Clem asked Cody to come to the front.

When Cody came up, Cameron looked serious, as hearing his son share from his heart would easily choke him up. Cody did just that.

"Dad, we have a surprise for you—actually, I have a surprise for you, but I couldn't have done this without some help from many here at the church. I know you have a tough life trying to take care of Mom and me, the church, and well, really the whole country." Cameron began to tear up and clear his throat. "Dad, we all want to say how much we love you, and I want to show you how much I love you by something that you need to see outdoors."

Cameron looked at Deni, and she shrugged her shoulders with an upside-down smile.

"Come on up here, Pastor!" Clem shouted out. "Look out that window!"

Cameron moved to the windows in the fellowship that paralleled the parking lot. When he looked out, he thought he was seeing a mirage. "What—what—"

"The speechmaker is speechless!" Clem shouted.

Everyone in the room laughed, but some were holding back tears as their pastor stared out the window looking so seriously and without speaking a word. Tears were streaming down one side of his face.

"Code, how is this possible? Where did you find Old Blue?"

Cody hugged his dad. "Dad, it's not Old Blue. It might be his brother." The gathered crowd laughed again. "I've been working for Brother Jeff. He gave me a job in his garage. He has been teaching me how to work on engines and bodywork. He had this car in his garage and helped me rebuild this car. It's for you, Dad. When I saw how it hurt you to have Old Blue stolen, and I knew it was the devil that did it too." The crowd laughed. "I was bound and determined to beat old Ser Pentino at his own game."

Cameron squeezed Cody and cried into his shirt.

"Dad, I'm getting wet!"

He let go of Cody and hugged Deni. He turned to his friends and church members. "I have the best family a man could ever have. I just can't make a speech right now. I don't have words to express how wonderful this is."

Many smiled and applauded as Cameron could only keep hugging Deni and Cody.

Chapter Twenty One

THE CHURCH NEEDS SPIRITUAL DISCERNMENT

Cameron returned to Washington for a half week of meetings with the task force, and while he was in Washington, Cody was keeping busy with school, his part-time job at Jeff's Garage, and youth group at Mariah City Community Church.

One of the four associate pastors of MCCC was put in charge of the teen group, whose name was Davis Rundee.

Cody never felt comfortable around Pastor Rundee but never said anything to his dad about it. He thought that his dad had enough troubles. Pastor Rundee seemed like he was being someone that he wasn't, according to Cody. It was like he was wearing a mask. Cody couldn't put his finger on it, but Pastor Rundee wasn't real. He knew that was a heavy charge to make against any pastor, but Cody didn't judge him; instead, he prayed that God would reveal what Pastor Rundee was hiding. No one told him, but Cody was pretty sure he had the gift of discernment that his dad taught about from time to time.

One Wednesday evening before youth group, Cody was getting some art supplies out of a closet to bring to the youth room and could hear through the wall. On the other side was Pastor Rundee's office. He had some teens in his office and was telling them that he liked to do things differently than Pastor Kale and that Pastor Kale didn't like him as a pastor. Cody knew his dad had never said anything bad about Pastor Rundee, and it wasn't right for him to tell the teens what he thought. Cody was just a kid, but he had enough sense to know that what he heard was not right. Cody went to his mother, who was getting ready to lead a woman's Bible study.

"Mom, I need to talk to you."

Deni looked like a student cramming for a midterm exam as she was looking over her notes. "Cody, I am leading Bible study in just a few minutes. What is it?"

"I heard Pastor Rundee through the wall talking to the teens and saying bad things about Dad. Can I call Dad?"

"I am sure you must be mistaken about what you heard, but you can't call your dad. He is so busy in Washington, and it would just upset him if you tell him this."

"Mom!"

"I mean it. Leave it alone for now."

Cody felt a sense of urgency about what he heard. He felt like his dad's ministry was in jeopardy. His bout with Ser Pentino taught him a lot about spiritual warfare that he would have otherwise never learned. Cody knew that God would not be pleased with disobeying his mom, but he was afraid for his dad and felt like he needed to warn him. Cody's dad's cell phone had a special ring for him and Cody, the revving up of a racecar motor. Cody dialed his number.

Cameron was resting in his hotel room before attending a special dinner with some government dignitaries. His cell phone rang.

Rummmm, Rummm, RRRumm, RRRummm.

Cameron reached for his phone and saw that it was Cody. He knew Cody would never call him unless it was pretty important.

"Cody?"

"Dad, I'm sorry for calling, but I had to tell you something. Mom told me not to call you and worry you."

"What is it?"

"I never told you this before because you have enough things to worry about, but I have always had certain feelings about Pastor Rundee."

"What do you mean, feelings?"

"Well, he has just not seemed real. You taught us about discernment. I believe that I am discerning that something is not right about Pastor Rundee. I have been praying for him that God would show me. Tonight, I heard him through his wall talking to the teens. He was saying bad things to them about you."

"Are you sure?"

"Those walls are as thin as paper. I heard everything."

"I will be home tomorrow. I will handle it. Just don't say anything to anyone, okay?"

"I won't. I love you and miss you."

"I love you too, I will see you tomorrow."

Cody saw Pastor Rundee come out of his office, and several teens came out too but went the opposite way down the hallway. Cody couldn't help himself.

"I heard what you said."

Pastor Rundee folded his arms. "What did I say?"

Cody cocked his head sideways and dramatically opened his arms, pointing his right hand toward Rundee's office. "I heard what you said to some of our group about my dad. I heard it all!"

Pastor Rundee looked sideways as if to gather his composure and to see if anyone was listening. "Listen, Cody Kale, just because your dad is the senior pastor doesn't mean you know everything. I didn't say anything bad about your dad, but I hear you complaining a lot about him and how he makes you go to church. I know you hate church, and anyone who loves church, you have a problem with. Why don't I tell your dad that?"

Cody stood with his mouth wide open as if he had heard threats from the devil himself. "Mr. Rundee, tell my dad what you want, but I know him better than you. He is only interested in hearing the truth." Cody left and returned to his mother's room and asked her if he could sit in her study.

She knew he was upset. She could see him physically trembling. "Ladies, please excuse me for just one moment." The women in the room smiled as Deni affectionately put her arm around her son and walked out into the hallway. "Cody, what's wrong?"

"Mom, do you remember what I learned by being taken by Ser Pentino?"

"How could I forget?"

"Well, God has given me discernment. Pastor Rundee scares me."

Deni looked at Cody with concern. "I thought no one could scare you after dealing with God's enemy himself."

"Can I just stay in your Bible study tonight and we can talk about it when Dad gets home?"

"Sure, I hope you don't mind our discussion about using makeup and dressing nice for our husbands is not a bad thing."

"Great—you're not going to talk about Dad being your superman again, are you, and get all mushy?"

"No, Cody, you're safe tonight." Deni put her arm around Cody's shoulder again, and the two of them walked back into the room, Cody smiling all the way.

After the Bible study, Pastor Rundee came into the room where Deni had held the study. "Mrs. Kale, can I talk to you?"

"Sure. Cody, I will meet you outside."

Cody responded, "Okay, Mom," but looked at Davis Rundee as if he knew that he was up to no good. Cody walked into the hall, closing the classroom door behind him.

"Mrs. Kale, I am very concerned about Cody," Davis Rundee said. "I don't want to alarm you, but he has been skipping out of my classes. I never know where he is going to go. I confronted him once, and he just mumbled that he is tired of his dad making him attend. I think he called them 'stupid meetings.' This is difficult to say, but whenever I praise your husband among the teens so that they know what a good leader this church has, Cody rolls his eyes as if he has a problem with your husband. I am so sorry to tell you all of this."

Deni could not believe what she was hearing but sensed there was something deeply wrong with what Rundee was telling her. He was not describing the Cody she knew. She held her tongue, wanting to wait until she could talk with Cameron.

"Thank you, Davis. I appreciate you coming and sharing this. It must have been difficult for you."

"Yes, ma'am, it was."

—◦◊◦—

Cameron's plane landed at Reno, Nevada, Airport. The long ride home to Mariah City allowed Deni and Cameron to talk about the situation concerning Cody and Pastor Rundee. Deni shared with Cameron the conversation she had with Rundee.

"Cam, I don't have a good feeling about Rundee. He told me some things about Cody that I find hard to believe."

"What did he say?"

Deni was looking down toward the car's floorboards and snapped her head up toward Cameron. "He said that Cody has been saying bad things about you and your ministry to the teens."

Cameron became emphatic, which is what Deni called "his preaching voice," in his reply. "I can't believe that. That is not Cody."

"I know."

Cameron shared that he believed that something was not right about Rundee and that he was going to get to the bottom of it.

Cameron and Deni pulled into the drive at their home. Cody came out to welcome his dad.

"Hey, Code," Cameron belted out with a smile. "How are you, son?"

Cody tried to smile but managed to answer. "Good."

"You aren't bummed out about this Davis Rundee thing, are you?"

Cody replied, "A little," but he didn't want to discourage his dad or share just how much this was affecting his spirit.

"Son, don't worry. I am going to take care of things. Your mother and I had a talk, and we both know that you are not responsible for what has happened. Just know that it is our job to protect you and to handle things God's way."

Cody smiled. "I know, Dad. You have always been Mom's and my superman."

Cameron bear-hugged him by his side. "You bet I am!"

Cameron called Davis Rundee to meet with him that afternoon at the church at Cameron's office. It was ten minutes before 1 p.m., the time for Cameron and Davis Rundee to meet, so Cameron took time to pray before the meeting.

"Lord, I praise You because we can come to You and trust that You know everything. I know You know what is going on with Davis Rundee. This is having an impact on Cody. I believe he is under attack, Lord. I pray that You will expose whatever is going on with Rundee. Give me discernment in this, Lord, and the wisdom to know how to deal with Rundee. I pray this in the name and power of Jesus's name. Amen."

Davis Rundee knocked on Cameron's door. Cameron could see Rundee through the glass in his door.

"Come in, Davis."

Davis walked in and sat down. "Pastor."

Cameron stood up and shook Davis's hand. "Davis, how are you?"

"I am doing fine, sir, but am troubled about Cody. I am sure that Mrs. Kale has filled you in."

Cameron looked sternly. "Yes, she filled me in."

Davis sounded apologetic and tried to defend himself by expressing the problems he said Cody was expressing. Cameron listened carefully and was praying silently that God would expose what Davis was trying to do.

"Pastor, I am so sorry to tell you and Mrs. Kale all of this, but Cody has been complaining a lot about coming to youth group and about you and your ministry. He has told the teens that you make him come and that he hates coming to church. He is creating quite an upset with the teens. I am concerned how this will negatively impact our youth ministry here."

Cameron decided that he would take Rundee on boldly and assert what he knew to be the truth. "Davis, you have never given me a reason to doubt you until now. I know Cody, probably better than anyone, and I can tell you that what you are telling me doesn't match up with who Cody is. As far as hating church, he probably understands theology more than most of my pastors. I mean, he understands deeply and personally about things that most of my leaders have not experienced."

"Pastor, are you telling me a sixteen-year-old knows more than I do?"

"I am not questioning your knowledge, but if I was a gambling man, I would put my paycheck up that Cody has more spiritual maturity than most of my leaders."

Rundee stood to his feet. "Kale, you are crazy. I can't believe you are even a pastor yourself. I feel like you are calling me a liar."

Cameron could tell by Rundee's response that he was not a spiritual man and that he was hiding behind a facade. Cameron pushed harder. "Well, Davis, I have to say that you surprise me. I don't know what you are hiding, but you are not a spiritual man. You are dismissed as of this moment as a pastor of our youth. I have to think of their welfare."

Davis Rundee leaned over the desk. "You will regret this Kale." Rundee's disrespect of Pastor Kale was evident, and his agenda had been exposed. He was now acting like a frantic animal lashing out because it was trapped.

Two other associate pastors came to Pastor Kale's office as they heard Rundee's raised voice. They opened the pastor's door.

"Pastor do you need any help?" they asked.

"No fellas, just having a chat with Davis. He seems to be offended by something I said."

"Liar, you fired me!" Rundee retorted. "You just can't face it that Cody is not a Christian and is a problem in this church."

The other pastors knew that what Rundee was saying was not true but listened in shock at the blasts of this outraged youth pastor.

"The truth is, Rundee, you are out of line and not walking in the Spirit. You need to leave. You are not who you say you are, and I prayed that God would expose you this morning for who you are."

Just as Cameron boldly exposed Rundee for who he was, Rundee snarled at the pastors in the room and said, "You have no idea who I really am," and pulled at his face like someone writhing in pain. Suddenly, his fingers dug into his skin at the top of his forehead, and Rundee tore from his face a mask, revealing a hideous face that had been badly burned and disfigured. His face was so disfigured it was difficult to know who he was, but he had the presence of Jepson. Could it be him? Everyone was sure that there was no trace of him from the car explosion.

The scarred man growled, "Cameron, you will pay, you will pay!" and ran toward some large windows in the foyer of the church.

Cameron ran after him while shouting to his associates, "Call Clem Mager and Chief Bormand—tell them hurry, a man I think is Jepson is in the church!"

Just as the man claiming to be Davis Rundee neared the huge glass windows that ran from the floor to the top of the cathedral ceiling, he smashed through the glass and kept running. Cameron climbed through the window and began running across the property and down the street just yards behind Rundee.

Chief Bormand and Clem Mager showed up at the church. The two associate pastors that witnessed Rundee's threat on Pastor Cameron showed them the broken window that Cameron had run through chasing Rundee. As Clem looked through the window, he saw Cameron running a hundred yards across the church campus. Rundee was in front of him by just a few yards. Bormand and Mager ran to catch up to the running men. As they reached Cameron and moved closer to Rundee, a driver of a car that had no license plate picked him up. Bormand radioed a squad car parked behind the church, and as the car pulled up, Bormand, Clem Mager, and Cameron Kale got into the car and chased the driver who picked up Rundee.

Both cars ran down a one-way street toward a lift bridge. As Rundee's car reached the bridge, the gate was going down, and the road on the bridge was being raised. Rundee's driver crashed through the bridge gate and bounced into the side rails and went over the rails into a lake.

Police teams arrived at the bridge site with cranes and divers. The car was lifted from the lake, but neither the driver nor Rundee were found. As investigators searched the vehicle, they could only find a pinstriped suit jacket in the backseat.

As Bormand, Clem, and Cameron head back to the church campus, Bormand asked Cameron what led up to his chasing Rundee.

"It was Rundee, our youth pastor, or I think he was Rundee," Cameron explained. "He was wearing a mask."

"What type of mask?" Bormand inquired.

"It was a very professionally made mask. I would have never known Rundee was wearing it." Cameron pulled it out of his jacket. Bormand examined the mask as Clem looked on.

Bormand started his typical investigative procedure. "When did you hire this guy?"

"It was just about four months after Jepson disappeared."

"What are you trying to say, Pastor?" Clem asked.

"I think it was Jepson in disguise."

Bormand spoke up. "Cameron, here we go again. Where is the proof?"

Cameron stood up straight. "Chief, his face was disfigured. He sounded like Jepson, and his face had been badly burned."

Clem interrupted. "Chief, it had to be Jepson. No one else would fit that MO and come after Cameron."

"But there is still no evidence!"

"He's gone. I have no proof."

Bormand and Mager took Pastor Kale's statement and left. Clem put his arm around Cameron and told him to go home and get some rest. Cameron drove home and shared with Deni what had happened. Deni fixed Cameron some hot tea and encouraged him that God was still in control. She could tell that this affected Cameron and that he was exhausted both from the chase and from spiritual warfare too. Neither Cameron nor Deni told Cody anything about Rundee at this time because they did not want to worry him. They prayed for the right time to explain to Cody about their youth pastor.

The youth group and their parents would also need to be debriefed by Pastor Cameron about what had happened concerning Rundee and for them to keep their children under close watch since he fled the police.

That Sunday, Cameron was at home and in his pulpit. Just following a debriefing of the youth group and their parents about the pastor who had deceived them, Cameron shared with the church about those who may wear a mask and deceive the church. It was a great illustration about how there are "wolves in sheep's clothing" in the midst of the church and we have to be discerning. He talked about discernment and how important it is that we know the real thing so that we are not misled or led astray by a counterfeit. He praised Cody, who had enough discernment to warn his mother and Pastor Cameron about Davis Rundee. While this was a shocking episode for everyone, Cameron had the opportunity to share that living the Christian life is not boring. His congregation laughed. He also shared that our Christian experience is an adventure and that as we serve the Lord in the kingdom, we will come into spiritual warfare.

He shared from Ephesians chapter five how that we are children of light and one of our responsibilities as believers is to expose darkness. He encouraged the flock that God is always watching us and that He has set his angels to guard us, lest we should dash our foot against a stone.

On the way home, the Kale family was heading to their favorite ice cream place for soft-serve ice cream. Cody brought up something from his dad's sermon.

"Dad, I laughed when you said angels will guard us if we should dash our foot against a stone. It sounds like God will give you an angel to protect you even if you are about to stub your toe."

Cameron laughed. "At least He may have mercy and only let you stub your toe for disobeying your mother by calling me in Washington."

Cody responded, "You're right, Dad," but continued the humorous line of thinking. "You also said that we entertain angels unaware. So do angels sit up in the clouds and watch us make all kinds of mistakes that entertain them and then God smacks them on the heads and says, 'Get down there and help them out'?"

Cameron laughed again. "Well, not exactly. It means that we may be talking to or visiting with or in the presence of angels without our knowing it. They are all around us, Code."

Cody smiled and chuckled. "That's cool."

Cameron was wrapping up his work in Washington with the task force for the Surgeon General. It had been a successful campaign of talks and national ads supporting life issues. Poll rates of Americans changing their minds to support life for the unborn and support of the elderly were increasing. Several Washington movers and shakers were talking with Cameron about being a part of the new movement that would oppose the new Democratic League. Some Democratic Washington insiders warned Dr. Kale to not get involved with the new party, as it would end his effectiveness in Washington and limit his impact on the nation. Cameron was careful whom he shared his thoughts with as he learned that you couldn't trust everyone in Washington.

Two Democratic state senators—Jim Kraft and Bill Barton of New Hampshire and Massachusetts, respectively—made it clear to Cameron Kale that they would do everything they could to stop his national campaigns if he decided to support the new Independent Party. As Bill Hanson and Cameron Kale sat in a lunch meeting with Jim Kraft and Bill Barton, as well as some other politicians Cameron worked with over the past year, in a heavy discussion about the new Independent Party, Bill and Cameron seemed to be outvoted by those who were against it and its conservative platform.

Bill Barton, the senator from Massachusetts, leaned across the table and pointed his finger at Cameron Kale, deeply desiring to persuade Kale with his politics. "Kale, I don't want you to think about moving over to this new party. Yes, I know your views and values, but think about the impact you have made working with a Democratic administration. You won't get things done in Washington under that party. If you want my opinion, you will become a laughing stock instead of making an impact on your constituents."

Jim Kraft from New Hampshire and several other Democratic politicians chimed in. "Think about it, Cam. It won't get any better than it has with this task force on health issues under our administration."

Republican and Independent leaders who were at the luncheon where shaking their heads and making grimacing faces at Barton and Kraft's comments. Bill Bright, a young Republican senator from Texas, was at the table and expressed his thoughts in real Texan style.

"Jim, Bob, or is it Jim Bob? You must think we are just a bunch of backwoods boys who don't know anything. Have you been reading the polls and seeing what Americans are talking about and what they are supporting? This new party is making waves, my friends, and I don't know about you, but I want to catch the wave, if you know what I mean."

Some of the group applauded. Jim and Bob just grunted.

As the boys were exchanging their ideas, someone walked up to the table and put her hand on Cameron's shoulder. "Hello, Dr. Kale. It is so good to see you again."

Cameron wheeled around to see who was talking to him. As he turned he opened his mouth but nothing came out at first. "Uh, Dr. Canthrop!"

"Joan to you, Dr. Kale."

Jim Kraft and Bob Barton stood up, and the rest of the men at the table followed suit.

Bob Barton said, "Gentlemen, this is Dr. Joan Canthrop, a very prominent supporter of the Democratic Party and a mover and shaker in Washington who came from very humble beginnings, a schoolteacher and a college professor in a small town in Nevada."

All of the men said their "hellos" and "glad to meet yous." Bob Barton continued to speak.

"And I believe she is from your home town, Kale."

Cameron spoke up. "Yes, that's right. Dr. Canthrop and I have had opportunity to meet and to become friends."

Kraft offered Dr. Canthrop a seat at the table and waved the waitress over to give her a menu.

"No thanks, Jim. I've already eaten. I will have a latte, though."

Bob Barton continued to chide the conservatives in the crowd. "Well you guys are in trouble now. You haven't heard Dr. Canthrop's views on this ridiculous Independent Party."

Dr. Canthrop looked over at Jim and Bob and smiled as if she was ready to say something shocking. That was no surprise to them. They were prepared for whatever she might say, as she was known as "the tiger lady" in DC. Joan looked around the table, glanced at Dr. Kale and smiled. She then turned to look at her Democratic associates.

"Gentlemen, have you guys ever listened to Dr. Kale's lectures?"

They looked at each other, nodding. "Yes, sure." They were expecting Cameron Kale to get a blasting from Joan Canthrop, and they were ready for the highlight of the luncheon.

"Well, if you have listened to him even a few times, you know that what he says makes a heck of a lot of sense."

They all laughed, looking at each other, thinking she was ready to set Cameron up and drop the punch line but wondered where she was going with this. Dr. Canthrop continued.

"Fellows, for a long time now, I have heard that we are the party of change, but we are the party of exchange. We have *exchanged* our old American values for the newest form of liberalism yet in American history—Marxist ideas and socialism. I gotta tell ya, gentlemen, I'm not buyin' it."

Kraft leaned over to Barton and whispered, "It sounds like the tiger lady just lost her teeth!"

Bob dared to speak up. "Joan, you aren't suggesting that that you are buying into the platform of the new Independent Party?"

Joan fired back. "I am saying that I am buying into what is decent and right for this country and am no longer willing to play into the old politics of pragmatism. If it works, let's do it. I have deeper values now."

Kraft snorted out, "What, you got religion now?"

Joan looked at Kraft like she had never before looked at someone. It was eyes of compassion, not of revenge for challenging her ideas—it was the eyes of Jesus. "No, Jim, I have found Jesus."

Kraft got his back up. "I just said you've got religion."

Joan raised her body to perfect poise and continued to look at Jim with compassion. "No, Jim, Jesus isn't religion. Religion is everybody's idea about God. There are as many religions as there are individual people and their different ideas as to whom or what God is. Christianity is God reaching down to man. Jesus was and is the Son of God, who came to earth more than two thousand years ago and died on a cross. He came to take our punishment for sin that we deserve. He died so that you and I could have life and be a part of the family of God."

"Come on, Joan!" Bob shouted. "This is ridiculous. You are going to sit there and preach to us? You are going to turn our lunch into some sort of freaky church service?"

Cameron boldly spoke up on Joan's account and on account of Christ. "Jim, Bob, give the lady the freedom to express herself, since you do believe in the freedom of speech—the Constitution. That is what you have been telling us."

Both Jim and Bob settled down but looked like they had been beaten up in an alley by some thugs. The Jesus-talk hit them out of left field.

Joan Canthrop continued. "Gentlemen, all I can say is that before, I thought I understood life, but I was miserable and living in a prison of my own making. I always seemed angry and particularly with Christians because they seemed to know where they were going. They had zeal and a confidence about life and death that I didn't have. Instead of desiring to follow their Jesus, I mocked and ridiculed them. One day Cameron Kale came to visit me. I didn't ask him to. He just came. I was a threat to him and his family, but he came to see me because he cared about me. I had never seen that kind of unconditional love until I met Cameron Kale. It was his love for me when I thought he should have hated me for threatening his family that led me to want to know his God. I accepted Christ as my Lord and Savior and have become a Christian. It is because of Him that I can no longer accept some of the policies you guys have been selling Americans for years."

Jim Kraft got up and muttered, "I have had about enough of this stuff," and left the restaurant. Several other Democratic politicians got up and left too.

Cameron and Bill smiled as they looked at Dr. Canthrop.

"Joan, you make me proud," Cameron said. "You are a walking miracle. I had no idea that you had clout in Washington, and now God has saved you to become a voice for Him in Washington."

"Let's get a team together and do what we can to help the new Independent Party," Joan said.

"I'm in," Bill said.

Cameron shared in Bill's thinking. "I'm in too."

Bob Barton had been standing at the front desk, appearing to be paying his bill. As Cameron, Bill, and Joan were walking up to the front desk, Bob said, "Joan, can I have a word with you?"

Bill Hanson was shaking his head and whispering *no* to Joan, as he feared Bob would continue to blast her about her conversion.

"Sure, Bill, as long as whatever you have to say comes from your heart and not blurting from your head," Joan responded.

"It's a deal."

Cameron and Bill told Joan that they would wait for her outside. Bob and Joan sat back down to the table where they had been sitting.

Sitting in the midst of busboys anxiously cleaning up the table for new guests, Bob spoke up. "Joan, I have always thought Christians were just uneducated people with some crazy ideas about life. Until today, I didn't know that educated people, people who have some savvy in the world, know Christ."

"What about Dr. Kale? He's no dummy, you know."

"Of course not, and Dr. Kale was an enigma to me. I saw, as you said, that much of what he says makes sense, but I could not put it together with the fact that he is a Christian minister and an evangelist. But when you shared what you did with us today, I realize I have been wrong. Please tell me how to know your Christ."

Joan Canthrop shared with Bob how he could trust Christ as Savior and how becoming a Christian would allow him to understand spiritual things, things about God and Christ that he could not see. She explained how he was blinded to these things because God has an enemy who desires to keep people's eyes blinded to spiritual realities and not give theirs to Christ and become part of the family of God. Bob bowed his head and asked

Christ to come into his life. Joan told him that he should go and share his newfound life with others.

"I will not only tell my family and friends, but also I will share this with the constituents of my state."

Joan hugged Bob. As Bob walked out of the restaurant ahead of Joan Canthrop, he approached Bill and Cameron. Bob stopped and smiled.

"Kale, she is still the tiger lady, and I am a new Christian."

Cameron grabbed his hand and shook it with a smile that stretched from ear to ear. Bill shook Bob's hand too.

"Let's get together soon and talk about what this nation needs to hear!" Bob said as he was leaving.

Both men said, "Amen." Joan walked up and put her hands on Bill and Cameron's shoulders.

"Joan, praise God!" Cameron said. "You are making disciples just like Jesus said in Matthew 28:19-20."

"Thank you, Cameron Kale, for discipling me so that I could disciple others."

"That's the way Jesus meant it to work," Cameron said.

Joan, Bill, and Cameron talked about setting up some meetings soon to talk about the new Independent Party and how they could be a help.

PART III

Triumph over Evil

Chapter Twenty Two

THE NEW INDEPENDENT PARTY

C ameron had made many new friends, as well as co-laborers in the gospel, through his work in the nation's capital. During Cameron's work with Virginia Bassman and the task force for health issues, the Democratic administration they were working for was in its final quarter of the year before the election. The Democratic Party had already been campaigning as the "new party with the same old trusted values." Of course, there was nothing you could trust about this party, and it was a lot of the same old ideas but carrying them to their destructive end.

—⟨∞⟩—

A new grassroots movement emerged throughout the country that held to similar values. All of them wanted the United States of America to be like the country it was founded to be. They said they were the holders of the true family values and true American patriotism. It was a party who believed in small government and one that truly represented the people, not big lobby groups and special interest groups. It was a party that was opposed to almost everything the Democratic League proposed: socialism, taxing—not just the rich but anyone who worked hard for their money in America—government jobs, social programs that further burdened the taxpayers, loss of personal privacy, religious freedoms, as well as the right to bear arms.

Cameron had met many of the people in Washington who were for this Independent Party, and he was inclined to support it. One of the leaders of this grassroots movement that Cameron met while in Washington was Sandra Dalin. Dalin had gained widespread support across the country as an avid spokesperson about family values and American freedoms.

Many leaders were springing up all over the country from this movement and drawing massive crowds to hear what they had to say. Rallies were filling football stadiums and drawings thousands to events in nearly every state of the union. This new movement bragged support of Democratic, Republican, and Independent voters. Pollsters and political analysts were predicting that this new movement would become an Independent Party and win the coming election. With the economy still struggling to rebound from one of the toughest recessions since the 1930s and a national debt of nearly 15 trillion dollars, the new Independent Party was sure to find support, as its platform focused on downsizing government and big government spending. Gallup polls were showing a rise in the nation of people supporting a pro-life stand over pro-choice supporters. This new party supported the sanctity of life. Freedom issues, such as rights of privacy, freedom of free speech and religion, as well as the right to bear arms, are all part of the platform of this new party.

———◦◦◦———

While Cameron was still in Washington, he used some free time to meet with Bill Hanson for lunch. Bill invited Cameron to talk about some concerns he had politically. Bill and Cameron met at Central, a popular bistro in downtown DC. Both of them enjoyed a lobster burger.

Bill reached over the table and grabbed Cameron's upper arm. "Cam, we gotta talk."

Cameron responded with sincerity. "Go ahead, Bill. Share whatever is on your mind."

"Politics are not what they used to be in the Democratic Party. I have to say, I don't like the direction things are going with this new Democratic League."

Cameron was glad to hear what Bill was saying. "Bill, knowing you, I knew you would be concerned with the direction the Democratic Party is going in. Does it surprise you?"

Bill shook his head with a look of disappointment. "No, not really. I am just disappointed with some of my constituents who are wearing party blinders."

"What do you plan to do?"

"I am thinking about participating in the new Independent Party that is emerging."

Cameron smiled. "So am I!"

Bill smiled. "Good, then we are on the same team."

The waitress came with their lobster burgers. Bill took a huge bite and, out of DC restaurant decorum, spoke with his mouth full. "This is good!"

Cameron taking a bite of his burger grunted. "Mmmm."

———

Cameron was back home, and Deni typically fixed Cameron and Cody's favorite dishes when her husband came back from Washington DC. She decided to fix Cameron and Cody one of their favorites, beef stroganoff.

While she was in the kitchen preparing supper, Cameron and Cody were tossing the baseball in the front of their home. In typical form, Cody would inquire about his dad's life.

"Dad, what is it like working with the president of the United States?"

Cameron tossed a slow pitch. "Well, I don't actually work *with* the president but with people who work with the president."

Cody, throwing a fast pitch to his dad asked, "But you've seen him right?"

"Sure, I have met him."

Cody stood throwing the ball into his own glove. "Why didn't you say something about it? You met the president of the United States!"

Cameron raised his glove, signaling Cody to throw the ball back. "Well, I met him in passing at a gathering in the White House. I was not formally introduced."

"Still, that's cool! But I see your point. It's like if we were at a Packers game and I was near the field seats and Aaron Rodgers waved and said, 'Hi, kid!' That would be cool, but it wouldn't be like he invited me over to his house or something."

Cameron smiled. "You got it."

The boys enjoyed a great meal, and the Kales watched one of their favorite reality shows, *America's Got Talent*. It was a great pastime trying to guess who would be the final winner.

It was ten o'clock in the evening, and everyone would be turning into bed soon. Cameron gathered Deni and Cody closer and shared a thought from the Scriptures. It was the last phrase from Matthew 28:20 where Jesus said, "And lo, I am with you always even until the end of the age."

Cameron read the phrase and then commented. "We have had a pretty challenging past several years, haven't we?" Deni and Cody nodded affirmatively. "Sometimes life can throw us curves."

Cody piped up. "Yeah, like the one you threw me earlier, Dad!"

Cameron smiled. "Yes, but I mean life's curveballs." Cody nodded. Cameron continued. "Not everything that happens to us every day or week, month, or year are things that make us feel good. Some days, weeks, months, or years are difficult."

Cody spoke up. "Like when Ser Pentino kidnapped me, and when Jepson LaPlant shot you in the shoulder at the Fire and Ice restaurant!"

"And when your mother was rushed to the hospital, and we thought she might not make it," Cameron added.

Cody emphatically added, "And you lost Old Blue!"

Cameron nodded. "Yes, exactly. Those were difficult things. But here is my point. When Jesus was leaving the disciples to ascend to His father in heaven, this was a difficult time for the disciples. They would greatly miss their friend, teacher, and the one who made them feel safe from the world's troubles. And Jesus said, 'I will be with you always'; that is what He wants us to know. He is here with us and won't leave us without His help, protection, and comfort. We need to keep that in our head and in our hearts." Then Cameron prayed. "Lord, thank You for how You have blessed the Kale family. Thank You for calling us into Your work. Thank You for the many souls that have been brought into Your kingdom through our ministry. We praise You. Keep your watch over us as we sleep. Bless us that we may be a blessing to others. In Jesus's name I pray. Amen."

Cody came over to his dad and gave him a big hug. He loved hugs, and Cameron hoped that Cody would never outgrow this.

"Cody, make sure you brush your teeth, and Dad and I will be in before you go to sleep."

Cameron hugged Deni as she was yawning.

"I am tired tonight, Cam. I need a good night's sleep."

Cameron couldn't help but yawn too. "I hear you. I could use some sleep too."

Both went in and hugged and kissed Cody again and turned in for the night.

⎯⎯⦚⦚⎯⎯

Early the next morning, Bill Hanson called Cameron. "Cameron, you don't need to come to Washington this month."

"What's up, Bill?"

"Washington is coming to you. Joan Canthrop has made it so that the Independent Party's rally is going to show up in Mariah City at Central Park. She wants you to speak at the rally."

Cameron was overjoyed. "Wonderful, Bill. That is great news!"

"We'll get together and go over some of the details. Keep it in prayer!"

"Amen!"

That night, the Kale family attended their first-of-the-month prayer meeting. Cameron would share a devotion from the Scriptures, and while a CD or a live musician played, members of the church would find places to sit alone all over the auditorium. Cameron would often go to the very top row of the balcony so that he could look over the facility and pray for God's oversight and watch care of the ministry. Sometimes as Cameron prayed, he would sense God's angels perched up in the upper parts of the sanctuary to guard the church from God's enemy coming in. On one particular evening, a lady in the church who was clearly playing the part of Jezebel in her life and acting out this temptress spirit in the church climbed the steps to the balcony and sat in the top row opposite Pastor Cameron. He knew this spirit in her was challenging his authority under Christ. He prayed for God's protection and authority and felt God's power moving mightily over the church, answering the pastor's prayer. Ser Pentino had not materialized to Cameron in a long time, but Cameron knew that he was active behind the scenes. Cameron also knew that many Christians are deceived because they don't realize the extent that we experience the effects of spiritual warfare in our lives. While we do not need to fear, Cameron would always say "We need to be aware and know how to fight God's enemy with spiritual weapons."

Within a few days, a new political party would be sharing truth in Mariah City. He asked God to use him and his speech to change people in Mariah City. He also thanked God for changing Joan Canthrop's life and for the impact that she was making for righteousness in the community and in the nation. Cameron was not sure how he would be used in this new party, but he knew God had a plan to use him. He was thankful that there was a healthy and righteous alternative to the Democratic League.

Bill had returned a call to Cameron the next day and shared that the rally would be held in two weeks at Mariah City's Central Park. There would be enough room for a crowed nearing 20,000.

———⟨ω/ω⟩———

It was the day of the rally, and TV crews, vendors, and thousands of supporters of the new Independent Party poured into Mariah

City for the rally. Bulletins were passed out with the day's agenda and a list of the speakers. Many of the hometown supporters were excited to hear what Dr. Kale would have to say at the rally. It was exciting to Cameron as many from his church turned out for the event, but also many of his political colleagues from Washington were there as well.

As Cameron, Deni, and Cody were shaking hands with folks in the crowd, Dr. Canthrop came up to Cameron and tapped him on the shoulder from behind.

"Dr. Kale, I want you to meet a good friend of mine, Sandra Dalin. She may be our next president."

Cameron smiled and reached out to shake her hand. "Is it Miss or Mrs. Dalin?"

Smiling, she responded, "Mrs."

Cameron bowed his head as he shook her hand. "It is a pleasure to meet you, Mrs. Dalin."

"Likewise."

Cameron held the back of Deni's arm. "And this is my better half, Deni."

Sandra Dalin reached to shake her hand. "It's good to meet you. I have heard much about your husband and was looking forward to meeting him today." Addressing Dr. Kale, she said, "Word is out that you may become more involved with this party."

Bill Hanson stepped up next to Cameron and Deni, interrupting. "You bet he is. Hi, I'm Bill Hanson, the mayor of this fine city…and interested in your party too."

Sandra Dalin shook Bill's hand. "It is nice to meet you too, Bill, and I am happy to hear that you are a supporter of this party. We need you."

It was near time for Cameron to speak. By this time he had shaken many hands and talked with at least sixty people.

The organizer for the event called some names of people who were participating in the event to come to the tent behind the platform. Cameron's name was one of them.

A briefing was held for several minutes with those who would be participating on the platform. Cameron would be introduced as the opening speaker, but before he would speak, the crowd would be led in the Pledge of Allegiance.

Everyone was asked to remove any head coverings and to join in the pledge. The pledge leader spoke as the crowd began to speak. "I pledge allegiance to the flag of the United States of America and to the Republic for which it stands. One nation under God, indivisible, with liberty and justice for all." The crowd lit up with patriotism with shouts and applause.

Bill Hanson was the man who would introduce Cameron Kale. He came to the podium. "Ladies and gentlemen, fellow Americans, and citizens of Mariah City, Nevada, it is with great pleasure that I introduce to you our speaker, our own Dr. Cameron Kale!"

The crowd went ballistic with applause and whistles. Signs were being raised reflecting the new party's platform. Bill Hanson continued his introduction.

"For many of you, there needs to be no introduction to our speaker. He has been a resident of our city. He has been our doctor. I always say that Dr. Kale straightened me out. A little chiropractic humor there." The crowd laughed. "He has also been a pastor and community leader in this city and even greater in our nation as he spearheaded with our nation's Surgeon General, Dr. Virginia Bassman, a task force for better health on issues like abortion and euthanasia. He has straightened me out because Dr. Kale was the one who changed me from a Democrat to the American values and views of this new party. He is a good family man who deeply loves his wife, Deni, and son, Cody, and lastly, he is a good Christian. He deeply loves his God." The crowd roared with approval and applause. "Ladies and gentlemen, I give you Dr. Cameron Kale."

Cameron briskly walked to the podium wearing khakis and a blue shirt with his sleeves rolled up, looking presidential and full of energy and passion. Smiling, he shook Bill's hand and gave him a bear hug. All the time, the crowd continued to roar with applause, whistles, and shouts until Cameron spoke into the microphone.

"Good morning!"

The crowd was in tune as they answered back. "Good morning!"

"It is great to be here. To quote Dorothy from *The Wizard of Oz*, 'There is no place like home'!"

The crowd laughed and cheered and applauded. Most people would have expected his opening words to be profound and found his humor refreshing and personable. That was the nature of Cameron Kale. It didn't matter where Cameron was—he was real.

"Some of you who don't know me very well might be interested to know that several years ago I was primarily serving the community as a small-city chiropractor and living a pretty normal, typical American lifestyle. In addition to my practice, I helped out with local mission teams at our church, Mariah City Community Church, helping folks with needs in the community, and Deni has been working at the pregnancy center also, helping women and men through crises with their unexpected pregnancies. We are just a typical American family. That is what I appreciate about many of you attending this event, because that is what you are too!"

The crowd applauded and was waving their signs and American flags. Cameron continued his speech.

"That is what I respect about this party, because it is about typical American families that believe in the values established in this country when it was founded several hundred years ago!" Again, the crowds rang out in applause, shouts, whistles, and sign waving.

"I don't think I was asked to come here because of any political ambition on my part. I just want you to know that. I don't have a lot of political ambition. What I do have is a desire to tell the truth. I have a desire to truly help those who are helpless in our country—the unborn, the elderly, victims of human trafficking, and private citizens who are losing their personal privacies and freedoms!" The crowd raised the decibel level with the applause and shouts. "I know that this is what this party is all about, not relying on Washington politicians to tell us what they think, but raising up true representatives of the American people and telling Washington what we think!"

Cameron paused while the crowd continued to respond. Cameron was effective as a political spokesperson and always was a person who could adapt to his environment, but while he could express appreciation for his fellow citizens, his real passion was to express God's heart on matters of life.

"I am sure that most of you know by now that I am a minister of the gospel. That offends some folks and especially some in Washington. Most of you who know me know that I am not a person who seeks to offend anyone. I am a peacemaker. But I want to share my heart with you, and I can do that more readily since I am not a political candidate." Everyone laughed. "I am not ashamed of the gospel of Jesus Christ because it is God's power to everyone who believes on Him." Applause continued. "God called me to share the gospel—the good news of Jesus Christ. Many people think that is some religious fanatic's crutch or excuse for bad behavior. But because God called me to be an evangelist and a minister of the gospel, I have a heightened desire and responsibility to help the society I am a part of. God has called me to minister to the hurting and bring healing to the brokenhearted. I believe the greatness of this country is that we have a Judeo-Christian heritage, and we have many other religions in our land protected under our Constitution that stand for helping our fellow citizens. We need to stand united in this and protect our Constitution that protects us. We need to stand for the privacy of our people and not more power to government. We need to truly help the impoverished and not impound them by higher taxes. May God save America!"

The crowd cheered and came unglued with enthusiasm. Streamers were shot into the air, and red, white, and blue balloons were released into the air as the crowd applauded. It was as if Cameron Kale was their presidential candidate. When everyone thought Dr. Kale was finished with his speech, he continued further.

"I may get kicked off this platform or told I am inappropriate or even asked to never speak for this party again, but I want to make something clear today. If we are going to be one nation under God, then let's not be so glib or ignorant about what this means and be one nation under God! Contrary to popular belief, God did not create us and then put us here to figure out this world He created for us. That makes no sense. No, a loving God would create people for fellowship for interaction and help them know how to interact. If He was the creator of the world of those He created, He would also kindly give instructions about how to be benefited living in this world and point out the traps that are around us so that we get the most out of life. He would tell us how to care for each other like He cares for us. He has done that. He wants us to follow Him and trust Him and stop trying to do things the way we want—things that never work out anyway. He shows us the way through His Son, Jesus Christ.

"If you do nothing else today, if you had never trusted Christ and never given your life to God, do that today before you leave. For anyone who wants to criticize a presentation of the gospel at a political rally, let them first understand that government was never intended to prescribe a religion, but it was never intended for government to be untouched by the power of true religion either. I believe many in this party know that and believe that."

The crowd again raised the volume of their cheers and applause. Television cameras panned the crowds as people were actually getting on their knees, crying, praying, and repenting. Many were praying out loud, asking Jesus to take control of their lives. Reporters were giving live coverage to their network that a revival was taking place, something that looked like the times of George Whitfield and Jonathan Edwards.

That evening, the Kales were at home relaxing, enjoying some of Deni's famous homemade Yorkshire Pizza. It was Cody's favorite. As they sat in their family room watching the news, a clip of the party rally was shown.

"Hey, Dad, you're on TV!" Cody shouted.

Cameron jokingly responded, "Yeah, but they didn't get my good side." Deni tossed a couch pillow at him.

Cameron, Deni, and Cody started a friendly pillow fight when Cameron caught something on his television. Cody saw the distraught look on his dad's face.

"Dad, what's wrong?"

"Cody, give me the clicker!" He paused the recorded newscast and rewound it back a few frames and paused it again. Cameron raised his voice, "Look, Deni, look!"

Cameron, Deni, and Cody recognized what Cameron was making all of the fuss about. A small man with a pinstripe suit was walking back and forth through the crowd with no apparent destination, as if he was pacing off territory. It was Ser Pentino.

"Cam, he's everywhere!" Deni said, shaking her head.

"No, he can only be in one place at a time, but lately he wants to be where we are, that's for sure!" Cameron responded.

Cody spoke up. "Dad, it's just like the Bible says, 'He is like a roaring lion seeking whom he may devour.' Look, he is pacing just like a lion looking for his prey."

"Or marking his territory," Cameron said.

"What does that mean?" Cody asked.

"It's what cats do when they want to be the dominant male cat," Deni answered.

"Oh, I get it. Ser Pentino was marking the territory near Dad and all of the believers at the park and claiming that territory for himself."

"You got it, my young theologian," Cameron said. "He hates it when we speak out for righteousness and so many people get to hear the truth. He also hates it more when people give their lives to Christ like they did at the rally."

Cameron gathered his family together to pray.

"Lord, we are stopped once again to take note of reality. We are faced with a very real enemy, but we are not shaken. We are in awe of what You are doing in Your kingdom. We pray that You will protect us from the evil one and that You will continue to use us for Your glory. May many come to know You as their Lord and Savior in Mariah City and in the nation. In Jesus's name we pray with thanksgiving. Amen."

The Kales smiled at each other, and Cody blurted, "This just makes me more hungry. Who wants more Yorkshire Pizza?"

Cameron was in his office at the church the next morning and was making some phone calls. A knock was at his door. It was Scott Benson and Clem Mager.

"Pastor, are you in?" Clem asked.

Cameron stood up and shook his close friend's hands.

"Congratulations!" Scott said. "I saw the piece on the news. It was actually pretty positive, considering—"

Cameron pressed his lips together and nodded affirmatively, finishing Scott's statement. "—considering that the gospel was given."

"Yes, considering that!" Scott answered "Praise God for the response."

Cameron smiled. "Amen. How have things been, fellows?" Cameron sat back down and offered them both a seat.

Clem looked at Scott and then at Pastor Cameron. "Pastor, it's been tough. We don't want to be bearers of bad news, but while you were gone, the mice sort of played."

Cameron chuckled. "What do you mean?"

"Attendance was low at the Bible study, and some of the elderly folks complained about everything they could think of instead of praising God for what He is doing in our midst."

"What were they complaining about specifically?"

Scott spoke up. "You, Pastor. Some of the elderly folks are complaining about the time you have spent in Washington."

"Well, at least they were complaining about something legitimate."

Both Scott and Clem were surprised by Pastor Cameron's answer, but they knew not to expect a typical answer from him.

"Fellas, I know that, even going from time to time and making sure things are covered here, many people want their own senior pastor to be close by all of the time. I guess I am going to have to cut back on some of the time I have been spending in Washington and ensure that God's flock is my focus."

"That isn't why we came here, to tell you that you should be here more," Scott said. "We just were concerned about the attitude that some of the congregation had. And those who complained the most were not people we consider walking in the spirit of God. They are just complainers."

Cameron spoke up. "Nevertheless, this could be God's way of reminding me of what my first responsibility is. It is this church, not the nation."

Scott and Clem were blessed by their pastor's humbleness and his love even for those who complained in the church. He seemed to exude the love of Christ. He was what they needed in a pastor, a true under shepherd of Jesus Christ.

As Scott, Clem and Pastor Cameron were fellowshipping, Bill Hanson walked into the office. "Cameron."

Cameron stood up, as did Scott and Clem.

Clem reached out to shake hands with Bill. "Mr. Mayor."

"It's okay, Clem," Bill responded. "I know you have police business here."

Clem laughed. "Yes, sir."

Cameron asked Bill to have a seat, but Bill insisted on standing.

"Cameron, I just came to tell you some great news. Sandra Dalin has asked me to ask you if you would be willing to give the speech at the National Convention for the Independent Party and be the one to introduce her as the nominee for president of the United States."

Cameron was more excited about the news that she would be the top nominee than he was about his part. "Absolutely, it will be an honor!"

Bill reached out to shake Cameron's hand again. "Good, then I will get back to Sandra tonight and let her know you're in."

Cameron shook his head with surprise. "Wonderful!" Scott and Clem congratulated their pastor.

Clem laughed and said while nudging Scott, "Pastor, what was that you were saying about less involvement with Washington?"

Pastor Cameron smiled. "Well, maybe after the election."

They all laughed.

Chapter Twenty-Three

THE ENEMY'S PLAN TO END CONSERVATIVE CHRISTIANITY

Ser Pentino emerged again with a plot to end Christian practice in the United States by having the new Independent Party's candidate assassinated. If this assassination was accomplished, it would have major national and worldwide impact on peace and security of the nation and financial stability.

The opposing major political party was finding favor with radical leftists and the pop culture of society to remove Social Security, take the life of elders at seventy years old to reduce national debt, and the responsibility to care for their debts, to reduce the population of jails and prisons by 20 percent and decrease prison sentence times. It would increase measures to limit families to only two children and would require abortion-on-demand for any additional children. This new radical leftist party called the Democratic League would reduce the concept of capitalism and would embrace Marxist ideology. Karl Marx was an economist who promoted the idea that the wealth of a nation should be shared. This is the basis of socialism. The idea that everyone should have the same things even though they do not work for them while those who work hard for what they have should be limited to what they have is the heart of socialistic doctrine. The Democratic League would promote even bigger government and less control of the economy in the private sector. More programs would be set up to give to the poor what they have not earned, and those who are rich would not only be taxed higher taxes but also must give up a portion of their earnings for these social programs. This new party or formation of an old party will remove much of the privacy laws and allow government to monitor what people are doing in their businesses and homes by the use of bugging devices. They would also enforce gun control and would not allow any citizen to have or use firearms for *any* circumstances.

This new form of government would more usher in the end-times more quickly. Of even greater concern to Cameron Kale and his conservative colleagues was the Democratic League's position on the nation of Israel. President Othama was working diligently to bring about a peace treaty between the Arabs and the nation of Israel. Israel had been pressured to give up a portion of their land that God said in the Scriptures belonged to Israel. Cameron often shared with his congregation that those nations that bless Israel, God would bless, and those that did not, God would not bless them. Cameron also taught his congregation that the Prophet Daniel spoke about a future peace treaty that a man would have the Arabs and Israel sign, but it would be a pseudo peace. The man who would sign this treaty would be the antichrist. While Cameron would not say that the president was the antichrist, he did believe that the signing of this treaty would be an indicator of the signs of the times. He could not say that this treaty was exactly the treaty Daniel wrote about but could be the beginning of a series of treaties that would be signed leading up to the time the Bible calls the "tribulation," when the antichrist will make a covenant between the Arabs and Israel. While we know that God is sovereign and takes down and sets up kings for the purpose of His bringing about His plan of redemption, there are evil men who want to control the powers that be and usher a lifestyle that is contrary to the kingdom. We must fight social injustice even though God will use it to bring to pass His will. He will call us faithful servants in the end when we stand for what is righteous and good and His perfect will. He will judge the earth for their wickedness and their planning to destroy the kingdom of God.

Churches would need to go underground as freedom of religion was now seen as politically incorrect and treason to the rights of the state.

———*∞*———

Cameron had been asked by the party to deliver a speech and introduce the new presidential candidate for the party at the convention center in Reno, Nevada.

Cameron was sleeping soundly next to Deni in his bedroom and woke up to sounds of footsteps. While Cameron lifted his head from his pillow, he thought it would be strange to have one of his dreams again, as it had been years since he had his encounters with Ser Pentino. Looking into the corner of his bedroom where he heard the sounds, he heard a voice say, "Cameron Kale, you are right. I know what you are thinking. It is Ser Pentino."

Cameron sat straight up. "I can't see you."

"Very well." The strange glow of green light that Cameron had seen before allowed Ser Pentino to be visible in the dark room. Cameron looked over at Deni, but as before, she appeared as though she had been drugged so she would not wake up.

Cameron did not attempt to speak with Ser Pentino but immediately called out to God. "Lord God, rebuke the evil one. Come to my rescue and save us in this hour of jeopardy—handle this evil one, I pray and plead by Your precious blood, Lord Jesus, Lamb of God. I stand behind Your cross."

Ser Pentino vanished, but Cameron got to his knees beside his bed and began to pray. He knew that if Ser Pentino appeared after so many years that something big was about to happen for the glory of God, and Ser Pentino was there to see that it did not happen.

As Cameron knelt beside his bed, he was ministered to by the spirit of God. He felt strength in his inner man and a peace that was so peaceful that human understanding could not explain it.

As he prayed, he could hear the spirit of God. A voice told him to look on his nightstand. He turned his head and looked to find a peace of paper with very strange cursive handwriting. It said, "I have spared my warrior. He has risen again and will destroy you and your nation's leader." Signed Ser Pentino.

Cameron knew that this riddle was serious but not something that he could take to the police. It was something that he and those closest to him in the church, Scott and Clem, would need to pray about. Cameron went into the kitchen to make a cup of hot tea with milk. As he sat in his den, he read the note and continued to pray. He wrestled with the idea of who had done business for Ser Pentino and would rise again.

"I got it. Ser Pentino didn't want this to be too difficult for me to figure out! Jepson had been his warrior doing business for him like a military commander. Everyone thinks Jepson is dead, but Ser Pentino enables him to 'rise again,' or reappear, to carry out his work.

Cameron figured out that Ser Pentino wanted him to know that Jepson would reappear and destroy Cameron but also the new presidential candidate, Sandra Dalin of the Independent Party.

He knew that no one would believe him, other than his family and his close associates. If he were to speak openly about this, many would see him as a bumbling conservative that didn't know what he was talking about. It would give rise to a shift in people seeing more credibility with the Democratic League. Cameron knew he could not allow this party to control the White House and the nation.

In addition, Cameron knew that his family and close friends would be placed in danger if he attempted to say anything publicly about an assassination plan. Cameron resorted to prayer and dependence on God for answers. He knew he must fight this battle with spiritual weapons, not physical ones. He knew God's enemy could not win the war but could claim a major victory.

Chapter Twenty-Four

CAMERON'S CONTEMPLATIONS ON GOOD VERSUS EVIL

After Cameron's last dream about Ser Pentino, he realized even to a greater degree how important it was for him to be regular in his prayer time. If he believed it before, he grew to believe it more now that we are in a continual spiritual battle while we are here on earth. Some have compared heaven to Canaan, the promised land. However, Cameron always believed that Canaan is on this earth. Canaan is not a place of rest and ceasing from sorrow but of battles and victories. It is a place where we take what God has given us for the kingdom.

Cameron was also very contemplative of this real battle we experience on Earth of good versus evil. He was more convinced than ever that too many Christians do not take seriously the spiritual realities that are close to them.

He knew that Paul's words to the Ephesians to "stand in the evil day and having done all to stand" were as applicable as ever in his present day. He knew that he needed to live it and that he had to warn his congregation of it. These were indeed evil days, and Christians needed to redeem the time. He knew that he must preach the things that he had spent much time thinking about.

"Good morning, ladies and gentlemen."

The congregation answered Pastor Kale back, "Good morning."

Cameron grabbed both sides of the Plexiglas pulpit and leaned forward, as he was about to speak soberly and emphatically. "I want to share with you something that has been a burden on my heart for not just days or weeks but several years now. It is something that affects every one of us who know Christ as Savior. I don't have to tell you that we are living in troubled times." A few *amens* echoed throughout the auditorium. "I hope it never becomes cliché to say that we are near the time of Christ's return!"

While those words might ring in some ears of cliché spoken by other men, they came across in the power of the Spirit when Pastor Cameron spoke them. Many in the congregation clapped their hands and said, "Amen."

"Folks, I feel somewhat prophetic this morning as I am pressed to share the deepest burdens of my heart, and I believe these burdens are the heart of God. Because I want to speak from my heart, I am hesitant to give you a three-point sermon. But I know that some of you like an outline, so I have provided one for you. What God has burdened me about can be shared with you as three commands. One, be connected, fellowshipping with Jesus; two, be cognizant, focusing on heaven; and three, be communicators, fishing for men.

"I don't want what I am to share with you to seem like I am scolding you. I know that many of you have a desire to serve God and build His kingdom. But I want to tell you that I believe that we are not always doing that because we are not prepared to hear or see the truth. Let me tell you why.

"It is difficult to hear the voice of God and to see the trends of God because we can't see through the smoke and mirrors put up by God's enemy." Again, the congregation was moved verbally in agreement.

"First, we have to be connected—that is, have fellowship with Jesus. First John chapter one tells us that we have fellowship with God the Father and with His Son, Jesus Christ, when we become Christians. If we have never repented of sin and confessed Jesus to be our Lord and Savior, then we are not connected to God, right? Jesus said, 'I am the Way, the Truth, and the Life, no man comes to the Father but by me.'"

"Without coming to Jesus, we cannot be connected to Jesus. But being connected to Jesus is more than just salvation; it is having fellowship with Him every day. It is building an intimate relationship with Him. I want to tell you that without building intimacy with Jesus, we are powerless against evil. If you can't overcome sin, if you can't overcome habits, if you can't overcome a bad attitude, if you can't overcome worry, if you can't overcome using foul language or even overcome addiction, if you can't overcome laziness, you are not connected to Jesus. Jesus conquers all of those things.

"When we spend quiet, alone time with Jesus in prayer and in His Word, we develop a fellowship with Him, and it gives us power in our lives that we must have to conquer sin. Jesus enabled us to continue to walk with Him through confession. He said in First John chapter one verse nine that if we confess our sins, He is faithful and just and will forgive us our sins and purify us from all unrighteousness. Jesus wants us to continue fellowship with Him, and we can do that when we confess; admit; or, according to the original language, say the same thing as God says about our sin. He will cleanse us of sin, and we will keep our fellowship open with the Lord. Staying connected to Jesus is essential, dear hearts, if we want to have victory in our lives as believers. We can only stand against God's enemy, who prowls around like a roaring lion seeking whom He may devour if we stay close to Jesus."

"Now we can also win over evil by being cognizant—that is, having our focus on heaven. Let me explain how we get off focus. The truth is that we get caught up in too many things around us, and while we think we are more educated and broadened and wise, we are deluded, weakened, and blinded by those things we put into our minds. I am going to say something that may get me into trouble, but here goes. I love the contemporary music as much as most of you do. You all know that I love the hymns I grew up on, but I love the upbeat and praise tempo of contemporary music too. We can get caught up in the bands, music, and praising but simultaneously miss what God is doing. I think there is a lot of that going on. I know many of you come to church because you know that is what God wants you to do. You also know you need to hear the Word to get you through the week."

More people said, "Amen."

"But isn't it true that we can come into church regularly and get into a habit just like we do with many things and going through the motions? We are not really worshiping but thinking about what we are going to do when we get home."

The congregation was feeling the sting from Pastor Cameron's words. He was pressing something on the congregation, and everyone was listening carefully.

"Folks, I am not just preaching this to you. I am preaching to myself. I believe that we can become so focused on what is happening around us that we are missing what God really wants to do in our lives. We may be planning to have lunch out this afternoon and take in the movies this evening. We may be planning a vacation and going shopping for some cool clothes for the vacation this week, but even in the middle of all of that, a raging battle is taking place between major players, believers in Jesus Christ, and the forces of hell!"

Cameron's last phrase made a crescendo that raised the hair on the back of his congregation's necks.

"Folks, we are living out the reality of the battle of the ages, good versus evil! Every moment, every day, every month, every year, we are making decisions that seem just like simple things in our scheme of things but have eternal outcomes. I heard a popular musician say that we often think we have to be on a stage or speaking in a crowd to make an impact for the kingdom of God, but it is often the little decisions we make every day that builds God's kingdom. It is the little things we do every day in obedience to God that gives Him the glory and moves us all closer to His return. It is also the little bad decisions that we make that can work against the kingdom advancing for Christ and His glory. What are you and I doing to advance the kingdom or retard its advance? What decisions are we making—big or small—that are either hindering or helping the kingdom of God? I have been thinking a lot about that. Don't misunderstand. I am not telling you to not enjoy your recreation or not to fellowship with your family and friends. I am not saying that a vacation trip or even shopping is evil. No, not at all. I can shop along with the best of them!"

The congregation laughed, mostly the ladies.

"It is just that God wants us to keep our focus. So we must be connected, fellowshipping with Jesus, and be cognizant, focused on heaven. That's what Paul said.

"Listen to Paul, he said, in Colossians chapter three verse two, '…Set your minds on things above, not on earthly things.' *Why* did he say this? He said it because our time here on Earth is short—isn't it? Many young people here think that life is going to go on and on. As we get older, we get wiser about time. Growing older gives you perspective on time, because you now can ask, 'Where did the time go?' Three score plus ten is the life span that the Bible gives us for an average life. Seventy years. I get amazed at the Smucker's Jelly report from Willard Scott of elderly folks with birthdays above one hundred. But they are not the norm. We live seventy years, and then our Spirit leaves the earth. It is a vapor, as James tells us. But why so short? You all know the answer to this. It is because we are preparing for the future. Life here on Earth is for the future. It is to get ready for eternity. Are you ready? Are you prepared?"

Cameron knew there were always people in attendance who did not know Christ and spoke both to the believer and the nonbeliever. It was difficult for Cameron to not share the gospel since God had given him the gift of evangelism.

He went on to say that he had recently attended the funeral of a Christian man but that many family members were not believers. He shared with them how he had asked the question when people gather for funerals. The most common understood reason we gather is to pay our respects. Human life is valuable, and the contributions of a family member, friend, or associate cannot be underestimated. So we pay our respects. Cameron went on to share another reason we gather is to say good-bye. We know that we may not see a person for a long time, so we say our last good-byes. But then he shared another reason.

"There is another reason I believe God intends for us to gather together when a loved one passes: God wants to tell us, the survivors, about the temporariness of life and importance of eternity.

"Life is a vapor. It comes and goes. Those of us who are older understand how fast time goes by. It does. I remember when I could say, 'I have the rest of my life.' Now that I am nearing forty, I will count myself fortunate if I have thirty more years. Life is short. Life is fatal. I don't want to shock anyone here, but this day will come for each one of us. I am convinced that God wants us to be able to answer this simple question: 'Am I ready?' When most people think about being ready for death, they think, 'Well, there are things I haven't done yet, so I guess I should start doing those things,' so they make list and try to accomplish them, such as: I have always wanted to take a trip around the world, so I better get my finances in line and make some plans for that trip. It may be that on your list, you say, I have always feared heights, so before I die, I am going to plan to bungee jump and then parachute out of an airplane. Maybe you want to learn an instrument and play in a band somewhere, or maybe it is to find all of the people you have offended and, one by one, call, or write, or visit them and make amends. Wouldn't that be a great thing to do before we die?

"Many people think of preparing for death by doing some of these things. But that is not what I am talking about. I am talking about the fact that since our life was only meant to be temporary, all of us from birth are preparing for eternity. Too often we spend much of our time focusing on earthly things, but eternity comes too quickly.

"The Apostle Paul, inspired by God's spirit, said in our text, 'Set your minds or affections on things above not on earthly things.' The writer of Hebrews said that we are pilgrims on Earth looking for that heavenly city. Jesus wrote that we should not treasure the things that moths can corrupt and can be corroded, like metals. He said that whatever we treasure is what we have given our heart to. Where is your heart? What is it you treasure? These verses of Scripture are all saying the same thing: that we should focus on eternity while on Earth and be prepared for what is to come.

"What should we learn here? What should we come away with as we leave here today? We often don't think about this unless we attend a funeral, and sometimes we don't think about it then unless the pastor points it out. But the lesson we learn at funerals is that the death of a loved one is a clarion call to each one of us that life here is temporary and comes to an end. It is not the end of life, just the end of life here on Earth. Life continues. God created man as an eternal being. Man was created to live eternally. Man will live eternally either with God in the joy of His presence or separated from God for eternity in anguish and darkness away from God's presence.

"Listen to Jesus's words before He ascended bodily to heaven. He said these words to His followers who had put their faith and trust in Him: 'Do not let your hearts be troubled. Trust in God; trust also in me. In my Father's house are many rooms; if it were not so, I would have told you. I am going there to prepare a place for you. And if I go and prepare a place for you, I will come back and take you to be with me that you also may be where I am. You know the way to the place where I am going. Thomas said to him, 'Lord, we don't know where you are going, so how can we know the way?' Jesus answered, 'I am the Way, the Truth, and the Life. No one comes to the Father except through me.'

"You may not have been seeking the Lord, but He is seeking you. It is because the Lord loves you that He is seeking you. That is Christianity. It is not religion of man reaching to some god of his making. Christianity is God reaching down to man because of his unconditional love for him. He loves you this morning. And because of His great love for you, He asks you to come to Him and trust Him because He not only wants to prepare you for the life that is to come but also for this life here on Earth. He wants to help you manage this life better and bring His joy and blessings into this life that you are living now. Those of you who know him know this to be true. They have learned to love and trust Jesus, and as someone so aptly said, 'The prospect of meeting him face-to-face and being with him forever is the hope that keeps us going, no matter what life may throw at us.'

"So we must first be connected to Jesus—that is, have fellowship with Him—and then be cognizant—that is, having focus on heaven—and finally, we must be communicators—that is, fishers of men.

"Jesus's last words were to go out among the nations and make disciples. Disciples are followers of Jesus. When you become a follower of Jesus, you are a disciple. God wants you to make other disciples. The best way to do that is to communicate to others what God has done for you. Jesus said to His disciples, 'I will make you fishers of men' (John 21:1-17).

"Folks, God's enemy is trying to keep others from seeing the gospel. He will put up a smoke screen so they cannot see the gospel. It is our job to be lights in the world so that others see and hear Jesus."

Cameron also shared how the enemy is winning many battles when believers choose to not communicate what God has done in their lives. Finally, Cameron was winding down his message and emphasized that it was not easy to speak out for Christ in an unbelieving world but that God would bless the believer who dares to be bold in this day and share the gospel. He went on to say that the battle to keep men and women out of heaven and to keep Christians from focusing on heaven is out of control. He shared how too many who claim Christianity are not in the battle but on the sidelines, watching our wounded fall. He challenged every believer to engage in battle and be good soldiers of Jesus Christ.

Three things were necessary as the days were getting close to Jesus's return: be connected, be cognizant, and be communicators. He promised if we would do this, we would live as revolutionary believers. He believed that God would work supernatural miracles in our lives if we dared to trust Him in simple faith. He knew by his own experience that when anyone dares to just believe God, God makes simple men and women into superheroes of faith.

Cameron knew God was not finished using Him for His glory and for the building of His kingdom. He hoped that many more would join him in putting simple faith in Jesus.

Cameron had just finished his sermon and asked if any wanted to come to meet him or the other pastors in the front and dedicate their lives to Jesus Christ. Hundreds came forward, both receiving Christ and dedicating their lives to Jesus Christ. God was working miracles before His eyes. The greatest miracle of all is one whose life is transformed by the saving power of Jesus Christ.

Chapter Twenty-Five

CHRIST THE VICTOR OVER THE ENEMY

Cameron Kale often taught his congregation that good ultimately wins out over evil. While evil sometimes prevails for a time, it is finally overcome by good. Cameron had grown to discover that our power resides in the reality that God is the victor, whether we believe He is or not. Our belief in His ultimate victory aids us in becoming victorious with Him.

Cameron desired that everyone know Christ is victorious in the battle against the enemy of the ages and that everyone who is a believer is in this battle, whether they believe it or not.

Cameron's interpretation of Ser Pentino's note was correct. Jepson was alive. Jepson was ready with a small mob of political dissidents who were really goons that looked more like preppy college boys than Mafia. They were ex-military snipers who were trained as al-Qaeda under Osama Bin Laden in Afghanistan. These men were trained as translators and were utilized as security during the convention. Placed in key positions within the grand hall, they would be able to easily take out the potential presidential candidate.

Jepson would radio the order on a secured frequency on his radio. The signal would be Cameron shaking hands with the candidate as she approached the podium.

Cameron knew that he must preach the message God had given him to bring. He must be clear why this new party must take over Washington and how the old America would be gone if they handed over their values and freedoms to the Democratic League. Cameron knew that he must appeal to the hearts of those in the country who still believed in God, needed God, and wanted God to be their Ruler, their King, and their Leader. Cameron wanted the people of the nation to know that it was not about religion but being decent, honest, good, and loving our neighbors again. He wanted people to know that Christian ethics were not scare tactics. He wanted people to strive for freedom, not loss of privacy.

Cameron's message brought the house down and vocal levels of praise and applauds at decibel levels unheard of. The chants rang out through the hall, "Put God back in government! Put God back in government! In God we trust! In God we trust!"

Chief Bormand was still struggling with his thoughts as to why Jepson would try to hurt Cameron Kale, or Amy Benson for that matter. Cody had been interested in criminology since the case opened with Jepson. He wanted to help Chief Bormand, but the chief kept telling Cody that he was too young to get involved. The afternoon Cameron left for the conference center, Cody wandered over to Jepson's garage. It had been closed up. Earlier it was taped off, as investigators were looking for clues as to Jepson's whereabouts. No one investigated the earlier charges of his alleged murder of Amy Benson because the chief thought Jepson shot Cameron because of being charged with a murder he did not commit.

Cody made his way into a small door in the back of the garage that was only locked by a small hook. Cody knew no one seriously looked for clues proving Jepson as the murderer of Amy Benson. What was he looking for? What could he find that would help?

As Cody looked around the garage only lighted by one window, he began to feel like maybe he was just trying to be a hero, like his dad. Cody remembered what his dad often said: "We can all be heroes when we are obedient to God." Cody began to pray.

"Dear Lord, I know You know where there may be a clue showing us if Jepson hurt Amy Benson. I know it would sure help Mr. Benson if he knew how his wife died. Lord, I don't want any credit. I just want to help. I guess the best way to help is to pray. Thank You for listening. Amen."

As Cody finished praying, his eyes fell on a glove that was sticking out from under the workbench. It had a lot of dark fluid on it. Cody remembered that the brake line had been cut on Amy Benson's car and wondered if this might be the glove Jepson wore when he cut her lines. Cody grabbed the glove and wrapped it in an old plastic bag he found in Jepson's garage. He took it to Chief Bormand and explained what he did. Chief Bormand was not happy with Cody sticking his nose into police business. Cody apologized but insisted it would not hurt to have the glove tested.

Chief Bormand looked at Cody and then the glove. "Well, I don't have to test the glove to see that this is brake fluid all right, but everybody's garage has a glove with some kind of auto fluids on it. This doesn't prove anything."

The chief picked up a file that had been on his desk with Jepson's name on it. He opened the file and quietly flipped through the pages as Cody stood there like a statue.

"There is a lab report here mentioning a fiber that was found near the brake lines and was believed to be a common fiber found in a work glove. Let's get this over to lab."

The lab reports came back, and sure enough, the fiber matched the glove Cody found in Jepson's garage. This would provide the needed evidence that Jepson had cut the brake lines on Amy Benson's car.

With this new information, Chief Bormand somehow believed that Jepson was not dead. He didn't know how he could be alive, but he knew that no intense fire could burn through flesh and bone so quickly leaving no trace. Somehow Jepson had to be alive.

"I have to see your father," Bormand told Cody. "Didn't he go to the convention center in Reno? I am afraid he may be in danger. I have to get there and warn him."

Bormand got on the phone and called his lieutenant.

"Lieutenant, I need some back up. We need to get to the convention center in Reno. Get me a couple of suits. I don't want to raise alarm at the convention with uniformed officers."

After he got off the phone, he turned back to Cody.

"Cody, you go home. Don't say anything to anyone. Let your mom know what is going on and that we are on our way to help her husband." The chief turned his back and headed toward the door and then wheeled half around and looked at Cody. "Kale, good job. You might make a criminologist yet!"

As the chief left the police station, Cody knew he had to help somehow. He knew his dad was in danger and couldn't take the risk that the chief would miss something. Cody knew how dangerous Jepson was and was wise enough to know that Ser Pentino probably had something to do with this.

———

Cody rode his bike back to his house and sneaked into the garage. Fortunately, the door had been left open since Deni had been organizing some boxes there earlier. Cody had a set of keys for the blue Camaro. He was sixteen now and had driven the Old Blue look-alike many times with his dad in the car. He thought, *This is probably not the smartest thing I've done driving on just my permit, but Dad is in trouble. It is a matter of life and death.*

Cody climbed into the Camaro and rolled out of his steep drive in neutral so that his mom would not hear him. He rolled into the street and started the engine. Cody spoke a prayer.

"Lord, not sure You want to hear my prayer because You don't like breaking the law. But I pray You keep Dad safe, and me too. Amen."

Cody knew he would have to drive through the hills in Northwest Nevada to get to Reno. He had a map but was not sure of the way. There were twists and turns in the road, and to an unfamiliar driver, it was a scary adventure. Cody was not self-assured being an inexperienced driver, but somehow this Old Blue, like the old one, seemed to know the way. He had listened to his dad talk about the first Old Blue like the Camaro had human characteristics, and he tended to believe it. Cody was more willing to accept that the spirit of God was guiding the way for him.

He was able to drive to the Conference Center Hotel in Reno, Nevada, without much trouble. He breathed a prayer again.

"Thank You, Lord, for protecting me and getting me here. I know You are helping me in spite of myself. I don't deserve Your help. Please help me find Dad. Amen."

Cody parked the car and ran into the hotel. He went to the front desk to ask where he could find his dad. The desk clerk told him he would have to wait, as it was near time for his dad to go on stage and give a speech.

———

Chief Bormand and several undercover cops had already arrived and tried to find Cameron without bringing too much attention as to why they were there. Bormand realized that the future of Mariah City Community Church and even the nation might be in jeopardy if Jepson had planned to destroy Cameron at the convention. Steve Merson, the fireman, and Deputy Mager came along to help the chief locate Cameron and try to help in some way.

Bormand arrived and checked in with his undercover officers. While Steve Merson and Deputy Mager found their rooms, Bormand decided to have some coffee at the café in the Convention Center Hotel. As Bormand was paying his bill, he noticed a man walking past the glass windows as if he was going to a fire. It was Jepson. He knew it. Jepson was alive, and Bormand knew exactly what he wanted to do.

Bormand called up to Steve and Clem's room and told them he saw Jepson and that he was right about what Jepson is going to do. He was trying to locate Cameron, but it was getting too close to the time Cameron would be entering the platform to give his presentation. Steve and Clem arranged to meet Chief Bormand in the lobby.

The hotel concierge helped them find the convention schedule and when Cameron would come on to speak. They could not give them locations of participants. The chief was insistent that this was a matter of police business, even though he knew he had no jurisdiction there.

The three men split up and walked the aisles and floors of the convention center, looking for someone suspicious. They saw three security men but did not think anything suspicious about this until they noticed Jepson talking with one of them.

Bormand figured out that these men were plants and not real security men. These were the assassins. Bormand, Steve, and Clem decided to each take out these men, although they realized they would be coming up against trained operatives and that they were endangering their own lives. What else could they do? How else could this be stopped?

Cameron came to the podium. He was all too aware that Jepson would attempt to use this occasion to destroy Cameron as well as the new presidential candidate. As Cameron was ready to give his speech, he uttered a prayer: "Lord, only You can protect us and Your nation too." He gave his speech. Echoing through the great hall, Cameron's voice could be heard. "Welcome to Nevada!"

Applause sounded like rumbles throughout the hall as the crowd held signs bouncing up and down with phrases like "Dalin for President," "A New Party for a New Day," and "Uphold America."

Cameron spoke into the mike again with typical Cameron Kale humor. "This is Reno, and what happens here does not stay here!"

The crowd broke into laughter and anticipated his following words. Cameron took thirty seconds to continue his phrase.

"What happens here does not stay here because what is happening here is going to be heard in the nation and moving us into the Capitol!"

The roars of the crowd in the hall were at deafening decibels. As the crowd quieted down some, Cameron spoke again.

"Thank you for inviting me here to speak about something and someone that will change America. I am excited to be a part of all of this. Several years ago, I was just practicing chiropractics in the small town of Mariah City, Nevada, enjoying my family and serving in our local church. Life was simple then." Everyone laughed. "As Deni, my wife, and I and Cody, our son, stepped up to serve more in our church and in our community, everything skyrocketed from there. We would have never imagined sharing our thoughts, ideas, and our hearts for those who hurt in Washington, DC, with the help of Virginia Bassman. Thank you, Virginia. What has been exciting is that we have seen many people with the same vision and passion for this country and care for the innocent, the hurting, and the needy from both sides of the aisle. We have seen much bipartisan work to help meet needs in this nation. I am thankful for that. But I am here to tell you tonight that Republicans and Democrats alike, as well as Independents, are joining together in this new party to finally get things done in Washington!"

The crowd began to roar again. Signs were waving across the hall. Many new party hopefuls were pointing to the large monitors with Cameron's image as he pointed his finger heavenward. Cameras panned the large hall, zooming in on the faces of small children, with their parents, trying to see what their parents were pointing to. Even with typical traffic of people walking to and from various areas of the hall, an amazing number of people kept still and focused on what Cameron Kale was saying.

"I want to tell you tonight why I believe things are going to get done in Washington. It is because we have the support of people who don't want to just talk about turning this country back to the America it was but are committed to doing it. It is time that we have a party that will honestly embrace life issues. It is time that we have people who have figured out that if we choose to terminate pregnancies, we have no future society. It's time that we stop using government to raise your taxes and fund the abortions of private citizens. It is not right that you have no choice but to pay for the choices that many women are making. It is about time that we recognize, according to the Gallup poles, that more people in this country choose life than to support abortion. Since that is the case, let's support someone in Washington who agrees with the majority of Americans!"

Again, the crowd went ballistic in shouts and a chant of "New party now! New party now! New party now!"

"I want to tell you that it is time for Americans to wake up and realize that we are losing our rights. Government has become so big that it is controlling how you and I live in the private sector. Government is telling us what school our kids must attend. Government is telling us what insurance or health care we must have. Government is telling us that we can't pray in public or talk about Christ in public places. Our Judeo-Christian heritage is being under-minded, and we are told we cannot serve God the way we want. You are losing your right to free speech. Our Constitution, defended by the blood of those who have fought for our freedoms, is being questioned and looked at by liberals as an archaic document that has no application to our modern America. Shame on those who believe this. Shame on those who would try to take away the America that you and I know and love."

As Cameron was attentive to the reality that Jepson was in the crowd, it came to him that, as people were standing and shouting, it would be near impossible for the shooters to get off a clear shot on the possible presidential candidate. The Spirit whispered to Cameron to continue to get the applause and cheers as he introduced the person who would lead the nation to accomplish those goals. People did not sit down. Cameron kept them cheering.

As the shooters were signaled by Jepson on their radios to commence firing, they could not get a clear shot with so many people standing between them and the candidate.

Meanwhile, Bormand, Steve, and Clem reached the security men, by a wing and a prayer and no doubt some divine direction, and grabbed the men from behind. Several shots rang out, but only to the ceiling of the hall. Masses of people fell to the ground, including Cameron, shielding the presidential candidate from the spray of bullets to protect her.

Secret police and other authorities rushed in to assess the situation and see who the shooters were. Convention security arrived and shouted for the shooters to lay their weapons down.

The security men shouted, "We were jumped by these guys! We have clearance to protect the candidate!"

They obviously had other plans. Bormand, Steve, and Clem showed their identification and showed the report to the security commander that Jepson was involved in a murder case and had fled an arrest the previous year. The security men were taken into custody and Bormand, Steve, and Clem were released.

Meanwhile, Jepson was able to get away and worked his way through the convention center without being noticed except by one person, Cody Kale.

Cody stood frozen as he saw the man everyone said was dead, Jepson LaPlant. As Jepson was making his way out a side glass door of the convention center, Cody followed him. Jepson was making his way through the parking lot, no doubt heading for his vehicle. Cody ran between parked vehicles and found the blue Camaro.

"Please God, tell me what to do!"

Cody started the car and began to back into the parking garage. As he turned one of the corners of the garage, he could see Jepson run across the roadway.

"Forgive me, God, but this has to happen." Cody stepped on the gas and knew the blue Camaro was able to rev up super speed in a matter of seconds. "Here we go!"

As Jepson stepped into the roadway, Cody and the blue Camaro raced around the corner at top speed. The Camaro caught Jepson in the hip and threw him over the hood and onto the street. Cody slammed on the brakes and came to an immediate stop. Cody got out of the car and saw Jepson struggling to get to his feet, but he was obviously injured. Cody could hear Chief Bormand and his undercover cops running toward them from a distance. Just for a moment, Cody felt safe. It would all soon be over.

Just as he thought all was well, his eye caught a strange sight of something in the shadows clinging to the girders supporting the upper deck. As he focused in, he could see that it was the half-man, half-lion Drawg. Drawg growled as he fixed his eyes on Cody. As Drawg was about to lunge toward the young man, intending to end Cody's life and freeing Jepson, Cody's voice echoed through the garage.

"God, I can't do this. Only *You* can! I trust You. I believe You have the power to overcome Drawg!"

As Cody's words of faith reached the ears of Spirit who was at Cody's side, the power of the Spirit moved to save Cody Kale. The roaring lion was now crawling across the upper deck beams as though he was wounded and weak. Each howl released the demon spirits from his mouth that seemed to be screeching and wailing as though they were in pain.

"Spirit of the living God, don't destroy us, don't destroy us!" they repeated. Finally, the demon spirits and Drawg disappeared as quickly as they had appeared. Cody had trusted the Lord to do what only the Lord could do. The Spirit of God vanquished the enemy in the twinkling of an eye.

Chief Bormand and his officers came running through the garage with guns drawn on Jepson. Bormand, surprised to find Cody, just shook his head and grinned.

"And now you caught Jepson?" Bormand growled. "Son, you are your dad's son for sure—a hero! But don't think you are not in trouble for driving on just a permit."

"Yes, sir!"

Bormand and the suits grabbed Jepson, who appeared to have only broken his hip and had a few bumps and scrapes.

"Come on, Jepson, we are putting you away for a long time, not only for the murder of Amy Benson and the attempted murder of Cameron Kale, but also for the plot to assassin the next president of the United States. Read him his rights, boys, and chain him and get him in the car. And don't take your eyes off him."

The papers released a story the next day saying that this attack was set up by the Democratic League to destroy the new party candidate. Popularity points went up for the new candidate, and Sandra Dalin was elected president of the United States.

Cameron and Cody were hailed as superheroes. When Deni was asked about what she thought about her men being superheroes, she said, "I am used to it. We are all superheroes when we listen to God."

"I am just content with bringing the evangel, the good news to men and women," Cameron said. "It is my highest calling."

Cameron, Bormand, Steve Merson, Deputy Mager, and Cody Kale were all honored with special medals of honor and heroism for their capture of the assassins and saving the life of the presidential candidate.

Mariah City, Mariah City Community Church, and the nation were experiencing better days—for now. Ser Pentino lost a battle but desired to win the war. As far as he was concerned, it wasn't over.

Sandra Dalin came back to visit Cameron, Deni, and Cody, her friend Bill Hanson, and her new friends Scott Benson, Clem Mager, and Chief Bormand. Everyone met at the Fire and Ice restaurant. Cody thought it was pretty cool with a presidential limo parked outside, security, and the president's own Secret Service everywhere. Sandra was discussing with the group how hopeful she was that there would be a great turnaround in the country and a move away from the extreme positions of the Democratic League. The group was upbeat and enjoying the best cuisine Fire and Ice had to offer—on the president! Everyone was enjoying their meal and talking about the hopeful things they believed they would see come about in the nation that would also impact their states and cities.

Suddenly, a finely dressed man came into the restaurant, seemingly in a panic. The Secret Service took note of his erratic behavior and kept their eyes on him. He was asking, "Where is the prophet? Someone told me the prophet is here. Where is the prophet?"

The manager came over to quiet the gentleman down, as he was not only concerned about his customers but also not wanting this to disturb the president of the United States. It didn't appear that the man was carrying any weapon or wanted to hurt anyone but seemed like he desperately needed to find this person called "the prophet."

"Sir, I don't know who this person is you are looking for," the manager said. "Who is the prophet?"

The man gazed into the manager's eyes and spoke words that were confusing to the manager: "The days are evil. Our lives are in jeopardy. Everyone says, peace, but there is no peace until the Messiah of God rules on Earth. I was told there is a prophet here by a man who appeared to me, spoke kindly, and then disappeared. He told me I would find him here."

The manager realized that he needed to get help for this man who seemed to have lost his mind.

Cameron Kale's family, friends, and Sandra Dalin could hear the ruckus from the table and wondered what was going on. A Secret Service agent came over to Sandra Dalin and whispered into her ear. He told her there was a man looking for someone and seemed somewhat desperate to find him but seemed as though he was mentally disturbed.

Cameron overheard the Secret Service agent tell Sandra Dalin that the man was told that there would be no more real peace until the Messiah came and that a man appeared to tell him to look for the a prophet who could explain this to him at this location, and then the man disappeared. Cameron was concerned about what the man said and wanted to talk with him. He asked the Secret Service agent if it was okay to talk to this man. He gestured to Cameron affirmatively.

Cameron came up to manager still trying to calm the man down. "May I talk with him?"

"Yes, if you think it will help," the manager said.

Cameron looked concerned about this man and put his hand gently on his shoulder. "Sir, can I help you? You were asking about a prophet?"

The man hugged Cameron and was crying. While everything about this man made Cameron want to think that he needed some psychological help, the words he spoke were witnessing to his spirit. The man stopped crying and became very lucid and self-controlled.

"You are him," he said. "You are the one the man told me about. He told me that when I found you I would know you. Thank You, Jesus. Thank You, Jesus."

Cameron asked the man what the man said to him.

"He told me I would find a man who looked like you and that you would be with your family and friends here at this restaurant. I knew it was you when you spoke to me. You have the voice of a prophet."

Cameron continued in his typical investigative way. "Suppose I am this prophet. What can I do for you?"

The man grabbed Cameron's forearm. "My children have families of their own and are busy, and I was feeling alone. I have also been sick from diabetes, and my medications were making me sicker. I was depressed and thought about taking my life. I was sitting by the north bridge and was ready to jump when this man appeared out of nowhere and called my name.

"'Samuel Aquino,'—that is my name—he said. 'Don't do it. There is much to live for.'

"I stopped and turned and asked him why I should live. He told me about Jesus and that Jesus would take away my sorrows. He explained about how Jesus came and taught on Earth that the way to the heavenly Father was through Him. Then He went up to the Father but is coming again for those who trust Him. I asked him how I could know more. He told me about a man named Cameron Kale, the prophet. He told me that God had gifted him as an evangelist but that he was a prophet of God too. He told me you could help me understand God's will for my life and how I should live until this Jesus comes back. He said that is what a prophet does."

Cameron stood in awe and with his mouth practically wide open. God had witnessed to him that what the man heard was from Him. He didn't know who the man was that saved this man's life but was pretty sure it was entertaining an "angel unaware," as the Scriptures says. He witnessed in his spirit that God sent the angel to bring a message to this man, saved him in the process, and then sent him with a message to Cameron about another area of gifting.

Cameron knew that God not only wanted him to win men and women to Christ with the evangel but also that God wanted him to continue at Mariah City Community Church boldly preaching the prophetic Word. Cameron wondered and pondered in his heart what God would do next to show His amazing power through a simple servant.

Ushering Samuel Aquino over to his table, he introduced him to his family, friends, and Sandra Dalin, the president of the United Sates. Cameron reassured everyone that there was nothing to worry about. He shared that he believed that Samuel was saner than most people and that God had used him that day to say something to him.

"What did he tell you, Dad?" Cody asked.

"That I am not only an evangelist but a prophet."

"We knew that already!" Cody replied. Everyone laughed, including Cameron, who was scratching his head, wondering why he was often the last to know what God was doing in his life.

Sandra Dalin turned to Cameron. "Well, Cameron, what is your next assignment as the prophet of Mariah City?"

Cameron, who never had trouble finding words, could only say, "When God tells me, be sure I will let you know!"

Sirens rang out in the streets, screeching past the Fire and Ice. You could see Steve Merson in the one of the trucks on the radio. Chief Bormand radioed the Secret Service attending to the president so as to not alarm the president but to get a message to Cameron Kale. A Secret Service agent took the call and walked up boldly to Cameron.

"Dr. Kale, I'm sorry, but I was just informed to let you know that there is a serious fire at Mariah City Community Church. Much of the new additions are engulfed in flames."

Cameron told everyone, "I apologize, Mrs. President, but I need to get over to the church." He turned to the Secret Service agent, "Do they know how this happened?"

"I believe it is arson, sir. They saw a small man in a business suit on the property just before it happened. They are looking for him now."

Cameron knew his work on Earth would not be over as long as God's enemy was on the prowl, and that would be the case until Jesus Christ came back for His saints. He knew the good news is that Jesus Christ has already won the victory over evil. We just need to really believe Jesus and obey Him. When we do, we will see the mighty and miraculous things that He will do in our lives.